A lesson in history…

"Millie and Mitchell…so that's what the Double M stands for."

He gave an affirmative nod. "I'll have to show you a photo of them sometime. They were a pretty striking couple."

"I'd love to see it. I thought the name of your ranch had to do with your last name having two Ms."

"Nope. My great-grandparents' last name was Stanford. They had Gran, who married Daniel Alger, and they had my mother. Dad is the McMillan."

"Got it." Summer picked a stem of red clover and twirled it beneath her nose, a little in awe—and a little envious. "You're a fascinating guy, Reese McMillan. Wish my life had been half as interesting."

"You say 'had' as if it's over. You're barely in your twenties, woman. You have a lot more living to do."

She peeked at him through her lashes. "It's certainly gotten more exciting since I met you. Though, I'm still not sure if that's good or bad."

He leaned in toward her and caressed a slow path from her knee, up her thigh, and back again. "Maybe it's a little bit of both."

Praise for Donna Marie Rogers

GOLDEN OPPORTUNITY

"Deliciously sweet…with plenty of heat!"

—*USA Today* bestselling author, Norah Wilson

THAT MAGIC TOUCH

"Sheer genius. I will now put all future books by this author on my must read list."

—5 Stars, Amazon Reviewer

THERE'S ONLY BEEN YOU

"Love lost and found is the basis of this wonderfully heartwarming read. Throw in a years-old lie and a strong sense of family and it only gets better and better."

—4 Stars, RT Book Reviews

MEANT TO BE

"The plot kept me spellbound throughout the entire book. Rogers has the ability to keep her readers on the edge of our seats."

—5 Hearts, The Romance Studio

"The material is tightly written, well plotted and fast paced, and the characters are unforgettable."

—5 Books, Long and Short Reviews

Donna Marie Rogers Titles

JAMISON FAMILY SERIES
There's Only Been You, Book 1
Foolish Pride, short story
Meant To Be, Book 2

LAKE SHELBYVILLE SERIES
That Magic Touch, Book 1

DOUBLE M RANCH SERIES
Golden Opportunity
Golden Dream

WELCOME TO REDEMPTION SERIES
A hometown series full of sexy romance, humor, and heart...

A Fair of the Heart, Book 1
The Perfect Blend, Book 3
Home Is Where the Heart Is, Book 5
Never Let Me Go, Book 7
Say You Love Me, Book 9
(Books 2, 4, 6, 8, 10 written by Stacey Joy Netzel)

Golden Dream

DOUBLE M RANCH SERIES, Book 2

DONNA MARIE ROGERS

GOLDEN DREAM

This is a work of fiction. Names, characters, places, and incidents are either the product of the author's imagination or are used fictitiously, and any resemblance to actual persons living or dead, business establishments, events, or locales, is entirely coincidental.

Copyright © 2019 by Donna Marie Rogers

Cover art by The Killion Group
Formatted by Author E.M.S.

ISBN-13: 978-1-941829-10-3
ISBN-10: 1-941829-10-4

Published in the United States of America

For Robin

An amazing sister-in-law, and even better friend.
I'm sorry it took me so long to finish this one.

Chapter One

$\mathcal{S}$ummer Hanson took one last look in her rearview mirror, fixed a small, black smudge in the corner of her eye, then opened her car door and stepped out onto the wet pavement. A slight mist hung in the air. A quick glance at the overcast, early September sky confirmed the rain would start pouring again any minute. Though she hated spending money on anything that wasn't an absolute necessity, she made a mental note to pick up an umbrella next time she was at Target.

Mustering her confidence—while suppressing a familiar twinge of self-doubt—Summer shut the door and threw her shoulders back. She had an interview for a receptionist position at Henderson & Smythe, and nothing was going to stand in her way of getting this job.

After checking both ways, she took a deep, calming breath and started across the street.

Blaring music drew her attention. She shot a look to her left as a huge gray pickup pulled up to the light and made a swift right turn. She got a quick look at the driver—the very handsome driver—a split second before a stream of muddy water pelted her across the face and down the front of the only suitable business attire she owned.

Dammit!

She jumped back, sputtering, as the clueless idiot drove off down Washington Avenue, the twang of country music fading into the distance as he disappeared from sight.

Panic set in, and she raced back to her car to get a look at the damage. Maybe it wasn't as bad as she feared. But a glance at her reflection in her driver's side window confirmed her worst fears—she looked like she'd just crawled out of a swamp. Sludge dripped from her face, and bits of Lord only knew what clung to her blonde curls. She reluctantly lowered her gaze and groaned. The smart peach blouse and gray, pleated dress slacks were both soaked as well.

Tears burned her eyes. A small sniffle escaped as she flung the door open and slid inside. A swift yet thorough search of her car didn't produce a single thing she could clean herself off with—no Wet Wipes, tissues, or fast food napkins to be found anywhere. She was the mother of a five-year-old, her glove box should be jam-packed with such things.

Thinking about her little Katie Bear brought on a fresh wave of tears as the enormity of the situation hit her. Panic morphed into despair. She needed this job, desperately. Lord only knew how much longer she could keep up the rent if she didn't start earning a regular paycheck.

She started the car and sat for a minute with the heater blowing. What the hell should she do? Give them a call and try to reschedule her interview, or hurry home to get cleaned up, then rush back and apologize for being late? Choosing the former, she dug her cell from her purse, searched her caller list, and dialed the number.

"Henderson and Smythe."

"Hello, my name is Summer Hanson, and I have an interview with Mr. Smythe at ten o'clock. But…I'm afraid I had a family emergency. Would it be possible to reschedule?" She crossed her fingers as she awaited the woman's reply.

"One minute, please."

Elevator music filled her ear, and she waited with baited breath, her heart stuttering as she sent up a silent prayer. This position paid much better than the barely above minimum wage she earned at Johnson's SuperMart. But more importantly, it was full-time, included health insurance, dental, and paid sick days.

The music stopped. Her pulse sped into triple time.

"Miss Hanson?"

3

"Yes, I'm here." Her grip on the phone tightened.

"I'm sorry, but Mr. Smythe is a stickler for punctuality, and the other applicants were here on time. He said there is no point in rescheduling."

Her heart sank, her chest burning with disappointment. "I understand. Thank you."

She ended the call, leaned her head back, and stared numbly through the windshield as the weight of this latest blow made it difficult to draw air into her lungs.

What the hell am I supposed to do now?

Even if she could talk her boss into giving her some extra hours, it would be nights and weekends, when she had no one to watch Katie. Evening and weekend childcare cost an arm and a leg.

With a muttered curse, she swiped at both cheeks with the heels of her hands, threw the car into drive, and headed home.

A long, hot shower took the edge off her anxiety, but she still had a huge dilemma when it came to keeping a roof over their heads. Not that the roof in question was anything special. As she glanced around the sparse, one-bedroom apartment, a yearning for something better nearly overwhelmed her.

She'd had such big dreams when she and her ex first arrived in Golden, Colorado. She'd been three months pregnant, madly in love…and sadly naïve. Tall, dark, and sexy in that macho-Italian, bad boy way, Nico Moretti had swept her off her feet from the moment he came through her line at her parents' grocery store back home in Redemption, Wisconsin. The smooth-talking New Yorker had flirted his way past the defenses she'd erected after the boy she secretly dated senior year of high school dumped her when she refused to sleep with him. She'd been seventeen, vulnerable, and thoroughly infatuated.

Within days, they were dating. Within months, she was pregnant.

Horrified, her ultra conservative parents insisted she go live with an aunt up in the U.P. of Michigan until the baby was born—then put it up for adoption. When she'd refused, truly shocked by their cold-hearted demand, they threatened to press statutory rape charges against Nico, who begged her to run away with him. He'd painted such a wonderful picture—them against the world, starting a new life together somewhere far away, getting married, raising their kid, living happily ever after. And so, she'd packed her meager belongings into two ratty tote bags and never looked back.

Eight months later—and still unwed—her dreams were obliterated when the police showed up at their door and arrested Nico for dealing drugs, possession, and a whole host of other charges. Unbeknownst to Summer, he'd had a criminal record a mile long back in New York, a cocaine habit, and a secret girlfriend in Golden. The day the judge slapped him with a ten year prison sentence was the last time she'd laid eyes on him.

Torn between heading back to Wisconsin with her tail between her legs to beg her parents' forgiveness, or trying to make a go of it as a single parent, she'd chosen the latter, knowing in her heart she could never be happy again in that environment. Not that she'd experienced much of that particular emotion in the first seventeen years of her life. Without a doubt, her parents would throw her mistakes in her face every chance they got, while looking down their judgmental noses at Katie. Maybe they'd eventually warm up to their beautiful granddaughter, maybe they wouldn't. But that wasn't the way she wanted to raise her child. She had plenty of self-esteem issues thanks to Jim and Betty Hanson, no way in hell would she let them inflict the same damage on her daughter.

Forcing her attention back to the present, she made herself a cup of tea, then sat at the kitchen table and flipped open the classifieds, determined to find something that paid better than her current job. Plenty of part-time openings filled the pages, but with no college degree, there were very few full-time positions she qualified for. A couple of assisted living facilities had openings for both second and third shift, and a repackaging plant— which claimed to have a great benefits package— was also looking to fill several evening positions.

If only she could find affordable daycare. Most places wanted fifteen to twenty bucks an hour for night and weekend hours, which was probably more than she would make at any of these jobs. And with no family and few friends in town, her options were definitely limited. The only person she felt comfortable enough with to watch Katie was Mrs. Langley, the elderly widow who lived directly above them. But the poor woman could barely walk anymore, let alone chase after a five-year-old.

With a sigh of despair, she flicked a glance at the clock—and shot up out of her chair. *Eleven forty-five! Holy crap.*

Nearly an hour had flown by in what seemed like minutes, and Katie's kindergarten class let out at noon today thanks to a teacher's workshop. She grabbed her purse and keys, yanked on her jacket, and ran out the door.

As if validating her earlier prediction, a light, steady rain started as soon as she slid in behind the wheel. Summer forced herself to maintain her speed as she drove down Rubey Drive, not wanting to take any chances with the way her luck was going. Not that she was especially superstitious, but neither did she believe in tempting fate.

Just as she figured, the lot was packed—her usual spot taken, dang it—so she drove around back and parked near the dumpster. After slipping her keys into her purse, she threw the door open and stepped out onto the wet pavement.

Recognizing Angela McMillan, whose daughter, Molly, was in Katie's class, and who she'd chatted with many times while waiting for the dismissal bell to ring, Summer tossed her hood up and quickened her pace. The pregnant redhead held a huge, royal blue umbrella, and waddled slow enough that Summer caught up to her within seconds.

Angela turned, a smile spreading across her face. "Hi! I'm glad I ran into you."

"Me, too. How are you feeling?"

Her new friend moved in close to share her umbrella, then placed her free hand against her expanded belly and gave a noncommittal shrug. "Tired. And a little beat up. Boy or girl, I think this kid is going to be a linebacker."

Summer grinned empathetically. "I was sure Katie was a boy. She kicked me so hard once, I thought she broke a rib."

"Molly was a breeze. I had such a good pregnancy with her. They say that's how it goes sometimes." The redhead cast a quick glance up at the dreary sky. "So, any chance you're free this Saturday? Molly'd like to have Katie over for lunch and a playdate, and I could sure use some grown-up female company. Don't get me wrong," she quickly amended with a hand to her chest, "I love Meara dearly. But she's more of a mother figure than a confidant, if you know what I mean."

Angela had raved about Meara on more than one occasion. The lady, who had helped raise Angela's husband and his brother, had been taking care of the household and family ever since their grandmother died. But Summer could understand why it might be difficult to confide in the older woman about certain things.

"We're free, and we'd love to." She smiled with genuine excitement. It had been so long since she'd had a real friend—and truly, she'd never needed one more than she did right now. "I can tell you all about the idiot who ruined my job interview this morning."

Auburn brows sunk together. "Oh, no! What happened?"

The bell rang before she could respond, signaling the end of the school day. Within seconds, the front doors burst open and a sea of children poured out in two endless waves of bustling enthusiasm. Once the lines thinned, the younger kids started out, and she smiled as Katie and Molly strolled out together, arm in arm. They rushed forward when they spotted her and Angela.

Summer bent down and scooped her little munchkin into her arms, while Molly wrapped an arm around her mother's hips.

"Momma, can we go to Molly's house for a playdate?" Katie's eyes widened dramatically. "They have horses!"

"You bet. In fact, we were just talking about that when school let out." She met Angela's gaze. "We'll see you Saturday. The Double M Ranch, correct? Off highway ninety-three?"

"That's it. The entrance is about six miles past that little diner with the bacon and eggs-shaped neon sign in the window. Just watch for the huge, wooden arch. And the driveway is about a half-mile long, just so you know." She grasped her daughter's hand and grinned. "Looking forward to your 'idiot' story."

Chapter Two

$\mathcal{R}$eese McMillan gazed across the lush, emerald rolling hills to the majestic Rocky Mountains beyond, in awe of his beautiful home and surroundings. Why had it taken him so long to appreciate what most people would call heaven on earth? Hell if he knew, but as he watched a small herd of Double M horses galloping in the distance, he knew he would never take this place—his birthright—for granted again.

"Uncle Reese! Uncle Reese!"

He tightened his hold on the rambunctious little girl bouncing in the saddle in front of him.

His niece, Molly, smacked his leg, then pointed toward the horses. "Can you catch one for me?"

He chuckled softly. "Not today, munchkin. If we're not back to the ranch in time for your playdate, Meara'll have my hide."

"Katie's coming over today, she's my bestest friend! We're gonna have mac 'n' cheese, and peanut butter and jelly sandwiches."

His stomach churned at the thought. "Sounds yummy."

"You can have some, too," she assured him, craning her neck to make eye contact.

He smiled earnestly. "I appreciate the offer, Molls, but I promised Meara I'd run into town for her. Besides, I bet your daddy would love to join you guys for lunch." Lord knew there wasn't much James wouldn't put in his mouth. As kids, he'd have eaten almost anything for a dollar, including, but not limited to, goldfish, ants, a big spoonful of mayonnaise, and a whole jalapeno.

"But Daddy's not home. He took mommy to the doctor."

Reese frowned over the reminder. Well into her seventh month of pregnancy, his sister-in-law, Angela, had woken up with cramps, so James had driven her to Denver to see her doctor.

"I know, but they should be back in time for your playdate. If not, and if Meara doesn't mind waiting for her groceries, I'll be happy to have lunch with you and your friend."

"Yay! Meara's gonna make the mac and cheese, but me and Katie are gonna make our own sandwiches. I can make yours if you don't know how."

He almost laughed. Truth was he could barely make cereal, so a peanut butter and jelly sandwich could definitely hold a challenge. "I just may take you up on that, munchkin." With one last look across the valley, he tightened his arm around her, and galloped back toward the ranch.

Meara was waiting for them by the back door; the older woman's arched brow wouldn't bode well for him. Hell, they were only a few minutes late.

Reese trotted right up to her and grinned down. "Hey, beautiful."

"Don't you be trying to butter me up, young man. I told you to be back here by eleven a.m. *sharp*." She reached up and helped Molly down.

"We're like ten minutes late," he defended.

"I told you, she needs to take a bath before her company arrives."

He dropped the reins and slid from the saddle. "I'm sorry, Meara." Stepping forward, he wrapped an arm around her waist, effecting the wide-eyed look of remorse he'd been using on her for years—and which never failed to win her over. "Still love me?"

The annoyance faded from her keen gaze as a reluctant smile took hold. "Oh, go on with ya."

As the beloved housekeeper turned to escort Molly into the house, he asked, "Can that ride into town wait until later? If James and Angela don't make it back in time, looks like I may have myself a couple of dates for lunch."

She paused, then gave Molly a gentle pat on the head. "Why don't you head upstairs and choose which bubble bath you'd like. I'll be right in."

"'Kay."

Once his niece disappeared inside, Meara spun back around. "I didn't want to mention it in front of Molly, but James called about fifteen minutes ago. They're definitely going to be late. Angela got dizzy in the elevator at the doctor's office, and her blood pressure spiked, so they're running some extra tests. The cramps had eased by the time they arrived, though, so that's a relief. The doctor says he's just being cautious, but James is beside himself."

Son of a bitch. "I should give him a quick call."

"He said he was heading back into the exam room, so he probably turned his phone off. I'm sure he'll call back if there's any news." The older woman attempted a reassuring smile. "She's a tough young woman, I'm sure there's nothing to worry about."

"That she is," Reese agreed. He'd known Angela even longer than his brother, and knew firsthand what a tiger she could be. But it killed him, this fear of the unknown she and James were facing, and wished there was something he could do to help.

"Well, I need to get Molly bathed for her playdate. Since you'll be standing in for them"—she raked her gaze up and down him—"you may want to jump in the shower yourself."

He crossed his arms across his chest and arched a brow. "You saying I stink?"

"You work with horses," she reminded him. "I'll let you connect the dots."

He laughed. "That's cold, Meara."

She held his gaze for a moment, then pursed her lips and turned to head inside, adding over her shoulder, "I happen to know this young lady's mother is single. Just thought you might want to look—and smell—your best." With that, she disappeared into the house.

Meara and her matchmaking heart.

Reese gave his head a rueful shake as he led his horse into the barn. After hooking his reins, he got the brush out.

Sure, he'd love to have what James and Angela had. Someday. But it wasn't like he was ready to drop to bended knee anytime soon. He had business plans he needed to fulfill.

Though…he was damn tired of being alone. The semi-regular hookups he indulged in were becoming fewer and farther between, just enough to keep him out of the monk category. But he knew his weaknesses, and had spent nearly five years following the right path, putting his party boy ways behind him as he worked hard to shed his old reputation and build a new one. He had focus, drive, determination.

And dreams of opening a dude ranch.

He'd spent the last three years doing research and knew it would be a great investment. The only problem had been where to build. Some prime property had recently gone up for sale, but the hard part would be convincing James, who was as cautious as the day was long. He also knew his brother didn't fully trust him, though he'd never

15

come out and said so. But actions spoke louder than words, and big brother had ignored nearly every suggestion Reese made about the ranch. And because his sibling was the majority shareholder, he called the shots.

Reese gave his head a frustrated shake. James' mistrust and reservations were justifiable. He'd screwed up, bad—broke his brother's heart, and nearly lost him for good. But he'd been working his fingers to the bone these past years, keeping his nose clean, and doing everything in his power to earn back his trust. Soon, he planned to pitch him his idea for a working dude ranch, a resort unlike anything the area currently offered. But first, he needed to get James to agree to sell him the last one-percent of the ranch that prevented them from being full partners.

Feeling optimistic, he finished brushing Daisy and headed back to the house for that shower.

When Reese returned to the kitchen, Molly was seated on a stool next to the stove, her little face wreathed with excitement as Meara poured shredded cheddar cheese from a bag into a big pot. The mac and cheese, he assumed.

"Something sure smells good in here," he announced as he stepped forward and peeked inside. "I don't suppose it's ready for tasting?"

"It has to go in the oven first, Uncle Reese. And we gotta put the crackers on top. I helped crush 'em." She proudly pointed to the bowl sitting beside her on the counter.

He reached out and gently tugged one of her damp pigtails. "Looks like you did a fine job, too, Squirt."

"Yep. Meara said I'm the best cracker crusher *ever*."

"You're the best helper a gal could ask for, that's for certain." The older woman smiled at her young charge, then pulled the pot off the burner and waved toward the opposite counter. "Reese, can you grab that casserole dish for me, please?"

He did as asked, frowning when Meara struggled to lift the full pot. Knowing how proud the old girl was, he gave her a gentle pat on the back and said, "Here, let me make myself useful and hold that for you."

She blessed him with a smile of gratitude, and as he made good on his offer, she scooped the noodle and cheese mixture into the ceramic dish. After patting it down with the back of the spoon, she nodded at Molly, who reached into her own bowl for a fistful of the cracker and melted butter mixture. Once she'd sprinkled all the topping on the casserole—and a good amount on the counter as well—Meara opened the oven, and Reese slid the pan inside. Teamwork at its finest.

After setting the timer, she gave Reese an appreciative side hug, then helped Molly down from the stool and led her over to the sink to wash her hands. Meara normally lifted Molls up and held her on her hip, but she flexed her fingers and winced. In the last few weeks, her arthritis seemed to have gotten worse, though the stubborn woman refused to take it easy. And she'd nearly gone through the roof when James suggested they get her some help.

Thankfully, she didn't protest when he lifted Molly up and held her while she washed her hands. When he set her back on her feet, she hurried over to the table, oblivious to the older woman's discomfort.

"Look, Uncle Reese, we're gonna decorate cupcakes! Wanna help?"

"Sounds like fun. Count me in." A platter piled high with both vanilla and chocolate cupcakes sat in the center of the table, surrounded by two big bowls of frosting—one pink, one white—and every kind of sprinkle, candy, and colored sugar imaginable.

"Molly, why don't you go brush your teeth," Meara suggested as she put the pot in the sink and started filling it with water. "Your guests should be here soon."

"But I already brushed 'em this morning," she protested.

"Please, no arguments. You promised to brush your teeth again if I let you lick the beaters."

She let out a whopper of a sigh. "Fine."

As soon as she skipped out of the room, Meara said, "Son, I need you to handle the playdate for me. Just take the mac and cheese from the oven when the timer goes off and set it on the stove. Molly knows where I keep the peanut butter and jelly, the bread's on the counter. And everything you need for decorating the cupcakes is already on the table."

He stepped forward and placed a hand on her shoulder. "You okay, Meara? I can tell your arthritis is acting up again."

She smiled and waved off his concern. "Just old age, boy. And a little low on energy. Nothing to be frettin' about. I didn't sleep so well last night, so I just need to lie down for an hour or so. I'll be down to rescue you before you know it."

He studied her for a moment, not quite sure he believed her. But then he kissed her on the cheek and gave her shoulder a gentle squeeze. "Take as much time as you need. I'm sure between this girl's mother and I, we'll manage."

Meara patted his cheek. "You'll be just fine. And don't worry about cleaning up. I'll take care of all that later."

He grinned. "No arguments here."

Reese stood behind his niece a short time later as she peeked out the living room window. A vehicle slowly made its way up their long, winding driveway—an older, red, Chevy Malibu that had seen better days. He gave Molls hair a reassuring fluff as she bounced with excitement.

"They're here, they're here!" she needlessly announced.

He chuckled softly. "I can see that, squirt. You ready to have some fun?"

"We're gonna have the bestest time, Uncle Reese. Can we go for a ride? Katie said she's never seen a real horse, only on TV."

"Maybe we should save the riding lesson for next time. I mean, we already have so much to do."

She peered up at him. "But I promised she could pet Daisy."

Reese watched as the little red Malibu pulled up alongside his truck. "She can pet Daisy, sure. Maybe feed her a carrot, or a few sugar cubes."

"And peppermints!"

He chucked her under the chin. "Sure. But just a couple."

The driver's side door opened, and Reese stared with interest—*darn you, Meara*—as a thin, leggy blonde stepped from the car and stared at his truck for a moment. She wore skin tight blue jeans, white sneakers, and a powder blue hoodie. Long, wavy, pale gold hair hung several inches past her shoulders, and he couldn't take his eyes off her as she opened her rear passenger door, and leaned inside. When she stood back up, a little girl with long, nearly black hair climbed from the back seat and grasped her mother's hand. The woman reached back inside and pulled out a tote bag, slung it over her shoulder, then smiled down at her daughter before they started up the walkway.

Reese let out a low whistle as he let the drapes fall back into place. "Wow. Your friend's mom is a knockout."

Molly's nose crinkled. "What does that mean?"

"It means she's very pretty."

"But Uncle Reese, she's a *mommy*."

He grinned. "Yeah, but it's okay for me to think mommies are pretty."

"Do you think *my* mommy is pretty?"

He placed a gentle hand on top of her head. "Second only to you."

Before she could respond, the front doorbell rang. Reese gave his giggly niece's chin another chuck, then swung open the door. The little, dark-haired cutie raced inside and embraced Molly. He smiled as he turned back to greet her mother—and was taken aback by the fury flashing in those big blue eyes.

"*You're* the idiot!"

Chapter Three

Summer gritted her teeth. The moron who had cost her that job was actually laughing at her!

"I wish I could say this was the first time I've heard that."

She crossed her arms over her chest. "Why am I not surprised?"

He swiped a hand through his thick, dark auburn hair and held her gaze with what appeared to be confusion.

"I'm sorry, do we know each other? I have to admit, you don't look familiar, so I'm a little unsure of why you're upset with me."

She breathed deep in an attempt to calm her racing heart. What in the world was wrong with her? These people had invited her and Katie to their home, and though she was fairly confident Angela's husband was the guy who'd driven though that puddle, she was starting to think he had no idea what had happened.

A quick glance at her daughter's horrified expression had her schooling her features into a sheepish smile. She bent down and winked at her. "It's fine, peanut. Momma was just joking."

Molly gave Katie's arm a tug. "Come on, I wanna show you all the cupcakes we're gonna decorate!"

As her daughter was dragged away by her enthusiastic friend, Summer blew out a silent breath before turning back to face Angela's husband. "I'm sorry. A few days ago, I was about to cross Washington Avenue on my way to a job interview when someone in a gray pickup truck drove through a huge puddle right next to where I was walking. I was doused and had to miss my interview."

He propped his hands on his hips and looked down at his boots in thoughtful contemplation for a moment. "Ah, hell." He met her gaze. "I was in town making a run for Meara Thursday around ten a.m. Came down Thirteenth Street and made a right onto Washington. I didn't see you. I'm really sorry."

Well, shit. As she'd silently fumed over the past few days, nursing quite the grudge, it hadn't occurred to her she'd ever run into the guy. Or that he'd turn out to be her friend's husband. Talk about a small world. "It's okay. How could you have known?"

"I'm really sorry," he repeated, the remorse in his tone, and his eyes, genuine.

An awkward silence followed. Finally, she said, "So, did I hear correctly, we have cupcakes to decorate?"

He grinned, and she found herself unable to take her eyes off him. James McMillan was a very handsome man. And her friend, a very lucky woman.

"Sure do. A mountain of them. But first, we have lunch to eat." His eyes suddenly widened. "Shit! I need to take the mac and cheese out of the oven."

He raced off, and Summer followed after him, taking in the gorgeous log cabin as she made her way through to the spacious kitchen. The girls sat at the table chattering about how they were each going to decorate their cupcakes, while James grabbed a couple of pot holders and opened the oven door.

"Thank God…perfectly browned." He pulled the pan out and set it on top of the stove.

Actually, it was a tad past "perfectly browned," but since his relief seemed profound, she decided to keep her opinion to herself.

"So, where's Angela?"

"Daddy took Mommy to the doctor," Molly offered.

Daddy? She frowned as she studied the man she'd assumed to be Molly's daddy. "I… Aren't you James?"

24

He tossed the potholders on the counter. "Sorry, I meant to introduce myself, but we got…distracted. I'm Reese. James is my older brother. And you are…?"

"Summer." Heat scorched a path up her neck as she was struck by an acute sense of relief. At least she hadn't been ogling her friend's husband. "And this little munchkin is Katie." She gave her daughter a kiss on the top of her head.

"Nice to officially meet you, Summer and Katie."

She frowned. "Is…everything okay with the baby?"

His smile didn't quite reach his eyes, which worried her.

"Oh, yeah. Fine. Angela was having some cramps, so they decided better to be safe than sorry. They should be home a little later."

Knowing she couldn't ask for further details in front of Molly, Summer nodded. She prayed her friend and the baby were all right.

Reese clapped his hands together. "So what do you say we have lunch? Besides Meara's amazing mac and cheese, I've been told peanut butter and jelly sandwiches are on the menu, accompanied by tall glasses of milk—or sweet tea—with DIY cupcakes for dessert."

"Sounds good to me." She picked up one of the unfrosted cupcakes and examined it while fighting the urge to stare at the handsome cowboy like a lovesick fool. She knew Angela's brother-in-law was single, and she found herself eager to learn more about him.

"Uncle Reese doesn't know how to make a peanut butter and jelly sandwich, so I'm going to make his for him," Molly informed her. Next to her Katie Bear, the little redhead was the cutest thing she'd ever seen.

"I can make yours for you, too, Momma," her daughter chimed in with a questioning lilt.

Summer met Reese's gaze. "Wow, aren't we lucky." To Katie, she said, "I would love that, sweetie, thank you."

"All right, Molls, why don't you grab the peanut butter and jelly, and show our guests into the dining room. Meara already set the table for us."

"C'mon, Katie. We have grape jam, strawberry preserves, *and* orange mommalade."

"*Mar*malade," her uncle corrected with a smile.

"Will Meara be joining us?" Summer asked, setting the cupcake back down. "I've heard a lot about her, I was looking forward to meeting her."

"She was a little tired, so she's lying down for a bit. But she'll be down later." He grabbed the pot holders and picked up the pan of mac and cheese.

"I'd like to help," Summer told him. "What can I do?"

He smiled. "If you could grab the milk from the fridge, that'd be great."

Once they had everything moved into the dining room, Summer poured them each a glass of milk, while Reese scooped four plates of mac and cheese, and the girls made the sandwiches. Molly's uncle ate his food with what had to be forced enjoyment. He didn't even seem to mind there was more peanut butter and jelly on the outside of his sandwich than on the inside. He sure did adore his niece, that much was clear.

Her idiot, as it turned out, seemed to be a pretty nice guy. He was also incredibly good-looking, though she had little interest in hooking up with anyone. Sure, she was lonely, and…lonesome. But she'd never been the type to sleep around. Katie's father was the only guy she'd ever been with.

Which meant she'd been celibate for over five years. Her gaze inadvertently dropped to his hand. No wedding band…

She took a gulp of her milk, watching as the girls fed each other mac and cheese, and bites of their sandwiches. The two had become thick as thieves in such a short time, and she couldn't have been happier for her daughter. Summer hadn't been allowed to have many friends as a young girl, and she'd certainly never been allowed to go to anyone's house, or invite anyone over to hers.

Though, from what she saw of the ranch, grounds, and enormous, state-of-the-art log cabin home, the McMillans appeared to be pretty wealthy. Summer couldn't help but worry Katie might come to resent the fact her mother couldn't give her the same things her friend had.

"I promised Molly I'd let her and Katie feed Daisy some treats later, if it's all right with you?"

She glanced up from her sandwich and met those incredible, whiskey brown eyes. "Who's Daisy?"

"My mommy's horse," Molly excitedly explained. "She loves sugar cubes, and peppermints, too. Uncle Reese said we could feed her some, but only a few so she doesn't get a tummy ache."

A horse. *Great.* Already her fears were coming true. Summer could barely afford to let Katie ride a horse on the carousal at the amusement park, never mind come close to ever owning the real thing.

"Sounds like fun," she hesitantly replied. "Is it safe?"

"Of course," Reese assured her. "Daisy is the gentlest horse we own. She belonged to my grandmother, and now Angela. And in a couple years, Molly will be able to ride her."

"I've never ridden," Summer softly admitted. "Is it hard to learn?"

"Nah. But it does take some time. I'd be happy to teach you, if you're interested."

"Me, too?" Katie asked, her hands clasped together in pleading.

"Absolutely."

He smiled, reaching out to ruffle Katie's hair, and Summer's heart melted a little bit.

"My schedule is pretty flexible. Anytime you ladies are ready, just let me know."

Summer didn't know if she'd ever be ready, but she kept that thought to herself since Katie seemed quite excited by the idea.

She insisted on washing dishes after lunch, but Reese assured her that Meara would have both their hides if they didn't leave her something to do. So they put the milk, leftover mac and cheese, and fruit spreads in the fridge before taking seats at the kitchen table to decorate the cupcakes.

The girls appointed themselves the official frosters—Molly magnanimously let Katie have the pink frosting—and put Reese in charge of sprinkles, and Summer on colored sugar duty. It turned out to be the most fun she'd had in a long time, and by the time all forty-eight cupcakes were decorated, she was as excited as the girls were to dig in.

"Wait, let's get a selfie," Reese insisted as he pulled his cell phone—the newest phone on the market, from the looks of it—from the front pocket of his well-worn, snug fitting Levi's. He had everyone hold their favorite cupcake, and when they were all happy with their poses, he held up his cell and snapped a couple of pictures.

"I'll text you these later today," he said as he slipped the phone back into his pocket. "If you don't mind giving me your number, that is." He met her gaze for a brief moment, as if to gauge her reaction, before announcing, "Okay, let's eat!"

He took a huge bite of his cupcake, and Summer watched in fascination as he licked vanilla frosting from his bottom lip, the slow drag of his tongue the hottest thing she'd seen in a long time.

She gave herself a mental shake. "Of course not. Remind me before we leave."

He nodded, his grin a little mysterious as he polished off the rest of his cupcake.

After they'd all eaten their fill, Molly asked, "Uncle Reese, can we feed Daisy treats now?"

"You bet." He licked his finger, then wiped his hands with a napkin. "Why don't you grab the sugar cubes and peppermints and meet me out by the stables."

Summer had seen horses back in Redemption, but she'd never ridden one, or even petted one before. She was a bit nervous as they headed out the back door and made their way down the path that led to the stables. Katie ran ahead with Molly, both chattering excitedly while Summer slowed her steps. Reese said something to them she couldn't hear, but figured it out when both girls backed up and stood off to the side.

Reese disappeared inside, reappearing a minute later leading a beautiful brown horse. He waved her forward with a reassuring smile. "Don't worry, Daisy's a sweetheart. She takes from the hand real gentle-like."

Molly shook a couple of sugar cubes onto her palm and handed one to Katie. "Okay, watch, I'll show you how to do it." She held her hand out, and Daisy daintily nibbled her treat off her palm.

"My turn, my turn!" Katie took a step forward.

Summer held her breath as she fought the urge to leap in front of her little girl.

"First, let her sniff your other hand," Reese explained, holding his own out to show her what to do.

The breath eased from her lungs as she watched him demonstrate, his voice soft, his smile reassuring. He really was quite good with the girls, which upped his stock even more.

Katie followed suit, letting out a little squeal when the horse's muzzle touched her hand. "It tickles."

"Now, hold your palm out. Make sure your fingers are straight, and she'll take it nice and gentle." He showed with his own hand how to do it.

Katie fed Daisy her treat and immediately begged to do it again.

Reese chuckled. "We don't want to give her stomach ache, so just a few more. Why don't we try a peppermint." He met Summer's gaze. "C'mon, Mom. Your turn."

She gave her head a shake. "Uh, no, that's okay. Let the girls have their fun."

"Scared?" he teased, grinning.

Boy, does he have a killer smile. Standing with his arms propped on his hips like Superman, black T-shirt stretched taut over his muscular arms and chest, and that gorgeous auburn hair gleaming in the afternoon sun, Reese McMillan made one impressive figure. She came precariously close to sighing like an infatuated teenager.

"Maybe," she wasn't afraid to admit. And she was pretty sure he hadn't expected her response because he frowned slightly, stepped forward, and held out his hand to her, which she took without thought.

"Daisy won't hurt you, I promise. Just hold your palm out flat like the girls did." He pressed one of the unwrapped peppermint candies into her hand.

"Momma, it tickles. It doesn't hurt at all," Katie assured, her little face screwed up with earnest sincerity.

Well, unless she wanted to look like a big baby, she supposed she'd better do it. Summer held her slightly shaking palm out, and squealed nearly as loud as her daughter had when Daisy quickly lipped up the candy.

Reese laughed. "Daisy really loves her peppermints." He let each of them feed the gentle creature one more treat, and just as they were about to head back inside, Angela's dark blue sedan pulled up the driveway and parked on the side of the house.

A tall, dark-haired man got out of the front driver's side and came around to open the passenger door. He helped Angela out, then wrapped an arm around her and shut the door before they both started slowly forward.

"Mommy! Daddy!" Molly cried as she took off running.

James—and she was pretty sure it was her friend's husband this time—released Angela to bend and scoop up their daughter, and all three embraced.

Summer's heart swelled as she watched the loving scene before her. A small hand suddenly slipped inside her own, and she gazed down at her Katie Bear, who watched as her friend was engulfed in her parents' loving arms.

She knew Katie was thinking about her own father; she had just recently started asking about him as his picture was displayed in the living room. Summer hadn't been sure how to handle the questions, so she'd decided on the truth, explaining he'd broken the law, and unfortunately, had to go away for a long time to make up for his mistakes. She'd had no intention of bringing her infant daughter to a prison, even if she could have afforded to do so, which she couldn't. Most days, she was lucky to have enough gas to get to work, school, and home, let alone a facility nearly three hundred miles away.

And yes, part of it was plain, old-fashioned anger and resentment. He'd promised her marriage and a wonderful life together, and delivered poverty, drugs, and womanizing, leaving her to raise their daughter alone, with no family or friends to help her. As far as Summer was concerned, she owed him nothing.

The only decent thing he'd done was assure the court she'd had no knowledge of anything, thankfully saving her from having charges filed against her as well.

Summer forced away the unpleasant thoughts as her friend approached, smiling.

"I hear you guys had quite the afternoon," Angela said with a curious twinkle in her eye.

"I hear you did as well. How are you? I hope the doctor's visit went well."

"Everything is fine," her friend assured. "Summer, I'd like you to meet my husband, James. James, this is Summer Hanson, Katie's mom."

"Nice to meet you." He reached out to shake her hand.

She studied him as she returned his welcome.

James McMillan stood about the same height as his brother, putting them both in the six foot plus category, and while he was certainly handsome, he didn't hold a candle to his gorgeous younger sibling. His features were sterner, the angles of his tanned face a little sharper. They both had the same head of thick, reddish-brown hair, and the same amber-flecked brown eyes. But that's where the comparisons ended. There was a light about Reese she didn't sense in James, who seemed to hold the weight of the world on his shoulders.

Angela beamed as she stepped forward. "How would you like to keep me company while I eat lunch? I've been dying to hear your idiot story all week."

Grinning, she twined her arm with her friend's while casting Reese one last glance. "Turns out it has a surprise ending."

Chapter Four

Reese chuckled as Angela led Summer back to the house, the girls running ahead in a fit of giggles over Lord only knew what. He glanced over at his brother, who sported a frown the size of Texas.

"You okay, bro?" he asked.

James stared after his wife until she disappeared into the house before turning to face him. "Just peachy."

Since he knew the guy had a hell of a load on his mind, Reese ignored his surly reply. "What did the doctor say? How's the baby?"

His brother blew out a hard breath and crossed his arms over his chest. "They have no idea why her blood pressure spiked, no idea why she was cramping. They pretty much ruled out everything and sent us home with instructions for her to get plenty of bed rest, not to strain herself, or pick up anything over ten pounds."

He absorbed the information, which overall didn't sound like such bad news. "So, if they didn't find anything wrong, why do you look like you're about to blow a gasket?"

James cursed. "I just don't understand why they can't figure out what's wrong. It scares the hell out of me. And you know Angela. Bed rest? Fat chance. She spent the entire drive home telling me how ridiculous the doctor's orders were since she's apparently fine, and not about to spend the rest of her pregnancy lying in bed watching TV when she has a job to do."

"Didn't you point out she can simply work from her laptop and rest at the same time?"

James' scowl deepened. "Of course not. The doctor said no stress, and you know how stressful accounting can be." He dragged a hand down his face and took another deep breath. "I mentioned bringing in someone to take over for her, just until after the baby arrived, and she burst into tears."

Reese gave him a sympathetic thump on the back. "Sorry. As hard as this is on Angie, I know it hasn't been easy on you either. But she seemed happy when you guys pulled up."

A reluctant smile cracked his brother's lips. "A song came on the radio that reminded her of our wedding day, she asked if we could stop for ice cream at that place in Denver on Sixteenth Street, and she's been in a great mood since."

"She does like her ice cream."

James nodded, then stared toward the house as something else seemed to claim his attention. Out of the blue, he admitted, "I've also been a little worried about Meara."

Reese recalled how hard the morning had been on her. Though he hadn't planned on bringing it up to James since he already had enough on his plate. "Me, too. Her arthritis has been acting up and—"

"No, it's more than that. She's been tired a lot lately, and forgetful. The other day, she peeled potatoes for dinner, twice, because she forgot she'd already done it."

"She's almost seventy three years old, man. Aren't those things kind of normal at that age?"

"I don't know…maybe. I just wish she'd agree to see a doctor. But you know how stubborn the old girl is."

"That I do, bro. That I do."

Daisy whinnied, and James reached out to pat her neck. "If I could just get Angela on board with hiring someone to help her, it would be one big weight off my shoulders.

Remembering Summer's aborted job interview— and his own unfortunate part in it—an idea formed. "I think I may have a solution for you."

"I still can't believe Reese turned out to be your 'idiot.'"

They were sitting in the living room, with Summer relaxing on the most comfortable sofa she'd ever sat on, while her friend, resting on an equally comfortable-looking matching recliner, polished off a big bowlful of leftover mac and cheese.

"I know, right?" She laughed softly. "Talk about a small world."

Angela set the empty bowl on the end table with a sigh of contentment. "Well, as the very old saying goes, 'all's well that ends well.' I'm just glad you and Katie had a good time."

"We had an amazing time. Though I'm sorry we didn't get to meet Meara."

Her friend cast a glance over her shoulder. "Me, too. She must be coming down with something. It's not like her to nap this long."

Before Summer could respond, the girls raced down the staircase, both giggling.

"Hey, kiddo, you ready to head home?"

Katie's face fell, her bottom lip popping out in disappointment. She wanted to stay, and who could blame her? The McMillan's home was a mansion compared to their tiny apartment. Heck, it was a mansion, period.

Molly ran up to her mother's side. "Can me and Katie have another playdate tomorrow?"

"Honey, I'm sorry, we're busy tomorrow. But we can plan something for next Saturday." Angela met her gaze. "If you guys are free...?"

Katie stared up at her with those big, puppy dog eyes, and she couldn't help but laugh. "We're free. And thank you. Today was the most fun we've had in a long time. Right, peanut?"

Katie gave an enthusiastic nod. "Reese is funny. He showed me how to feed treats to a horse. He's awesome."

"The feeling is mutual, sweetheart."

Summer spun around at the sound of that deep, familiar voice, her pulse picking up speed at the sight of him as he and his brother strode into the living room.

James walked up behind his wife and gently gripped her shoulders. She smiled back at him with such love, Summer could feel their connection as if it were palpable.

Reese ruffled Katie's hair, and smiled at both of them before meeting his sister-in-law's gaze.

"Can we all talk for a minute?"

Taking that as her cue, Summer stood up and dug her keys out of her tote bag. "Katie and I were just on our way out. Thanks so much for having us, all of you. We had a great time." She slung her bag over her shoulder as she met Reese's gaze. "You were definitely an 'awesome' host. Thanks for the hospitality."

"My pleasure. You ladies saved me from an afternoon of hard labor."

James let out a soft snort, and Angela chuckled.

Smiling at their familial teasing, Summer grasped Katie's hand. "C'mon, honey. Time to let these nice people get on with their day."

"Actually, we wanted to run something by you as well," James explained, earning an odd look from his wife.

Summer paused, eyeing both McMillan brothers in surprise before looking over at her friend, who stared at her husband with equal curiosity.

"Um, sure. What is it?"

Reese waved Molly and Katie over. "Why don't you girls go pack up some of those cupcakes for Katie and her mom to take home. Otherwise, I'll end up eating them all myself and ruin my girlish figure."

Both girls laughed and bounced up and down in excitement before racing off for the kitchen.

Reese moved to stand beside his brother. "I explained to James what happened the other day when you were on your way to that interview, and the unfortunate part I played in it."

Angela chuckled. "I still can't believe *you* were the idiot who did that."

He sent her a quelling glance. She laughed even harder.

"My brother and I have several positions we need to fill here at the ranch," James said, casting a look between her and his wife. His gaze settled on Summer. "Most are outdoors, ranch hand, handyman, etcetera. But we've decided to hire someone to take over the bookkeeping duties for Angela while she's on maternity leave."

Summer sat quietly for a moment as she absorbed their offer of a job. Their very generous offer. It felt a lot like charity, but in her position, could she really look a gift horse in the mouth? They had to pay better than the grocery store, and if they gave her enough hours, she'd not only be able to keep up with the rent and bills, but also, maybe, put a little aside for the future.

Finally, she glanced at her friend, whose raised brow said it all. "You didn't know about this, did you?"

Angela eyeballed her husband for an uncomfortable moment before admitting, "No. But...James' is right. I'll need to start training someone to take over for me soon. Like I told you, the doctor put me on bed rest for the rest of my pregnancy, and while I'm not happy about it, I would never do anything to put my baby in jeopardy." She shot James another quick look. "But the position would only be part-time, *and* temporary, and I know you need something full-time and permanent. And with benefits."

"Look, I appreciate the offer of a job more than I can say," Summer told them with a smile of regret. She really would have loved to work here at the ranch. "But I'm pretty sure it's coming from a place of guilt on Reese's part, which is silly since what happened the other day was clearly an accident.

And Angela, this was all just sprung on you, and though you're being very nice about it, clearly you aren't exactly thrilled."

"This isn't charity, I promise you," Reese insisted as he sat beside her. "The women in this family tend to be as stubborn as the day is long." He cast a sidelong glance at his sister-in-law, and Summer had to bite back a grin. "James and I plan to run a want ad soon either way since we need to fill several other jobs before winter settles in. It just seemed to make sense Angie would rather hire a friend to take over for her—someone she likes and trusts—than someone from a temp agency."

Summer smiled apologetically at her new friend. "To be fair, Angela and I haven't known each other that long, and I hate that she's being put on the spot like this."

Angela's expression softened, putting Summer somewhat at ease.

"My brother-in-law is right about one thing, I can be pretty darn stubborn. But I also think I have good instincts, and I *do* trust you. But again, I know you need something full-time, and taking over for me will only give you about twenty hours a week."

"I have a suggestion." Reese shot a glance toward the staircase before lowering his voice. "Mornings have been getting hard on Meara, though she's too proud to ask for help. If you don't mind doing some light housekeeping, we can sell it to her as if we're doing *you* a favor. You could work with

Meara from about eight 'til noon, then Angie can train you on the books after lunch until school lets out. Monday through Friday. What do you think?"

What did she think? That they had to be the kindest, most generous people she'd ever met. She still felt a twinge uneasy over how the job offer came about, but she'd have to be a fool to turn it down. She looked at each one of them before settling her gaze on Reese. "I... Thank you. I gratefully accept your offer."

"Awesome, then it's settled," Reese declared as he rose to his feet. He grinned. "Hey, I don't suppose you'd be willing to wear one of those little French maid numbers?"

"Angie, I think you'd better be the one to tell Meara what we've done," Reese teased once he and Molly returned from walking Summer and Katie to their car. "She'd never hurt a pregnant woman, but James and I might not be so lucky."

"What did you do, Uncle Reese?"

He chucked his niece under the chin. "Nothing, darlin', I was just teasing." He made a mental note to get Summer's cell phone number from Angie so he could send her those pictures. He'd meant to ask, but had gotten distracted while watching her bend over to buckle Katie into her booster seat.

"Katie's mommy is going to come work for us," James explained as he waved his daughter over to sit with him. "She's going to be a big help to Meara, and to Mommy, too."

Molly climbed onto her father's lap, wrapped her little arms around his neck, and gazed up at him as if he were the only person in the room.

A twinge of envy came out of nowhere and hit Reese square in the chest, taking him by surprise.

"Can Katie come work for us, too? Then she could play with me all the time!"

James smiled indulgently. "I'm sure Katie will be spending plenty of time over here once her mom starts her job."

"And once Uncle Reese starts their riding lessons," Angela added with an odd glance in his direction. Though her facial expression gave nothing away, Reese was pretty sure he was about to get a warning.

"And what's that supposed to mean?"

"Come on, Molly," his brother said as he scooped his daughter up. "Let's go check on Meara."

He shot Reese a 'good luck' grin.

Yeah, thanks, bro.

"Are mommy and Uncle Reese gonna have a fight?"

"Of course not, sweetie," Angie assured her. "Mommy just wants to set up some ground rules for when Katie's mom works here. That's all. You and Daddy go make sure Meara is feeling better, okay?"

Molly nodded and tucked her head against her father's neck. James gave them both a pointed look as he carried her from the room.

Chicken shit, Reese thought.

"You know exactly what it means," Angela responded as soon as the door closed. "I saw the way you were eyeing her. Like she was a sixteen-ounce ribeye. Let me make myself perfectly clear right now. I am not going to spend weeks training a replacement only to have her quit on me because you broke her heart."

Slightly offended, Reese crossed his arms and leaned against the wall. "Where is this coming from? I haven't broken any hearts that I'm aware of. I haven't even dated anyone for more than a few weeks in the last... Hell, I don't even remember how long."

"*That's* what concerns me," his sister-in-law insisted. "Summer may not seem it, but she's vulnerable. She's been a single parent since Katie was an infant, her loser ex is in prison, so she doesn't get financial, or any other kind of help from him. She's estranged from her parents, who live in Wisconsin, so she's been completely on her own for over five years. To Summer, this job is a Godsend, and I don't want to see her get hurt."

"Look, I get where you're coming from, but you have nothing to worry about. She's pretty, and I'm attracted, I admit it." When her brow rose in warning, he held out his palm in supplication. "Let me finish. I promise, if we do start to date and it doesn't work out, I'll let her do the dumping."

She rolled her eyes as a reluctant grin broke free. "What a prince you are."

"Exactly," he agreed, relieved to have that settled. "So, why are you always giving me such a hard time?"

"I don't think you want me to answer that," she teased.

He shook his head, exasperated. He was about to head out to the stables to get some work done, but stopped as his curiosity got the better of him. "You said the other day you've only known Summer for a short time, so how is it you know so much about her?"

She shrugged. "I don't know, we just had an instant connection. I have a feeling she hasn't had anyone to confide in for a very long time."

For some reason, the thought of Summer alone and afraid bothered him more than he cared to admit.

Chapter 5

Summer's bad luck returned in a matter of two days. She'd just dropped Katie off at school and was on her way out to the Double M to start the first day of her amazing new job, when her car stalled at a stop sign and wouldn't kick back over. Thankfully, she managed to coast into the lot of some old, abandoned auto garage.

Talk about irony.

She pulled out her cell phone and stared at it, unsure of who to call, Angela or Reese. She needed to let one of them know what happened so they didn't think she'd flaked on her first day of work. Reese was probably out working on the ranch by now, while Angela was more than likely taking it easy, enjoying a cup of tea or something. She closed her eyes for a moment, then dialed her friend.

She answered on the second ring.

"Hello?"

"Angela, it's Summer. I am so sorry to do this on my very first day, but my stupid car just died on me. I'm not far, just a few miles down on Highway 93."

"No shit? Are you all right?"

"I'm fine. I managed to pull it into the parking lot of Singer's—that abandoned auto shop. I'll need to call a tow truck and then get a ride to the ranch. I have no idea when I'll get there." These people had taken a chance on her, and here she was, letting them down on her very first day. Frustrated, she fought back tears.

"Don't bother calling a tow truck. I'll send Reese out to get you. He and John, one of the hands here, can take care of having your car towed."

Unfamiliar with the notion of having friends to count on, she wasn't sure what to say or how to handle it. "I appreciate the offer, but...that's asking kind of a lot."

"Trust me, the guys around here are always happy to help a beautiful damsel in distress. Now, just sit tight. Reese will be there soon." And with that, Angela hung up.

Summer gave her head a shake and slipped her phone back in her purse.

As promised, Reese pulled into Singer's lot less than ten minutes later. He drove up beside her car and gestured for her to pop the hood. Once done, she got out and came around to stand beside him as he peered at her engine.

"Don't tell me you're a mechanic, too?"

He grinned. "Nope, sorry. But John's going to meet us here, said it might be the fuel pump. Soon as he gets here, I'll run you out to the ranch, then come back and give him a hand. His uncle owns an auto shop on the east side, and he owes us a favor or two, so don't fret about the cost."

Though grateful for his assistance, she felt a tad uncomfortable accepting so much help from someone she literally just met two days ago. Her gut told her Reese was a decent guy, but she couldn't help thinking he might have certain... expectations.

"I appreciate that, but I wouldn't feel right if I didn't pay him for the work."

He nodded his understanding. "I'll let you know what he says after he's had a chance to look at it."

"Thank you." Alarm set in as a thought suddenly occurred. She needed to pick Katie up after school, but how could she do that without a car? "Is Angela picking Molly up from school today?"

"No, she asked me to start picking her up. She's a little afraid to drive after Saturday. And James wouldn't allow it anyway."

James wouldn't allow it? She almost laughed. Angela ruled that particular roost, there was no question about that.

"I hate to ask for yet another favor, but if my car isn't fixed by then, would you mind if I tagged along to grab Katie as well?"

"You bet. Not a problem."

She breathed a sigh of relief. "Thank you. I really appreciate everything you've done for me."

He shrugged off her praise. "All I did was help out a friend."

"I know, but you've only known me for a couple of days, and, well…my life tends to be a nonstop train wreck. Just warning you."

"Darlin', you may call this a train wreck, but compared to where I was five years ago, this is just another great day to be alive."

She eyed him with growing curiosity, suddenly eager to learn all there was to know about Reese McMillan. When he didn't elaborate, just stared off down the road as if watching for his friend, she grew a little disappointed. Maybe the connection she'd started to feel was all one sided.

He strode over to his truck, leaned back against the driver side door, and crossed his muscular arms over his broad chest. The man sure did have a nice physique. When she met his gaze, she realized he was staring at her, intently.

"What? Please don't tell me I have something stuck on my face." She ran her fingers over her cheeks and chin, just to make sure.

He grinned. "Just curious."

"About…?"

His eyes narrowed thoughtfully. "You. Beautiful woman, single mother, far from home with no family to help you out."

"I see Angela's been telling my life story." She rolled her eyes, only slightly annoyed with his sister-in-law.

"She was warning me away," he explained. "My French maid comment made her nervous."

"Really? Seemed like a typical joke any man would make."

"Angie's a pit bull when it comes to the people she cares about. And she definitely cares about you. And Katie."

Deciding to open up a bit, she admitted, "Angela's the only real friend I have. I mean, other than Mrs. Langley, the elderly lady who lives in the apartment above us. And a few acquaintances from work."

"You have another job?"

"I've been working part-time at Johnson's SuperMart for a little over three years now. I don't mind the work, but Mr. Johnson won't give me enough hours to qualify for health insurance, and I can't afford it on my own. Most months, it's a miracle if I'm able to make rent, let alone anything else. That's why I was really counting on that position at Henderson & Smythe." She gave a rueful roll of her eyes. "Sorry. I didn't mean to go all 'poor me' on you. I know plenty of people have it worse than I do."

He watched her for a moment, and she would have given anything to know what was going on inside his head. What he thought of her. Besides, perhaps, envisioning her in a French maid's uniform.

"You haven't given your notice yet that you're quitting?"

She gave a hesitant shake of her head. "I was a little afraid to give up my position before I'd even started working for you. I mean, it didn't sound as if Meara was going to be too keen on having me underfoot."

"Don't you worry about Meara. She's stubborn as a mule, but as tenderhearted as they come. She's happy to have the help, we just needed her to think it was *us* helping *you*, and not the other way around."

She nodded, though a niggle of doubt still remained. If it's too good to be true...

"Go ahead and put in your notice. Or just quit outright. Doesn't sound like you owe the guy any consideration, if you ask me. He must know you have a kid. Three years and no benefits?" He gave his head a disgusted shake.

Her gut told her Reese McMillan was someone she could trust, so she decided to confide in him a bit. "He's not exactly the easiest guy to work for, but then, I didn't have a lot of options. No college education, no one to watch Katie. Other than Mrs. Langley, and she could only handle her for a few hours at a time. I was grateful to have her, don't get me wrong. But I was very limited on the hours and times I could work, and Mr. Johnson was kind enough to work around my schedule."

"Well, I can personally promise you have a job at the Double M for as long as you'd like. And I'll have Angela take care of getting you and Katie on our insurance plan. There might be a waiting period, I'm not sure, but it shouldn't be more than a couple months."

Tears burned her eyes. Two days. The man had known her all of two days, and he'd already gotten her a full-time job, helped with her broken down car, and now was offering to put her and her daughter on their health insurance. Her head told her this was all way too good to be true, that the bottom would fall out just as soon as she got too comfortable. But her heart ached to believe her luck had finally turned around. That good things did happen to those who waited. And waited, and waited…

"You okay?" he asked in a near whisper, reaching out to swipe away the lone tear that had escaped down her cheek.

His gaze dropped to her lips, and for a pulse-pounding moment, she swore he was going to kiss her. But just as he started to lean in, a beep rent the air, signaling the arrival of the tow truck.

Reese cleared his throat, gave her shoulder a gentle squeeze, and walked off to greet his friend.

Wow. She breathed deep while willing her racing heart to slow down to its normal pace.

His friend climbed down from the cab of the tow truck and strode forward with an amiable smile. Muscular, average height, with short-cropped, light brown hair and dark, nearly black eyes, John made a surprisingly striking figure.

After a quick introduction, he disappeared under the hood, and in a matter of minutes confirmed the problem was indeed her fuel pump.

"I'll give you a call as soon as I talk to my uncle," he told Reese. "They should be able to have it finished by the end of the day."

"Do you have an idea of how much it's going to cost?" Summer asked.

He shot an unsure glance at Reese, who nodded.

"Normally, you'd be looking at about five to six hundred dollars. But Reese has directed a lot of business my uncle's way, so he's going to take care of it as a favor to him."

Reese gave him a thump on the back. "Hey, man, I appreciate this. I'll see you back at the ranch. And tell Leo I said thanks."

"Will do. It was nice meeting you, Summer." John held up a hand in farewell, and then got to work hooking the car up to the tow truck.

With a hand at the small of her back, Reese led her over to his truck.

Summer held her tongue until they pulled out onto the highway, then said, "Listen, I don't want you to think I don't appreciate everything you've done for me, because I do. Very much. But I'm starting to feel a little uncomfortable with how indebted I am to you. Even if it's just a few bucks a week, I'd really like to pay for the repairs myself."

He cast her a side glance. "Not necessary. The fuel pump itself only costs about fifty to sixty bucks. The labor is what drives the price up. And believe me, Leo has made plenty of money off me, and thanks to me."

"Then I'll pay for the parts. At least let me do that much."

He smiled and gave his head a shake. "You sure are one stubborn woman. No wonder you and Angie get along so well."

"I'm going to take that as a compliment," she declared, holding back a grin.

"Fine. I'll take it out of your first paycheck, okay?"

"Thank you." She bit her lip to hide a small smile of satisfaction.

He let out a playfully exasperated sigh. "Dammit, woman, I'm trying to be all manly here, and you ain't making it easy on me."

"Trust me, you have nothing to worry about on that score." *Oh, no...* Did that really just come out of her mouth?

He turned into the driveway, drove under the arched Double M Ranch sign, and headed down the long-winding road until he pulled to a stop in the same spot he'd been parked in the other day. He turned the engine off, but didn't get out of the truck. Instead, he turned to face her, a playfully smug smile curving those lips.

"Is that right?"

"Is what right?" she demurred, giving her hair a careless toss. "I don't even remember what we were talking about."

"Uh-huh. You know what I think? I think you kinda like me."

She tried to deny it, but the words wouldn't form on her lips. So she feigned a 'get real' eye roll, and threw the door open. But as much as it scared her to admit it, he was right. She was growing to like him more by the minute.

Chapter Six

$\mathcal{R}$eese watched with masculine appreciation as Summer stepped down from the truck and started up the brick walkway that led to the front door, her hips swaying enticingly as she reached up to finger-comb her wavy, blonde hair. She tossed a quick look back, almost as if to make sure he was enjoying the show.

And damn if he wasn't.

Grinning, he gave himself a mental shake and followed after her.

Meara was just coming down the staircase when he entered the house, and she beamed broadly as her gaze landed on Summer.

"Well, hello, young lady." The old girl lumbered forward until she stood before them, that smile as vast and wide as the bright, blue sky. "Summer, I presume?"

"Yes, ma'am."

Reese held back a grin over the little girl tone of her voice. Though Meara was the sweetest woman on the planet, she could invoke a certain amount of intimidation when you first met her.

"I'm so sorry I missed you the other day, I was feeling a little under the weather. I trust you and your daughter enjoyed yourselves?"

Summer smiled. "We did, thank you so much. That was the best macaroni and cheese I've ever tasted. And the frosting was amazing. Had to be homemade, right?"

Wow, it was as if she knew exactly how to get in to the older woman's good graces. Color him impressed.

Meara beamed and nodded confirmation. "I simply can't abide the canned stuff. Tastes like plastic, if you ask me."

"I agree. Though my frosting doesn't even come close to yours."

"Oh, do you cook?" Meara cast a lightning quick look his way, which almost made him laugh.

"I do, though I'm self-taught, so I'm no gourmet chef or anything. I've lived on a pretty strict budget for years, so I've learned to make the basics. And Katie and I try to bake something every week, like brownies, or pineapple upside down cake."

"Very impressive." The shrewd woman tossed another knowing glance his way. "Maybe we should plan a baking party one of these days. I'm sure

Molly would love that. And Reese here would be happy to help taste test. Wouldn't you?"

"It would be my pleasure."

"What about Angela? Wouldn't she like to join us?"

Reese broke into a chuckle, and Meara joined him. No doubt she was also remembering the birthday cake Angela made for James several years back where she'd used salt instead of sugar.

"Angela has many talents," Meara clarified, "but cooking isn't one of them."

"Amen," Reese concurred.

"She tries, bless her heart. But most of her attempts have resulted in the fire alarm going off."

"She forgets to set a timer," Reese explained, grinning.

Between the unsure smile hovering on her lips, and the frown creasing her forehead, Summer's expression was a cross between amusement and confusion.

Thankfully, Meara clapped her hands together, effectively changing the subject. "So, why don't we get a routine set up for you. Are there any household chores you don't care to do?"

"No, ma'am. As a single mother, I've done it all."

Nodding her approval, Meara propped her hands on her ample hips. "Well, now, that's what I like to hear. Not that I'd have you do anything unseemly," she added with a laugh. "But there's plenty to do in this big house, so it'll be nice to have the help. We'll head upstairs first."

She gestured for Summer to precede her to the staircase before casting a smile Reese's way. As long as the old girl thought this was about helping out a young, single mother, all would be right in the McMillan household.

With Summer in good hands, Reese headed out to the stables and saddled Milo, the newest addition to their private stock of Quarter Horses. Spirited, yet easy to handle, the bay roan had quickly become his favorite to ride. He knew James was working with Steve and Franky today, so he hopped on Milo's back and headed out to join them.

The Double M had made some big land purchases over the past five years, giving them a total of just over ninety-six thousand acres, and making them the second largest privately-owned ranch in the state of Colorado. Their biggest single purchase had been a thirty-three-thousand-acre cattle ranch in Park county. Nearly bankrupt due to years of family infighting and mismanagement, they'd picked it up at a rock bottom price. Now, two years later, the McMillan Cattle Ranch was fully staffed and profitable.

They also became a full-service horse ranch, offering both boarding and training, as well as breeding and sales, the last of which had tripled in the last few years. The Double M was now worth close to a hundred-million dollars, more than his grandparents, and great-grandparents, could have ever imagined.

He found them loading hay bales in the southeast pasture. James worked harder than anyone Reese knew. The guy was determined to make sure the future of the ranch was secure, and that everyone he loved would never have to want for anything. The only thing Reese wanted was for James to be proud of him, and he knew that he was, even if he hadn't come to fully trust him yet. *Time and patience*, he reminded himself.

James gave him a welcoming nod as he rode up. "I thought you were gonna start saddle-training that stallion today for Ed Baker's boy."

"I postponed it until tomorrow. Angela got a call from Summer before I headed out." He filled him in on the details.

James straightened and stretched out his back. "What a shitty break. I'm guessing it's an expense she can't afford right now?"

Reese rolled up his sleeves and hefted one of the hay bales. "I told her not to worry about it, that Leo owed us and wouldn't charge her for it. But she insisted on paying for the parts, so I agreed to take it out of her first pay check."

"Sounds fair. And Leo does owe us with all the work we've sent his way."

"That's what I said. Though I'll pay for it myself if the ol' coot balks about it."

James grinned, but didn't say anything.

"What?" Reese demanded.

"I didn't say a damn word."

He grunted and tossed the bale into the truck. "Look, I just feel bad for her, okay? We've never had to think about where our next meal was coming from. She's been raising Katie on her own since she was a baby, no family or friends to help out. And her ex is in prison, so she's never gotten any help on that end either."

"Careful, little brother. You sound like a man dangerously close to falling."

Reese glared at him. "Christ, man, I barely know her. Is it so inconceivable that I just want to help out a fellow human being?"

James held up both hands in surrender, that infuriating grin fading as brotherly concern etched his brow. "Geez, calm down. Just making an observation. This is the first woman I can ever remember you taking a real interest in and, well…I just don't want you getting in over your head. She has a kid, which means she's a package deal. If you two start dating, and things don't work out, she's not the only one who'll get hurt. Not to mention it'll make for an awkward situation here now that she works in our home."

Frustrated, Reese dragged a hand down his face. He did feel a need to take care of her, and he'd never wanted to take care of anyone before. The thought was a little frightening. But if they did start dating, and things went south fast, as they tended to do for him, Katie could be the one who got hurt. He adored the little munchkin, last thing he wanted to do was cause her any pain.

Truth was, the occasional hook-ups he engaged in all ended the same way, with an *"It's been fun. It's me, not you"* phone call once he'd had his fill. Frankly, Reese had started to wonder if he was simply incapable of falling in love.

And then Summer Hanson walked through the door and called him an idiot, knocking his whole world off track. The attraction had been instantaneous, but more than that, he'd genuinely enjoyed spending time with her. And Katie. He found himself eager to learn more about the both of them. Hell, even knowing she was a "package deal" with ex baggage hadn't smothered his interest. It's not like he didn't have plenty of shit in his own past that could send her running for the hills.

He realized James was snapping his fingers in front of his face, and his neck heated with embarrassment. He'd been caught wool-gathering, as Meara would say.

"I'm fine. Let's just get this load finished."

His brother removed his hat and swiped his forearm across his sweated brow. "Not that we can't use the help, but I kind of figured you had something else on your mind…?"

He gave a curt nod, still a little troubled by the direction of his thoughts where the Hanson girls were concerned. "I was hoping you and I could have a conversation tonight after supper. I have a couple of things to run by you."

"Sure thing." James gave him a slap on the shoulder.

They'd just finished loading the truck when his cell phone rang. He dug it from his front jeans pocket and frowned curiously when he noted the caller—Angie. Why would she be calling his phone instead of her husband's? He cast a quick glance at James before answering.

"Hey, what's up?"

"The school called, Katie's sick. She's running a fever, and Summer's pretty upset. I offered to drive her, but she wouldn't hear of it. Wanted to know if you'd heard anything about her car…?"

He checked the time on his phone. "I haven't, but I doubt it'll be ready for at least a few more hours. Listen, tell her I'm on my way. I'm out in the east pasture helping James and the boys collect hay bales."

He disconnected and turned to his brother. "Katie's sick, the school just called. Summer needs a ride to pick her up."

"Go, we're good here."

Reese nodded and hopped on Milo's back. He made it home in record time, passed Milo off to the stable hand, and raced inside the house.

Summer and Angie were both sitting at the kitchen table with glasses of lemonade in front of them; Summer shot to her feet when he rushed in.

"I'm so sorry to bother you. I was going to call a cab, but Angela insisted we call you. I figured my car wouldn't be ready yet, but I was hoping."

"It's no bother, and Angie was right." He smiled reassuringly. "As co-owner, my hours are pretty flexible."

She nodded, and he could see she was fighting back tears.

"Come on, let's go pick up Katie. Do you have a regular pediatrician?"

She shook her head. "Her doctor moved her practice down to Colorado Springs last year, and without insurance…" She shrugged. "I've had a little trouble finding a new one."

He glanced at Angela, who said, "I'm already on it."

"We can always take her to urgent care," he told her as he escorted her from the house. "And before you worry over it, the ranch'll cover the costs. You can settle up once you've got regular paychecks coming in. Agreed?"

She didn't reply right away, no doubt doing inner battle with her enormous pride. "I truly do appreciate the offer. But I simply can't accept. I can afford to pay for the doctor's visit, if need be."

He opened the door of his truck for her, and waited until she was buckled in before slamming it shut. Once they were on the road, he said, "I live a pretty selfish lifestyle, Summer. I don't have any kids, no wife or girlfriend, no one to count on me besides James, Angie, Meara, and Molly." He cast her a sidelong glance. "So let me help you. I promise, I can afford it."

She nibbled her bottom lip—that delectable, pink lip—and stared straight ahead out the windshield. After nearly a minute, she turned to him and quietly asked, "But what would you expect in return?"

Chapter Seven

"*I'*m sorry." Summer immediately regretted the accusation. It's just…what else was she supposed to think? This was all so surreal to her. "I know that wasn't fair, but…we met Saturday, and already you've given me a full-time job with benefits to come, you took care of having my piece of crap car fixed, and now you're taking time out of your workday—second time today—to drive me to pick up my sick kid. You even offered to cover the costs of urgent care, *and* have them taken out of a paycheck I haven't even earned yet."

Reese made a left, then a quick right before giving her a sidelong glance. "Wow, I really am a prince among men," he teased.

"I'm just not used to having someone help me. I've never owed anyone before, and it feels foreign to me. I don't know what you're expecting."

"I'm not expecting a damn thing," he insisted.

His hands seemed to tighten on the steering wheel, and she prayed she hadn't completely overstepped.

He blew out a hard breath and cast her another quick glance. "Look, I hate that you've been on your own for so long that you feel uncomfortable accepting help from anyone. But all I've done, James and Angela, too, is help out a new friend."

A tear escaped, and she nodded as she quickly swiped it away. Mortified, on so many levels, she forced a smile and remained quiet for the rest of the drive.

Relief flooded her when they pulled into the school's parking lot. Reese walked her to the double doors, then pressed the button for the office, and twisted the knob when the buzzer sounded. The offices were immediately to their left, and he waited for her to lead the way inside.

A woman a little younger than Meara sat behind the counter, graying light brown hair pulled back into a tight bun, and eyes framed by overly large, black-framed glasses. She smiled kindly as they approached.

"Hi, my name is Summer Hanson, and I'm here to pick up my daughter, Katie."

"She's still in the nurse's office. I'll go get her for you." She rose from her chair before adding, "I will need you to sign her out, please." She pointed to the open attendance log.

Reese placed a comforting hand on her shoulder as she picked up the pen. Truth be told, she was grateful to have him there with her. She had just finished logging in the time of day when the inner office door opened and the same lady escorted Katie into the room.

"Oh, sweetie," Summer whispered as she stepped forward and wrapped her arms around her. "How are you feeling?"

"I'm sick, Momma," she unnecessarily explained. "The nurse said I should only eat ice chips until my tummy feels better."

Summer picked her daughter up and wrapped her in her arms. Katie laid her head on her shoulder and let out a soft sigh.

The woman handed Reese the purple flowered backpack. "The nurse has three more kids in her office or she would have walked her out herself. Apparently, there's a stomach bug going around, and a fever isn't unusual with this strain. She had Katie lay with an ice pack until you arrived, but she said to give her some children's ibuprofen when you get home, and once the nausea passes, make sure she drinks plenty of fluids, and gets plenty of rest." She smiled at Katie. "Feel better, hun."

"Thank you so much," Summer said, relieved. She'd feared the worst when they told her about the fever.

Reese smiled at the receptionist, then held the doors open while she carried her daughter outside.

"Should we take her to urgent care?"

Summer felt her daughter's forehead—definitely warm, but not hot enough to be alarmed about. "I think I'll just take her home, get some meds in her like the nurse suggested, put a cool washcloth on her head and see how she feels in a couple hours. You said my car should be fixed before the end of the day, so if I need to take her in later, at least I'll be able to drive her myself."

She buckled Katie between them in the seat, and smiled at him over the top of her head. "Thanks again, for everything. And I'm sorry for... questioning your motives."

"Forget about it." He returned the smile, then announced, "Just realized, I have no idea where you live."

She gave a soft laugh. "That would be helpful, wouldn't it? Follow Rubey down to Sixteenth Avenue and make a right. My building is the first one on the left."

"Got it."

He pulled out of the parking lot and followed her direction. They rode in companionable silence, arriving at her place in less than five minutes. She had a moment's hesitation at the thought of him seeing her tiny, sparse apartment. Reese had proven himself to be a gentleman, and would likely insist on seeing them inside.

As she'd silently predicted, he parked in the small lot, stepped out of the truck, then reached back in to unbuckle Katie. He paused. "If you'd like, I'll carry her inside."

"I...Yes, thank you. I'll grab her backpack."

As he lifted her daughter in his arms and cradled her against his shoulder, an overwhelming rush of emotion clogged Summer's throat. He gazed down at her with such tenderness it nearly stole her breath. She didn't dare dream they could have a future with a man like this, and she certainly knew better than to get her hopes up. But Katie deserved so much more than she could ever give her, and it was hard not to dream of a better life for her, especially when she saw how well people like the McMillan's lived. She couldn't help but worry if they continued to spend time with them, Katie would grow attached. Which could only result in heartbreak.

For both of them.

She led him into the building, and he waited while she dug out her keys and unlocked the door. Her apartment, thankfully, was clean, but she felt a rush of embarrassment when he stepped inside and glanced around. To his credit, his gaze betrayed nothing of his inner thoughts. But she could only imagine what he must be thinking when he lived in such a grand house himself.

Ignoring the instinct to preserve what little dignity she had left and send him on his way, she closed the door behind him, set Katie's backpack on the floor beside her brown patterned, threadbare couch, and headed into the small kitchen.

"Pretty sure I have a nearly full bottle of fever reducer leftover from last winter." She opened the small cabinet above the stove and smiled with relief. She grabbed it, thankful the dose cup was attached, and returned to the twelve by twelve box that was her living room slash dining room.

"Katie, are you awake? Momma has to give you some medicine."

She lifted her head and nodded, but when Reese tried to set her down she protested.

He smiled and readjusted her in his arms. "It's okay, I've got you," he promised. "Why don't we sit down on the sofa, and you take your medicine like a big girl."

Katie nodded, gazing up at Reese as if he were the moon and stars himself.

Swallowing down her concern, Summer poured a dose of the grape-flavored liquid. "Okay, are you ready?"

Showing her first sign of energy since they picked her up from school, she took the little cup from Summer's hand and waited for the magic words.

In a sing-song voice that mimicked the owl in the classic sucker commercial, she counted, "One, two-*hoo*, three."

Katie smiled at Reese as if sharing a secret with him, then downed her medicine like the little trooper she was.

He winked his approval. "That's a good girl. How's your tummy?"

"Good. I don't feel like I'm gonna puke anymore."

"Glad to hear it." He tucked a lock of hair behind her ear. "Now, I'm sure your mom wants to get you changed into pjs and tucked into your bed. The sooner you fall asleep, the sooner you'll start to feel better, right?"

She gave a solemn nod.

After setting the medicine on the table, Summer plucked Katie from Reese's lap and held her on her hip. "C'mon, kiddo, let's get some jammies on you." To Reese, she said, "Thanks again for all your help. I have no idea what I would have done today without you."

"I'm happy to help. You just concentrate on getting Katie well. I'll let Meara and Angie know you won't be back for a couple days."

Katie's head popped up from Summer's shoulder, a small frown knitting her little brow. "Don't go. I want you to stay until I feel better."

"Oh, honey, I'm sorry, but Reese has to get home. He has work to do. But we'll see him again soon, right?" She apologized with her eyes for the awkwardness of the moment.

He winked away her worry before smiling at Katie, who stared back with such longing, it was all Summer could do to hold her tears at bay.

"I'm sorry, darlin', your mom's right, I have to get back to the ranch. And you need to get some sleep so you feel better. But, if it's all right with your mother, I'll come back later tonight to check on you."

Summer wasn't sure it was such a good idea for him to be spending so much time with Katie, since her daughter was clearly becoming attached to the kind-hearted cowboy, but she couldn't bring herself to say no. The man's generosity was unfathomable, and she was far from comfortable with this growing need to be in his company.

She was starting to crave the sight of him.

"That would be great. Right, sweetie?" She brushed the hair from her daughter's eyes.

Katie nodded, her eyelids growing heavy. "We can watch a movie."

"Sounds like fun. Maybe I'll bring a pizza." He looked at Summer. "If she's feeling up to it, that is. I know Molly's stomach bugs usually pass within a day, sometimes less."

"That's…incredibly generous of you."

"I'll call you as soon as your car's ready. Maybe John'll be able to drop it off here so we don't have to go pick it up."

"I don't know what to say, that would be great. Thanks so much."

He nodded, holding her gaze for a moment before giving Katie a gentle chuck under the chin. "I'll see you guys later."

Summer stared at the closed door until the revving of his truck snapped her out of her head and got her feet moving.

She carried her daughter into the bedroom and helped her into her pajamas.

"Momma?"

"What, sweetie?" She pulled the pink, lace-edged comforter back, and waited for Katie to settle in before pulling the covers up to her chin.

"Does Molly's uncle like me?"

Shocked by the question, it took Summer a moment to find her voice. "Of course he does. What would make you ask such a question?"

She shrugged, but didn't respond. And since she appeared more curious than upset, Summer chose to let the conversation end on that note.

"I'm thirsty."

She headed into the kitchen for a glass of ice water. When she returned, Katie had her pink giraffe clutched in her fists and snuggled beneath her chin. The plush animal was the first gift she bought for Katie after she was born, and she liked to nuzzle it when she was feeling vulnerable. *My poor baby*.

"Here you go."

She held the glass while Katie leaned forward and took a couple of sips.

"Okay, time to close your eyes and go to sleep. When you wake up from your nap, we'll give you another dose of medicine and see if you feel up to eating some chicken noodle soup. Sound good?"

Another nod. Then she surprised her by asking, "If I don't puke it up, can I have pizza?"

A small smile broke free. "If you can keep the soup down," she agreed. She kissed her daughter on the forehead, which thankfully was only slightly warm compared to when they'd picked her up.

They. As if she and Reese were a team. Oh, God, what was she thinking? It would be way too easy to fall for the guy. Especially if he decided to pursue her. The man was charming, kind, and as handsome as they came. But she knew better than to get caught up in fantasies. She was still trying to pick up the pieces from her last one.

After tonight, she had to start keeping him at arm's length. She just couldn't risk her heart—or her daughter's—on a pipedream.

Chapter Eight

Reese had never before experienced such conflicting emotions. The Hanson girls had somehow found their way past his ironclad defenses, causing him to feel things completely foreign to him. And he couldn't seem to get Summer off his mind, which made it incredibly difficult to concentrate on anything else. *Not a good sign, my friend.*

In desperate need of a shower, he ran into the house and headed upstairs to his bedroom, his mind a jumble of thoughts.

Every woman he'd been with had been about sex. It started with sex, and it ended with sex—once he tired of them. And he always tired of them. He'd never once felt anything more for a woman than intense lust. Hell, he'd started to wonder if he ever would, if maybe there was some sort of defect in his brain.

And then Summer Hanson had stepped out of her little red car and flipped his entire world upside down.

If that weren't enough, he found himself completely enchanted by her daughter. It had been surprisingly hard leaving Katie earlier after being asked so sweetly to stay. He'd wanted to hold her in his arms until she fell asleep, provide whatever comfort it was she'd been looking for. A father figure maybe?

And why didn't that thought scare the living shit out of him? No way was he ready to be father…

But then, was any man ever truly ready?

He'd just finished getting dressed when his cell phone rang. He dug it out of his pocket and checked the display before answering. "Hey Leo. The car ready?"

"Yeah, and sorry for the delay. Two of my guys called in today, and I had a couple of jobs from last night I needed to finish before I could start on your girlfriend's car."

"She's not…" For some inexplicable reason, he decided not to correct Leo about his relationship to Summer. He glanced at the time: almost six o'clock. "Listen, the lady needs her car back ASAP. Can you have it dropped off at her apartment?"

"It was my last job for the day, so I suppose I could drive it over, have Mitchell follow me and bring me back."

"Great. I'll meet you there in about twenty minutes. It's not far from Dairy Queen. I'll text you the address."

He found Meara to let her know where he'd be, then hopped in his truck and headed off to Summer's place, the blood humming through his veins in anticipation of seeing her. A glance at his gas gauge reminded him he needed to fill up first, so he stopped at the convenience store a couple blocks from her apartment building.

Inside, his gaze landed on a soda display, so he picked up a twelve-pack of 7-Up, and a bag of peppermints, remembering Meara used to give the same to him and James whenever they had a tummy ache. A plush frog caught his eye on the way to the register, and on impulse, he grabbed one for Katie. He hesitated for a moment, unsure if Summer would approve. He didn't want to step over any lines before he'd even had a chance to see if the attraction was mutual.

By the time he arrived, Leo was leaning against Summer's car waiting for him. Mitch sat in an old, brown pickup with Gate's Auto and their phone number painted in white on the door.

Leo tossed him the keys, then took a drag off the cigarette hanging from the corner of his salt and pepper bearded mouth. "This makes us even, right?"

"Sure thing." He slipped her keys into his front shirt pocket. "Just let me know what the fuel pump cost. The lady insists on paying for that herself."

"I don't remember exactly, it was around fifty bucks. I can fax you an invoice in the morning, if you'd like."

"I'd appreciate it. Thanks, man."

The mechanic gave him a salute before climbing into the truck. Mitch pulled away from the curb and they disappeared down Sixteenth Street.

Reese grabbed the bag and twelve-pack of soda from his truck, then dug his cell phone out of his front jeans pocket to give her a call, let her know he was there.

"Hello?"

"I take it your phone doesn't have caller ID?"

There was a slight pause. "Reese?"

"It's me. I'm standing outside your apartment. Your car was just dropped off."

"Really? That's awesome, thanks so much. I didn't think it would be ready so fast. Not that I need to go anywhere tonight."

"Does that mean Katie's feeling better?"

"Much better, thank you." He could hear the relief in her voice. "I think it had something to do with a certain promise of pizza."

He chuckled when he realized she was standing there holding the security door open for him, waiting with what could only be described as a shy smile. He stuffed his phone back in his pocket. "Hi."

"Hi. Come on in."

Reese followed her through the hallway into her apartment, and as he stepped inside, he had the same thought as earlier. The place was much too small for them. Katie deserved a backyard, with a swing set, and a puppy running around. And Summer needed a kitchen large enough to move around in. Especially since he was hoping she'd invite him over for dinner one of these days.

Ah, hell.

He plucked her keys from his shirt pocket and handed them to her.

"Thanks. So, what's in the bag?" she asked as she shut the door behind him.

"Just in case Katie's stomach was still queasy, I brought 7-Up and a bag of peppermint starlights. It's what Meara always gave us for a tummy ache, and I figured if there were any leftover, she could bring them to feed to Daisy."

Summer smiled and eyed the bag. "That was very thoughtful, thank you." Her nosed wrinkled with rueful humor. "It seems I say that to you a lot."

He set the soda on the floor next to the door, then pulled the candy from the bag and handed it to her, but hesitated over the frog, a little worried he may have overstepped. "I, uh, bought a little present for Katie." When her eyes lit up with pleasure, he quickly added, "It's nothing major, just a little plush toy." He took it from the bag and held it out for her to see.

The smile she bestowed on him—as if he were some kind of hero out of a romance novel—hit him square in the chest, and he suddenly had to fight the urge to crush her in his arms and kiss her. God, how he wanted to taste those perfectly bowed lips.

He cleared his throat and forced a chuckle. "She'll probably think it's silly."

"Oh, no," she assured him, a slight frown marring her brow. "She'll love it. Katie loves frogs, that's why I was a little surprised."

He gave a self-conscious nod and glanced around. "So, where is she? I hope I didn't come at a bad time, but I just figured since your car was ready..." He shrugged.

"Your timing's perfect, actually. She slept for a good four hours, and woke up feeling much better. Her fever was gone, so she asked if she could take a bath. I'll just get her some fresh pajamas and let her know you're here."

She set her keys and the mints on the counter before heading into the bedroom.

Reese slipped the frog back in the bag and tossed it on the couch. He glanced around, curious to know more about the Hanson girls. A couple of framed photos caught his eye, and he moved closer to get a better look.

A very young-looking Summer held an infant Katie in her arms. The picture appeared to have been taken at the hospital...by Summer's ex, perhaps? She smiled down at her little girl, the love shining in her eyes so profound, Reese had an immediate physical reaction deep in his chest. Like a damn geyser surging up. *Fuck*. He closed his eyes for a moment, stretched his neck from side to side, then forced his attention back to the picture.

Her hair wasn't quite as long as it was now, and she had no makeup on, though she was just as gorgeous, maybe more so. He wondered about her age. He'd thought her to be in her mid-twenties, but he was starting to suspect it was the sexy eye makeup she wore that made her appear older. Because, in the photo, she looked young, sixteen, maybe seventeen, which would make her around twenty-two, at most.

The second photo had to be Katie's father. He looked Greek or Italian, which would explain the young girl's darker coloring since Summer was light blonde and fair-skinned. He picked up the photo and stared at the guy...and a sick wave of recognition dawned. No. It couldn't be... Nico Moretti?

Jesus H. Christ...

He set the framed photo down with such force it toppled over and landed on the floor. Thankfully, the glass didn't break, and he picked it back up and tried again.

"Everything okay in there?" Summer called out.

"Fine, sorry. I accidentally knocked over one of your pictures."

Reeling, he paced around the small living room. Nico was a drug dealer...*his* drug dealer back in the day. He'd met Moretti through James' ex-fiancée, Paige Martin, and her brother Mark, and since the guy had been sleeping with one of Paige's friends, he was shocked to discover he was Summer's ex.

He'd had no clue Moretti had a family. Which made the minuscule amount of guilt he'd felt over his part in the guy's arrest intensify to the point it nearly choked him. Not that he'd had any choice at the time. The sheriff—also known as Paige and Mark's father—had video recordings of them all partying and snorting up a storm in his basement. And on more than one occasion, they'd gone through enough blow to warrant some pretty hefty prison time.

If it had just been Reese, Sheriff Martin would have thrown the proverbial book at him. Didn't matter that he'd been clean for weeks by then after making one of the biggest mistakes of his life. The man despised him thanks to James and Paige's broken engagement—which he knew Reese had been partly responsible for. But, thankfully, he'd had no intention of ruining his own kids' futures, so he'd offered him and Mark a deal. Serve up the person who'd been selling to them and he'd destroy the recordings. Bigger fish and all that.

So they'd set Moretti up. Had him meet them at their usual spot for double their usual buy. The cops moved in immediately and discovered an ounce on him, and later that night, another half a kilo in his apartment…

This apartment? The one he'd shared with his girlfriend and their newborn baby? The thought made him nauseous. He swallowed hard and reached up to massage his temples.

"Hey, you okay?"

He spun around as Summer escorted a smiling Katie into the room. He dropped his hand and smiled back, seeing the beautiful little girl in a whole new light. She'd been deprived of a father for most of her young life, and while he knew he wasn't responsible for Nico's actions, Reese couldn't help but feel a certain amount of obligation toward the woman and child the guy had left behind to fend for themselves.

"Hi!" Katie ran over and gazed up at him. "Momma said you brung soda. I'm not allowed to drink it, but she said I could tonight 'cause it's a special 'casion. We're gonna have pizza!"

He squatted down until they were eye level. "We sure are. In fact, you have a fantastic Italian restaurant not far from here that delivers. Unless you have someplace specific in mind?" He glanced up at Summer.

"Alberti's is the only Italian place I know of close by."

"That's the one. You wouldn't happen to have a menu, would you?"

Her luscious lips puckered as she thought about it. "I don't order out very often, but I may have an old one in the kitchen drawer."

As she went to check for a menu, Reese stood and motioned for Katie to come sit with him on the couch. Once she'd hopped up beside him, he said, "I bought you a little get well present. Hope you like it." He picked up the bag and pulled the frog out with a flourish.

Katie squealed and clapped her hands. "I love him! Can I name him?"

Reese handed over her new friend. "Of course, he's yours."

She hugged the frog and looked up at him as if he'd just lassoed a unicorn for her. Reese's throat constricted. He struggled to hold his emotions in check as he held her worshipful gaze. This amazing little girl had wormed her way into his heart, and he decided right then and there neither her nor her mother would ever have to struggle again. They both deserved so much more than the little they had. And thanks to Nico's bad choices—and his own selfish ones—Summer and Katie barely lived above poverty level.

But that was about to change, whether the stubborn woman wanted it to, or not. Reese could easily afford to make sure they had everything in life they needed, and he planned to do just that.

"I'm gonna name him Jelly 'cause Molly has a stuffed turtle named Peanut Butter, and they're gonna be bestest friends, just like me and Molly."

"I think that's a perfect name." He gave the frog a pat on its head. "Hello, Jelly. I'm sure you're going to be very happy in your new home."

Katie gave a nod of agreement and hugged him to her chest. "He will, I promise."

Reese was a little surprised when she leaned into his side, casting a quick glance up at him as if to gauge his reaction. He made a funny face at her, and she blessed him with the most heart-tugging smile he'd ever seen. Damn if the little cutie didn't make him ache for things he'd never given much thought to before. Like having a family of his own. He'd always wanted a wife and kids...someday. *Way* in the future. But since meeting Katie and her incredible mom, the yearning had been growing stronger.

Whoa. Slow down, man. You don't even know how the lady feels about you, let alone whether she plans to stay in Golden, or Colorado for that matter. He knew she was from Wisconsin, and though her relationship with her parents was nonexistent according to Angela, they were still her parents, and things sometimes changed. He knew that firsthand.

There was also the ex-factor. Once she learned about the sordid connection between him and Nico, it's doubtful she'd want anything more to do with him.

He heard a drawer shut, and looked up in time to see Summer swipe at her eyes. Whatever it was about, he sure as hell hoped those were happy tears. Reese was as clueless as most men when it came to the opposite sex.

She breezed into the living room and waved the menu as if it were a prize. "Found it. Sorry it took so long. I really need to clean out my junk drawer." She sat on the other end of the couch beside her daughter and gave her a kiss on the top of her head before opening the menu. "I'd like to pay for the pizza to thank you for everything you've done for us," she said, casting a quick peek his way.

"I appreciate the offer, but the pizza was my idea, so it's on me. As a gentleman, I must insist."

She nibbled her bottom lip in that sexy way of hers as she sent him another sidelong glance. He knew she could hardly afford to spend money on dinner, let alone Alberti's, which was a little on the pricey side as far as pizza went. But she had pride coming out of her ears, and Reese understood exactly how it felt to be beholden to someone.

"I have a proposition," he said. "You let me buy the pizza tonight, and you two make me supper another night this week. Deal?"

"Yay!" Katie exclaimed, her head whipping around to confer with her mother. "We can make s'ghetti, Momma. And I can butter the bread, and we can make brownies, too.

Summer did the mouth twist thing again, as if not quite sure he'd approve. "Or we could try something new, maybe a roasted chicken?"

Katie's face fell. "But everyone loves s'ghetti."

Reese ruffled her hair. "She's right. I love s'ghetti, and Meara doesn't make it nearly often enough."

Summer gave him a grateful smile, which, for some reason, sparked an immediate reaction below his belt. Stunned by the completely unwelcome response—especially with her daughter snuggled up beside him—he leaned forward a bit and braced his hands on his knees, struggling to get his libido in check. Christ, what the hell was wrong with him?

"Then it's settled," she said, oblivious to his inner turmoil. "You spring for pizza, and we'll make you the best spaghetti dinner you've ever had…Friday okay?"

"Perfect. Now, why don't you order supper while Katie and I decide on what movie to watch."

"Sounds like a plan. What would you like on your pizza?"

"I like pepperonis," Katie told him. "But Momma likes sausage. And can we get French fries?"

He chuckled. "You bet." He looked to Summer. "If it's all right with your mother. And for the record, I like any kind of pizza, so why don't you order the largest size they have, half pepperoni, half sausage. And a large order of fries."

The beautiful blonde nodded, and he prayed to God she didn't smile at him again because he'd yet to recover from the last one.

Chapter Nine

Reese insisted on answering the door when the food arrived, and Summer figured he must have given the delivery driver a pretty impressive tip when she heard, "Cool, thanks a lot."

She was grateful to him on so many levels. He'd been wonderful with Katie, who was quickly growing attached to the handsome cowboy with a heart the size of Texas. And if not for him taking care of her car repairs—she wasn't so sure she believed his story about the guy owing him a favor—she'd be without a vehicle, and have no way to get to work.

The fact she was growing more attracted to him by the hour added a level of complication she couldn't afford to indulge in. Nico was the last man she'd been with—the only man she'd been with—

and that was over five years ago. She hadn't dated, though she'd been asked out here and there, she hadn't flirted, hadn't had any interest in a man since her cheating boyfriend had been taken away in handcuffs while their infant daughter cried in her arms. The mental image was enough to make her shudder, reminding her of how bad her instincts were when it came to the opposite sex.

"Man, this smells good," Reese said as he carried the pizza box and paper bag into the living room. "Should we eat in here while we watch TV, or do you prefer to eat in the kitchen?"

"We can eat in here, right, Momma?" Katie held her cupped palms together in a pleading gesture.

Since they only had two kitchen chairs, Summer agreed with a "Sure, why not?" and started clearing off the coffee table, which her neighbor's daughter had given to her after her father passed away, along with a dresser and nightstand.

She headed into the kitchen to grab plates and napkins, and when she turned around, she ran straight into a hard chest.

"Sorry." Reese reached out to steady her. "Thought I'd give you a hand."

She attempted to ignore the woodsy, masculine scent enveloping her as she handed over the plates. "Uh, thanks. Take these, and I'll grab glasses and ice for the soda."

Having Alberti's pizza for dinner was a luxury for her and Katie, and they both enjoyed their meal immensely while watching *Frozen* for the hundredth time. Reese turned out to be a real trooper, oohing and ahhing when Katie did. They had Popsicles for dessert, and by eight-thirty, her daughter passed out, curled against Reese's side with Jelly clutched in her fist.

"She really bounced back fast," he said in a low tone as he gazed down at her sleeping angel. He brushed the hair back from her face and asked, "Are you sending her to school tomorrow?"

Summer pressed her palm against her daughter's forehead. "She's not warm anymore, though I gave her a dose of medicine a few hours ago. I'll have to see how she's feeling in the morning. Katie loves school, so I hate to keep her home if I don't have to." She met his gaze. "And I'd really hate to miss my second day on the job after missing most of my first."

He waved her concern away. "Don't even worry about that. Trust me, both Angie and Meara would understand."

"You have such an amazing family," she told him. And he did. More kind, generous people she'd never met.

"Can't argue with you there." He slid another look down at her sleeping daughter. "Would you like me to carry her into the bedroom for you?"

She hesitated, his thoughtful offer taking her by surprise. The thought of this man cradling her little girl in his arms warmed her heart. But was it appropriate? Was it too much, too soon? "I appreciate the offer, but I can get her." She scooped Katie into her arms and slowly rose to her feet.

He got up and walked ahead to open the bedroom door.

"Thank you." She laid her daughter down and worked the comforter up and over her. Once she had her settled in, she pressed a gentle kiss to her forehead. As she stood back up, Reese leaned over and followed suit.

The surprise must have shown on her face, because when he straightened and looked at her, his expression grew sheepish.

"I'm sorry, that was a complete overstep. I'm just so used to tucking Molly in that I—"

She stunned him—and herself—by throwing her arms around his neck and kissing him on the lips. After a moment, he lightly settled his hands at her waist, as if taken entirely off-guard.

Or maybe, she'd read the signals wrong and had just made a complete fool of herself.

Summer dropped her arms and broke off the kiss, taking a few seconds to compose herself before gesturing for him to follow her out. Once in the living room, she forced herself to meet his gaze, praying the mortification burning in her chest didn't show on her face.

"I'm so sorry. I have no idea what came over me. It was just..." She shrugged helplessly, finger-combing her hair back, then wrapping her arms around her middle in self-preservation. "I sound like a broken record saying this, but it's been just Katie and me for so long that it felt...nice having someone to count on. Someone to show an interest in my daughter. And I guess I romanticized your kindness in my head and—"

In one fluid motion, Reese slipped an arm around her waist and pulled her flush against his broad chest. Suddenly it was Summer's turn to be stunned speechless.

But instead of kissing her, he admitted in a low, almost rough voice, "I've wanted to kiss you since the moment you stepped out of your car Saturday. And trust me when I say I've never been one to wait things out. But there's something about you, darlin'...it's messed with the way my brain works." He pulled back slightly and gazed down at her with a rueful grin. "And I'd started to fear the attraction was one-sided...until about thirty seconds ago."

"I've never made a first move before," she quietly confessed, her heart racing as long-buried emotions rushed to the surface. Wanting, longing, desire. Her body hummed with the need to feel his warm, soft lips on hers again. It had been so damn long... "It was just...seeing how kind and amazing you are with Katie, I guess...you aren't the only one whose brain is misfiring." A sigh of amusement escaped her, and she dropped her gaze to the floor in awkward embarrassment.

He slid his hand around to her face, softly caressing her cheek with his fingertips before gently tilting her chin up with his thumb, urging her to look at him. "So, what do we do about this…mutual admiration?"

The huskily whispered question both thrilled and terrified her. She wanted him, so much. Which seemed crazy since she barely knew the sexy cowboy. But she couldn't have pulled away if her life depended on it.

He leaned in slowly, as if giving her a chance to pull back. But she wanted to kiss him again more than she wanted her next breath. She grasped the collar of his shirt with both hands and met his lips with hesitant anticipation. Her pulse picked up speed as their mouths joined, the incredible sensation nearly making her light-headed.

His tongue skated along the seal of her lips, seeking entrance. She opened for him, gasping softly as he slipped inside and slanted his head for better access. The hand cupping her face moved to curl around the back of her neck, while his other slid down to the base of her spine and pulled her into the cradle of his hips, molding her against the hard proof of his arousal.

Ignoring the voice in the back of her head that warned they were moving too fast, she twined her arms around his neck and met the rasp of his tongue against hers with needy abandon. Her nipples pebbled against the hard expanse of his work-hardened chest. She ached to slip her hands beneath his shirt and run her fingers over the smooth planes of his muscular pecs. Having never been the aggressor before, the thought suddenly held a lot of appeal.

Funny how much older she felt than her twenty-two years. Jaded in ways she'd never expected, yet…awkwardly inexperienced when it came to love and sex. A small niggle of insecurity caused her a moment of hesitation. What the hell was she thinking…?

Reese's arms wrapped around her, and with a low growl, he picked her up off her feet and carried her to the couch, somehow managing to maneuver around Katie's pile of movies and the coffee table without tripping. He fell onto it backward, so that she ended up on top, straddling his hips.

He finally broke the kiss to whisper, "You okay?"

She pulled her bottom lip between her teeth and managed a nod. "Perfect. You?"

"Never better." He gave a reassuring smile before capturing her face between his large palms and reclaiming her lips.

Summer plastered herself against him, loving the feel of his mouth on hers, the reserved strength in his arms as he crushed her to him, his sexy, masculine scent as it surrounded her. His tongue teased its way past her lips and teeth, and she met it with slow, exploring, light touches.

It had been so long since she'd thought about her own wants and needs. Since she'd felt pretty, or desirable. For the last five plus years, she'd concentrated solely on raising her daughter, a role she cherished more than anything in this world. But it sure did feel nice to be the center of someone's attention for a change. And not just anyone, but the most incredible man she'd ever met.

His hands worked their way down her back, caressing and stroking until he cupped her backside with both hands. She gasped softly and Reese deepened the kiss even more, the stroke of his hot, wet tongue growing more demanding as he held her against the hard ridge of his erection. A slow throb flared to life in response—

A familiar beeping penetrated the sensual fog surrounding her brain. Reese broke off the kiss with a muttered curse.

"I'm sorry," he said as he worked his cell phone free of his front jeans pocket. He looked to see who was calling, muttered another curse, and answered it. "Hey, James, what's up?"

His brother…her *boss*. Hoping her expression didn't reflect the mortification that suddenly warmed her face, Summer extricated herself from his lap, and headed into the kitchen for a glass of water.

She didn't mean to eavesdrop, but because her apartment was so small, and quiet save for the humming of the refrigerator, she couldn't help but hear his half of the conversation.

"Ah, crap. I'm really sorry, man. I had dinner with Summer and Katie, and lost track of time." A pause. "No, I get it. Listen, I'll be home in about fifteen minutes. Otherwise, it can wait until tomorrow." Another pause. "Sounds good. Talk to you soon."

She strolled back into the living room, the water glass clasped between her hands. "I take it you have to go?"

He stood and stuffed the phone back in his pocket. "Yeah. I had asked James if we could talk tonight, and I completely forgot. Got a couple things I want to run by him."

As much as she wanted him to stay, she was pretty sure this interruption was a blessing in disguise. Another few minutes and there'd have been a good chance clothes would have started to fall off. The thought had her clamping her thighs together.

He strode forward and grasped her face, a gesture she found incredibly sexy.

He kissed her, a slow, toe-curling kiss, then stepped back and tucked his hands in his pocket. "I had a nice time tonight."

"Me, too. Thank you for dinner. And for Katie's present. She loves her new frog."

"Jelly the frog," he said with a half-grin. "I'm glad she liked it."

After a few moments of awkward silence, she chuckled softly, and so did he. Summer set her glass down and moved to the door. She hated for the night to end, but they both had to work in the morning.

Under the same roof.

What the hell was I thinking?

"So, I guess I'll see you in the morning. I mean, assuming Katie's well enough to go to school," he amended.

"I have a feeling she'll make it. If not, I'll give Angela a call so she can let Meara know." She opened the door and stepped back, giving a small wave.

He chuckled and gave her a quick peck as he walked by. "Good night, Summer. Sweet dreams."

"I don't know how *sweet* they'll be," she softly admitted, earning another chuckle.

She caught her bottom lip between her teeth as she watched him walk out of her apartment. A wistful sigh escaped her. She shut the door and leaned against it, closing her eyes as she sucked in a few deep breaths. Her lips still tingled from his kisses, and her body hummed with unfulfilled desire. She wanted him. Lord, how she wanted him.

After everything Nico had put her through, she'd had no interest in the opposite sex. Not that she'd had plans to join a convent or anything. But she'd done what a good mother does, and focused all of her energy on raising her daughter. The day to day struggle of being a single parent left very little time to focus on anything else—most especially dating.

She'd certainly been in no hurry to make the same mistakes again.

And it seemed her patience had finally paid off, delivering a good man into her life just when she'd all but given up hope they even existed. Now, here she was, daring to dream of a future that didn't involve growing old bitter and alone.

Smiling ruefully at her melodramatic thoughts, Summer turned the deadbolt, then headed into the bathroom to get ready for bed. She was only twenty-three, for goodness sake, even if all the heavy responsibility sometimes made her feel much older. It just felt good to know love could be in the cards for her after all.

Her sexy cowboy was the polar opposite of Nico, a womanizing, drug-dealing junkie who cared so little for her and their daughter he'd sold cocaine right out of their apartment, putting them all at risk. Not only from the police, but from anyone who might have tried to break in and rob them. How she could have ever fallen for such a man was beyond her.

Yep, Reese McMillan was a perfect example that good men truly did exist.

Chapter Ten

$\mathcal{R}$eese climbed into his truck and turned the key in the ignition, his mind spinning as the engine roared to life. He blew out a hard breath and leaned his head back as he struggled to get his racing heart under control.

Damn, this is bad.

He'd never had such a visceral reaction to a woman before, and it scared the living hell out of him. The primal urge to storm back into her apartment and take what she so lovingly offered nearly overpowered him.

"Christ, man, get it together," he muttered as he threw the truck into gear and practically peeled out of there.

Okay, so his feelings for Summer were stronger than they'd ever been for any other woman.

Combine that with need to make things right for her and Katie after discovering who her ex was, and he was experiencing some pretty powerful emotions. Once the newness of everything settled down, he'd be able to channel his focus back where it needed to be—the ranch, and his future.

But were Summer and Katie a part of that future? Hell, he had no idea. What he did know was they were both a part of his life now, and he had every intention of taking care of them for as long as they needed him. He owed them that much.

And, as the attraction between him and Summer was mutual and undeniable, there was no reason they couldn't enjoy each other's company in the meantime, right? While he had no real illusions they were going to live happily ever after, he wasn't averse to seeing where things led, whether they simply dated for a while, and ended up as friends, or, the more likely scenario, she found out about his past, and his part in getting Katie's father put in jail, and dumped him.

So why did the thought of not having them in his life bring an ache to his chest?

This was exactly why he'd always steered clear of emotional involvements. *Too friggin' draining.*

Pushing thoughts of the Hanson girls to the back of his mind, he forced himself to focus on his meeting with James, and how to start the conversation. He knew his brother didn't fully trust him, though Reese had done everything within his power to prove himself after the appalling way he'd betrayed him years ago. His regret ran deep, but he loved his brother and swore at the time he'd do whatever he needed to, no matter how long it took, to earn back his trust.

But five years later, James still wouldn't sell him the one percent that would make them full and equal partners, and Reese's patience was starting to wear thin. He knew his brother had been justified in making him prove his commitment to the ranch, and to his vow to stay off drugs.

The latter had been surprisingly easy. Ending up in bed with James' fiancée had been exactly the wakeup call he'd needed. Unfortunately, James had walked in on them, and the hurt and desolation in his brother's eyes had been more than Reese could bear. As children, they'd been as close as two brothers could be. But once they entered their teen years, their relationship slowly changed. He'd felt as if his grandparents began to favor James, and bitterness took hold and grew, until Reese's resentment led him to make a lot of bad choices. He'd started running around with a fast crowd, staying out late, partying, acting out.

Now that he was older and looked at life through an adult's perspective, he realized his resentment had stemmed from jealousy, and not favoritism. James rode better than him, learned faster, and frankly, showed more interest in the running of the ranch. It's not that Reese hadn't been interested in the ranch, he'd just wanted to have fun, hang out with his friends, be a kid. While James always had a certain maturity about him; his demeanor, even as a kid, had been thoughtful and reserved, whereas Reese had been a little wild and rambunctious.

At the moment, those days seemed like another lifetime ago.

Making it home in record time, he pulled into the garage and hurried into the house. James had said he'd wait up for him, even though it was close to nine-thirty, and the rest of the house was likely all asleep by now. He headed into the study, surprised to see his brother tossing back a couple fingers of bourbon. His hair was mussed, as if he'd run his fingers through it a couple dozen times, and his eyes bore distinct lines of worry. There was a weariness about him that bespoke of a man with a lot on his mind.

Reese took a seat across from him and rested his elbows on the arm rests. "You all right?"

"Fuckin' peachy." James poured himself another drink and gulped it down before offering Reese one.

"No, thanks." He gave his brother a second onceover. "Listen, maybe we should postpone this for another night. You don't look like you're in the mood to talk business." And frankly, Reese had hoped to have him in a good mood and at full attention when they did talk.

But James dismissed his worry with a wave of his hand and sat up a little straighter. "I'm fine. I just like to make sure Angela's sleeping before I head to bed so my snoring doesn't keep her up."

Though James *had* been known to snore now and then, Reese got the distinct feeling there was a little more to it than that. A sidelong glance at the couch, where a pillow and folded blanket sat, confirmed his suspicions—his brother had been sleeping in the study. But Reese knew their marriage was solid, so he wasn't worried, just…concerned.

James must have realized where Reese's gaze had landed as he gave his head an exasperated shake before admitting, "I'm just a little afraid I'll roll over and hurt the baby, okay? I told Angela I've been working on a new project, and slept in here the last few nights. Please don't make a big deal out of it."

"That leather sofa can't be very comfortable. Why not just crash in your old room? Or one of the spare bedrooms?" Because Angela had fallen in love with Gran's room, they'd moved in there after the wedding.

"Hell, I don't know. I guess it felt less like I was avoiding sleeping with my wife, and more like I just didn't want to wake her if I crashed in here. Not that she's complained." A rueful grin quirked his mouth. "Pretty sure she's happy to have the bed to herself these days. Plus, I didn't want to worry Meara. I don't know if you've noticed, but the old girl's been especially touchy lately. Like she's scared, but doesn't want us to know it."

Reese gave a nod as he settled back in the chair. He'd noticed, but had been trying not to dwell on it too much. Meara had always been their rock, the glue that held the family together even during the worst of times. The realization that she might be entering her twilight years was something neither of them wanted to think about. Losing Gran had been hard enough. Losing Meara, too, would be unfathomable.

"So," James began as he leaned back again and crossed his arms. "Something going on between you and our new hire you'd like to tell me about?"

Reese debated whether to tell him the full story, or just the bare basics. He decided on the latter. "I like her. And I like Katie. They're pretty much all alone in the world, so I've been helping out a bit."

"Like paying for the repairs on her car?"

Reese tried and failed to hide a scowl. "Leo owed me a favor. I used it on Summer. You got a problem with that?"

"'Course not. I'm just afraid you're gonna do what you always do—break her heart. The problem is," he continued, holding up a hand when Reese would have interrupted, "there's a little girl's feeling involved this time, and she happens to be Molly's friend."

"Look—"

"I don't give a shit who you sleep with," James quickly added, cutting him off. "But Angela's worried about her friend, and she was obviously right about your involvement with her. Summer's going to be working under this roof, and I don't want her quitting before Meara and Angela have even had a chance to train her. All I want is a little peace and harmony in my life."

"Man, if you start singing "Kumbaya," I'm outta here," Reese teased, hoping to bring the level of gravity down a notch. When James' frown deepened, he sighed and conceded, "Okay, look. I like her. A lot. I don't know where it's going, and I can't promise it's going to end with some fairy tale wedding like you and Ang. But…it's more than just wanting to sleep with her, I can promise you that."

James stared at him for a couple heartbeats before giving a slight nod of approval and leaning back again in the massive leather armchair—their grandfather's chair. "I'll take it. So, let's talk business. And quickly, please. I have to get up early tomorrow to oversee the breeding of that new mare."

Deep breath. Here it goes. "I think by now you would agree that I've proven myself to be fully committed to the Double M. I work hard, day after day, I've learned more about the business side, as well as the running of the ranch, than anyone ever thought possible, including myself. And I believe that if Gran were still alive, she'd agree the time has come. I'm asking you to sell me the one percent that would make us full and equal partners."

He waited, pulse speeding, as James mulled over everything he'd said. He knew throwing Gran's name in had been a little bit of a Hail Mary, but it was true nonetheless. And James had to feel the same by now. They were as close as they'd been in years, and no one could doubt Reese's dedication and loyalty to the ranch. Not to mention, many of their most profitable transactions and land purchases were deals Reese had been directly responsible for.

Maybe he should take James' silence as a good sign and forge right on with his proposition to open a dude ranch on the new property they—

"Is this about that resort you've been talking to the guys about?"

Reese's jaw clenched. John and his big frickin' mouth.

"Listen, it's not that I'm completely opposed. But we have so much else going on that I don't see how we can seriously consider such a huge project when we're spread as thin as we are. And if I'm being honest, this is exactly why I'm not quite ready to give up control."

He flexed his hands as bitter resentment surged through his veins. Five years ago, he would have stormed out of there in a fit of rage. But he wasn't going to revert back to the spoiled, angry idiot he'd been. He loved this ranch, and yes, he loved his infuriating brother. He'd sworn to James, and to himself, that he'd work as hard as he could, wait as long as he had to in order to win back his trust. So, once again, he tamped down on the disappointment, reined in his frustration, and rose to his feet.

"I'll see you in the morning." He turned and strode for the door. The squeaking of James' chair announced he'd stood, too.

"I was patient with you when you needed me to be," his brother reminded him. "Now I'm asking for the same in return. Okay? We'll talk about this again soon, I promise. It's just…I have so much on my plate right now, if I have to deal with one more thing, I swear my fuckin' head will explode."

Remorse hit him square in the gut, and Reese spun back around to face him. *Damn*. No one knew better than he did just how much stress his brother was under—and had been under for some time. And yet he'd chosen *now* to add to it?

He propped his hands on his hips and hung his head for a second. "Look, I'm sorry. You're right. I should have waited, at least until after the baby's born, to bring this shit up again. We'll table the subject for now. Get some sleep, we've got a long day tomorrow."

James gave a grateful nod. "Hope Meara remembered to add an extra scoop of coffee for morning. I'm gonna need it."

"I'll double check while I'm down there. I suddenly have a taste for a peanut butter and jelly sandwich."

James chuckled and shook his head. "'Night, bro. And…thanks."

Reese grinned before softly shutting the door behind him.

He headed down to the kitchen, not bothering to turn on the light since the nearly full moon shone bright enough through the back window to fully illuminate the spacious room. He took a peek inside the basket that held the grounds for the coffeemaker, added an extra scoop from the canister on the counter, then went in search of the peanut butter. Once he had his sandwich assembled, he wolfed it down in four bites.

Exhaustion seeped into his bones as the adrenaline rush from his passionate *encounter* with Summer finally dissipated. Though his need for her still simmered just below the surface. And as anticipation of seeing her again tomorrow took hold, he headed off to bed feeling happier than he had in years.

Chapter Eleven

$\mathcal{T}$hankfully, Katie woke up fever-free the following morning, chattering excitedly about their pizza and movie date with Reese, and eager to go to school and tell Molly all about it. She even begged to take her new "friend" along, though Summer reminded her to ask the teacher's permission before taking Jelly out of her backpack.

After dropping her daughter off, she headed out to the ranch. A small twinge of uneasiness hit her when she rolled up to the stop sign she'd stalled at the previous morning, but when she took her foot off the brake and eased down the gas pedal, the car pulled away and hummed down the road without incident. Hell, it seemed to be running better than it ever had. Since Nico bought it off some used car lot a couple weeks after they'd arrived in town.

Her thoughts quickly turned to Reese and of the incredible kisses they'd shared. The connection between them had been undeniable, the chemistry explosive…though she didn't want to get ahead of herself. They'd had a nice time, they were obviously attracted to each other. But, after being celibate for over five years, it would be way too easy to romanticize this, make it into something it wasn't. The last thing she wanted to do was assume they were dating.

She drove down the long-winding driveway and parked next to Reese's truck, which sat in its usual spot between the massive log cabin house and the separate six-stall garage. Humming, she got out of her car and headed up the walkway, surprised to find Meara standing on the front porch, as if she'd been waiting for her.

The older woman greeted her with a cheerful smile and waved her inside. "Good morning. And how is Miss Katie feeling today?"

"Much better, thank you for asking." Summer stepped past her into the gorgeous tiled foyer. "I just dropped her off at school."

"I'm so glad to hear it." Meara closed the door and turned a suspiciously knowing smile her way. "I'm hoping my boy had a little something to do with it. I hear he's quite fond of…her."

She lumbered past, and Summer shook her head over the not-so-subtle double meaning. She followed after her while quietly admitting, "She's pretty fond of him as well."

The older woman glanced over her shoulder, mischief dancing in her eyes. "Good to know."

Summer inwardly groaned as she followed her into the kitchen.

Meara clapped her hands together, as if signaling a change of subject. "I wanted to start washing windows today. Are you up for it?"

She held her arms up and flexed her nonexistent muscles, striking a bodybuilder's pose. "I'm able-bodied and up for anything you have for me to do."

"I like your attitude, young lady." Meara gave a decisive nod, lifted a couple of buckets from the floor filled with window cleaner and paper towels, and handed one to Summer. "We'll start down here in the kitchen and work around to the living room. It should be lunchtime by then, and I know Angela would love for you to join her out on the back porch. Then she can get started teaching you the books. We'll finish the windows tomorrow. Ready?"

"Yes, ma'am."

By the time noon rolled around, Summer was more than ready to break for lunch. She and Meara had managed to finish all the downstairs windows, which totaled twenty including the gorgeous bay window in the living room that overlooked the east pasture.

"You're a hard worker, my dear. I'm quite impressed."

Meara gazed at her with such adoration she nearly blushed.

"Thank you. I appreciate that. Though I have to admit, I'm exhausted and hungry."

Meara chuckled. "Well, I hope you like chicken chili and ham sandwiches. It's what Angela was craving yesterday."

"Sounds amazing. I'm not a picky eater. If I didn't like what my mother made, I didn't eat." Which was why she was such a skinny kid. The only meals her mother ever made were meatloaf, beef stew, and tuna casserole, and all were as bland as could be. Though she had a feeling everything Meara made was delicious. That macaroni and cheese was certainly to die for. "Can I give you a hand?"

"The chili is already simmering, so it won't take me but a few minutes to get everything else ready. Why don't you go up and help Angela downstairs. She's the last door on the left."

After washing her hands, Summer made her way up the grand staircase that led to the open style second story, then headed down to the end of the hallway. The door stood open, but she knocked anyway.

Angela, as cheerful and radiant as ever, smiled and waved her in. After casting a surreptitious glance out into the hallway, she closed the door and immediately demanded, "Okay, I want to hear all about your date with Reese."

"We had pizza and watched a Disney movie." She smiled. "It was really nice, but I wouldn't call it a date." Though it had certainly ended like one.

Her friend's mouth sagged, her expression saying, *gimme a break.*

Summer sighed, not quite ready to even examine the situation in the privacy of her own mind, let alone talk about it aloud. But then, she'd never had anyone to confide in before until Angela, who knew more about her than anyone else in this world. So, why not?

She walked over to the window, drawn there by the magnificent beauty beyond. "What an amazing view."

Angela waddled over and stood beside her. An arm wrapped around Summer's shoulders, surprising her, and she was nearly overwhelmed by the most ridiculous urge to cry. She breathed deep in an effort to pull herself together. Good Lord, what was it about these amazing people that made her such an emotional basket case?

"When I first arrived in Colorado," her friend finally said, "I was so focused on finding the ranch, it wasn't until James brought me up to this room— his grandmother's room—that I finally looked outside and realized just how beautiful this place is. Like Heaven on earth."

"I've been here for almost six years now, but…I don't know. I guess I never really took the time to look around me." Regret lay heavy in her chest. "Spent most of my time taking care of Katie and feeling sorry for myself."

Angela dropped her arm and made her way over to the bed to slip into her shoes. "Trust me, I can relate.

Felt that way most of my life. Wasn't until I landed here that I truly started living." She pressed a hand to her rounded belly and a wistful smile touched her lips. "Well, this baby is ready to eat. Shall we?" She extended her arm in a dutiful manner.

Summer grinned. "We shall. I'm so hungry I could eat a horse."

Angela slapped a hand over her mouth, her eyes twinkling with mirth.

When Summer realized her faux pas, she burst into laughter. "I can't believe I said that!"

They were still chuckling as they stepped out onto the back porch, which Meara had set up in a fairy tale manner. Sparkling glassware and shiny, white dishes with a pretty floral pattern. A crystal vase filled with an arrangement of the purple and yellow flowers she'd seen growing on the side of the house. And a table laden with enough food to feed a small army. If these people ate like this every day, they must work out religiously to all stay so slim. But then, she supposed the hard labor of running a horse ranch was enough of a workout for anyone. If Reese's muscular physique was any indication, they must put in some pretty long, strenuous hours.

She realized Meara had set four place settings just as Angela asked, "Are the guys joining us for lunch?"

Meara beamed as she poured them each a glass of sweet tea. "James called just after I'd sent

Summer up to get you." She turned toward the west, and that's when Summer heard the thundering of hooves. "In fact, that's them now. I'll take my leave right after I serve. And don't either of you even think about cleaning up out here," she warned, casting them both a look of caution.

"We wouldn't dare, Meara," Angela assured her before Summer could respond.

She had no idea why the older woman was so adamant about not needing help. Pride, she supposed. And since Angela didn't seem too concerned, she decided not to worry about it. Though it did go against the grain to leave a mess for someone else to clean up.

Familiar male voices announced the men's arrival, and she looked up just as they rounded the corner. Summer found herself sitting up a little straighter as they strode over to join them.

James rushed up and wrapped his arms around his wife, whose glowing eyes and beaming smile bespoke of the deep love and affection between them.

Reese didn't approach her, but he did send a secretive little wink as he sat across from her. Her cheeks warmed at the subtle reminder of the intimacy they'd shared the night before.

"This looks wonderful," James told Meara as he straightened, "but we can handle it from here. Why don't you go on and take a break." He kissed the older woman on the forehead and murmured, "You work too hard."

Meara fluttered as if she'd just been paid the mother of all compliments. "I don't mind serving, but if you're sure…?"

"We've got this. Please, humor me and go take a load off. Maybe a little cat nap."

She seemed to think about it, then gave a decisive nod. "I think I will. Enjoy your meal. And remember what I said." She cast a meaningful glance at both Summer and Angela. "Leave the cleanup for me."

Summer waited until Meara disappeared into the house, then asked, "How come she doesn't join us for lunch? I mean, she made all the food, it only seems fair."

"Meara's old school when it comes to that sort of thing," Reese explained. "She prefers to take her meals in the kitchen, except on holidays, when we insist she join us."

"Duty and station are very important to her," James added. "She was born into a family of servants for one of the richest families in Ireland, so it's how she was raised."

"I had no idea, and I guess that all makes sense. It just seems to me if she made the meal, she should sit down and enjoy it. Because it's pretty obvious she is way more to you guys than a housekeeper."

"Meara's as close to family as a body can get without being blood related," Angela explained, casting a cheeky grin over her shoulder at her husband.

Must be a private joke.

James kissed his wife and returned her grin. "That she is."

He stood and took the top off the crock that held the chicken chili. "Everybody hungry?"

Summer's stomach rumbled, though thankfully not loud enough for anyone to hear.

Feeling as if she should do something—these people were, after all, paying her to help Meara—she stood and picked up the plate of sandwiches. "Please, let me help. After everything you've all done for Katie and me, the least I can do is serve the lunch."

James smiled his appreciation as he set the lid down and picked up his wife's bowl. "How about if you serve the sandwiches, and I pour the chili?"

"Well, now, I could get used to this," Reese teased as Summer set a thick ham sandwich on his plate. To his sister-in-law, he said, "Tell me you aren't picturing James in a French maid's outfit right now."

Angela pursed her lips and thoughtfully studied her husband, while James shot his brother a *fuck off* glance. Angela gave him a pat on the backside, Reese laughed, and a comfortable conversation was struck up as they all ate Meara's delicious lunch.

Summer smiled. As she got to know the family better, she really came to appreciate what wonderful, caring people they were. She already knew Angela to be a great friend. And Reese, well, besides being the sexiest man on the planet, was kind and generous. James, while reserved, had a wicked sense of humor, and was fiercely devoted to his wife.

So why did she suddenly feel like an outsider? Like she had nothing at all in common with them…or maybe wasn't quite good enough to be in their company? Frustrated with herself for such negative thoughts, she swallowed her self-doubt and allowed herself to enjoy the incredible food, and even better company.

Finally, Reese wiped his mouth with a linen napkin. "That was tasty; another homerun for Meara." He stood. "Well, I guess we'd better get back to work."

James nodded. He leaned in close to his wife and said in a soft tone, "Are you tired? Would you like me to help you upstairs?"

Angela gazed up at him with such love and adoration that Summer felt as if she were invading on a private moment.

"I'll be fine, you worry too much," she gently admonished.

James settled his gaze on Summer. "Will you please make sure she gets upstairs without incident?"

"Of course, no worries." She smiled reassuringly, then asked Angela, "Are you going to start teaching me the books today?"

"I am. I have a desk in my room, so we can work upstairs."

James rose and helped his wife to her feet. "See you in a few hours," he murmured before giving her one last kiss.

Reese made a teasing face behind his brother's back, then said to Summer, "I was thinking, maybe I could give you and Katie a riding lesson later today. What'd'ya think, are you ready to get on a horse?"

"I don't know about me, but Katie certainly is, so thank you."

"Definitely better than eating one," Angela pointed out with a smirk, and both of them exploded with laughter.

He cast her a curious smile before following after James. Summer continued to chuckle as she watched him walk away.

Learning the books, as it turned out, was easier than she'd feared, and Angela, thankfully, was a wonderful teacher. The software she used wasn't hard to learn, and her system was easy enough to follow, even for a novice like Summer.

"You're a quick learner, though I'm not the least bit surprised," her friend told her, followed by a huge yawn.

"Thank you. I think it has more to do with how patient you are." She stood and nodded toward the bed. "But now it's time for you to take a nap." When Angela frowned in protest, Summer reminded, "I promised your husband, please don't make a liar of me. Besides, it's almost time for school to let out. I'll pick up both girls since Katie and I are heading back this way for that riding lesson."

"That would be great, thank you."

When Angela struggled to her feet, Summer hurried forward to lend a hand—and a shoulder.

"I feel like a little old lady," the pregnant blonde complained with a soft chuckle. "I'm not an invalid, you know."

"I know. But if you happened to lose your balance and fall, I'd never forgive myself. And your incredibly protective husband would have my head. So please, humor me."

"Sorry." Angela grinned. "He *can* be a little intense."

She almost laughed aloud at the understatement. "He loves you."

Summer helped her onto the massive sleigh-style bed.

Angela tucked a pillow between her knees as she got comfortable. She let out a delicate yawn. "Thanks for saving him a trip to the school."

"After everything your family's done for me and Katie, I'm happy to finally be able to do something in return. Now rest. I'll see you later."

After calling Reese on his cell to let him know she would be picking up the girls from school, Summer hopped in her car and headed out.

The dismissal bell rang at three-oh-eight, and the girls came strolling out arm in arm, chattering away in their adorably animated way. They were excited to be riding back to the ranch together, especially when she told them why. She smiled as she listened to Molly explain in great detail how her daddy and her uncle Reese were the two "bestest" riders in Colorado, maybe even the whole world. Katie squealed and clapped her hands, her face glowing with anticipation.

Seeing her daughter's eyes alive with eagerness filled Summer with such joy. It was the little things at that age that made life so amazing. She sure wished she'd had more of those moments as a child, and couldn't help wondering if her own mother had ever felt the same about her.

When they arrived at the ranch, James and Reese were waiting out in the driveway. The girls practically jumped out of the car and raced off toward them. Summer had to blink back tears when Reese caught Katie around the waist and tossed her gently into the air, just as James did with Molly.

She suffered a panicky moment of unease, wondering if her daughter was becoming way too attached to her friend's uncle, way too fast. While it warmed her heart to see her so happy, and though she appreciated the attention Reese showed her, deep down she knew it was foolish to let Katie form an attachment to the kind-hearted cowboy.

But she had nothing significant to justify her fear, only her own misgivings, so she tamped them down, pasted a bright smile on her face, and followed after her daughter.

Chapter Twelve

Reese picked Katie up and gave her a "fun toss," something he and James had learned from their grandfather as little boys, causing her to squeal with delight. He tried not to examine too closely why his heart swelled with excitement when she'd emerged from the car and raced toward him. The joy that transformed her little face as she caught sight of him triggered an ache in his chest that nearly brought him to his knees.

He set her on her feet and asked, "So, how was school? No more tummy aches?"

She gave her head an emphatic shake. "I felt really good. I think the pizza made me better. And I brung Jelly to school to show all my friends."

"I'm glad you like him. Is Jelly behaving himself?" His heart thudded as Summer approached—just as it had earlier when he'd laid eyes on her at lunch. He started to seriously wonder if these Hanson girls had cast a spell on him.

Another nod. "Yep. He's a real good boy."

Reese ruffled her hair. "Glad to hear it. So, I'm going to give you and your mom a riding lesson today. How does that sound?"

"Awesome!" She turned to her friend. "Molly, wanna watch me ride a horse?"

"Sure! But I'm gonna go see my mom first. She's gotta stay in bed a lot now cause of the baby."

"Okay."

James picked Molly back up in his arms. "We'll be back down in a little while."

"Sounds good. We'll go over the basics first anyway."

Summer held Katie's hand, so he grasped her other and led them both to the stables where Daisy was already saddled and ready to go. "Okay, safety first. Normally, I would suggest wearing a pair of boots, but sneakers are fine to start out with."

"Momma, can we buy cowboy boots like Reese?"

"We'll see, honey." She gently cupped her daughter's cheek, and Reese felt a twinge of guilt for putting her in such a position. He knew she could barely make ends meet, let alone afford a new pair of boots just for riding lessons.

"Also," he continued, "never wear shorts or capris for riding. You could get chafed pretty badly from the friction of rubbing against the saddle." He was glad they both wore pants today. "And always make sure to never stand behind a horse. They kick, and we wouldn't want to have an accident, understand?"

Katie gave a solemn nod, while Summer said, "Got it."

"So, now it's time to reintroduce yourself to Daisy. Let her sniff the back of your hand, just like you did last time."

Reese knelt down beside Katie and showed her again how to do it. She giggled when Daisy snuffled against her knuckles.

"See? She remembers you."

"Really?" Katie turned big, soulful brown eyes on him, and he had to fight the urge to give her a big hug.

"You bet. Now, how would you like to get on Daisy's back with me and take a walk around the paddock over there?" He pointed to the fenced enclosure set about a hundred feet behind the stables.

Katie clapped her hands together and bounced up and down. Summer met his gaze for a brief moment, her smile a little hesitant. Was she already regretting...whatever the hell it was going on between them? Because, man, just looking at her sent his heartrate skyrocketing. *She's just nervous around horses*, he reminded himself as he shook off his worry and forced himself to focus.

"Okay, I'm going to climb up on Daisy's back, then have your mommy hand you up to me. And don't worry, she's as gentle as a lamb." He said that more for Summer's benefit than Katie's, who didn't appear to be the least bit nervous.

He put his left foot in the stirrup and hoisted himself up, then said to Summer, "Just wrap your arms around her waist and lift her as high as you can." She did as directed, and Reese grasped her beneath her armpits and settled her on the saddle in front of him. With Katie cradled safely between his thighs, he picked up the reins and slowly walked Daisy toward the paddock.

Summer followed along—keeping a safe distance behind—and while he could tell she was a teensy bit anxious, she didn't say anything. Just grasped the fence with both hands and watched as he walked Daisy in slow circles around the enclosure.

At first, Katie sat quiet as a church mouse, probably a combination of both fear and awe. He remembered that's how he'd felt the first time his grandfather took him for a ride on a horse. But after a few minutes, she caught sight of a couple mule deer sprinting in the distance, and started bouncing in the saddle.

He chuckled and leaned down to whisper, "Try to sit still, darlin', we don't want to scare Daisy."

"They're so pretty! Can we pet one?"

"I'm afraid not. Those are wild animals," he explained, as they rounded back to Summer. "We'd never even get close enough to touch one. But maybe we can take a ride to a local petting zoo one of these days. How does that sound?"

"Yay!" She clapped her hands, and craned her neck, looking at her mother as if for confirmation.

Summer's smile didn't quite reach her eyes. "Sounds great."

He realized suddenly that maybe he should have run the idea past her before mentioning it to Katie. He'd have to be careful about that from now on, crossing those parental lines. He just wanted both of them to experience everything life had to offer. Molly wanted for nothing. She had been to every zoo, museum, and amusement park within a hundred mile radius. Reese realized he wanted the same for Katie. The thought of watching the wonder on her little face as she hand fed animals in a petting zoo, or splashed around at an indoor water park, brought what was becoming a familiar ache to his chest.

He walked Daisy over to where Summer stood with her forearms braced on the top rail of the fence and attempted an apologetic smile. "Sorry."

He could see some of her tension dissipate as she gave him a playful eye roll. "Don't worry about it. I know your heart's in the right place."

She left it at that, though the implied, *but we'll talk about it later*, was there.

After a few more turns around the paddock with Katie, Molly raced up to stand beside Summer, James not far behind.

"Look, Molly, I'm ridin' Daisy!" Katie needlessly pointed out.

Reese trotted Daisy over to them, earning a shriek of joy from his passenger. He laughed and gave her a squeeze. "Did you enjoy your first riding lesson?"

She nodded emphatically. "It was awesome! Can we do it again?"

"You bet. One day next week...as long as it's okay with your mother," he quickly amended.

Summer chuckled as she reached up to help her daughter down. "I think that would be great. And very generous, thank you."

"Wanna go play in my room?" Molly asked her friend. "I can show you where Peanut Butter sleeps."

"Yay! But I need Jelly. He's in my backpack."

"It's in the car. I'll get it," Summer said.

"Don't worry, I'll get it for her," James countered as Molly gripped his hand and started dragging him along. His brother shot him a meaningful glance and added, "You kids have fun with your riding lesson."

As soon as they were out of earshot, Summer crossed her arms over her ample chest and cocked her head to the side. "Got something planned other than an actual riding lesson?"

"Nah. That was just James being a shit. Well, and I might have mentioned I'd like to take you for a ride down to a special spot, and it would be great if he and Meara kept Katie occupied for an hour or so."

"Is that right?"

She playfully narrowed her eyes and pursed her lips to the side. Now, why was something so simple such a damn turn-on for him?

He dismounted and took a step toward her. "You got a problem with spending a little alone time with me?"

"What if I do?" she coyly teased.

He moved close enough so he could place his hands over hers, which still rested on the top rail. "You didn't seem to have a problem with it last night," he reminded in a low tone, unable to draw his gaze away from her luscious lips.

She cleared her throat and shifted her gaze to Daisy. "Well, maybe we should get started then."

He chuckled and brought one of her hands up to kiss. "All right, come on in, and I'll show you how to mount a horse."

Summer came around and stood beside the pretty sorrel mare, cautious, yet eager. Truth was she'd always wanted to learn how to ride, even back in Redemption. The opportunity just never seemed to present itself.

"Okay, first, let her smell your hand. Once a horse knows your scent, they'll never forget you."

"Really?" She tentatively reached her palm out beneath the mare's nostrils. "Then how come you had Katie do it again today? You had Daisy smell her hand when they fed her treats the other day."

"Just in case she was a little nervous. I knew Daisy would calm her fears with a soft snuffle." He gave the horse a gentle pat on the neck. "Now, stroke her slowly, just like this. Don't worry, she loves being pampered."

Summer slowly reached up and patted the soft fur. Relief flooded her when the gentle creature leaned into her hand.

"See? Daisy's one of the most tame horses we've ever owned. She belonged to my grandmother, but mostly Angela rides her now." He seemed lost in thought for a second, then said, "Okay, time to get you in the saddle."

After a few basic instructions, he adjusted the length of the stirrups, helped her onto the horse's back, then had her dismount, and mount again. Left foot in the stirrup, then lift right leg up and over. Always mount and dismount from the left.

"You know what surprises me?" she admitted as she sat in the saddle holding the reins. "They don't smell as bad as I'd thought they would."

Reese laughed. "I'm sure Daisy appreciates that. So, how do you feel? You sit well, nice and straight. That's important. Make sure the balls of your feet rest in the stirrups, and keep a firm grip on the reins, but make sure there's slack. You could hurt her mouth if you pull too hard."

"Crap, now you're making me nervous." Last thing she wanted to do was hurt this precious animal.

"Sorry." He took off his Stetson and swiped his forearm across him brow. "You'll get the feel for it soon enough. Just don't pull too hard, or use the reins to balance yourself. Keeping your balance is key, that's why it's important to keep the balls of your feet—the widest part of your foot—resting on the stirrups."

She took a deep, calming breath, and that's when she saw someone leading a big, grayish horse with a black mane and tail toward them. Reese met the guy halfway, thanked him, and expertly mounted the beautiful animal in one smooth motion.

Reese McMillan made one striking figure in the saddle.

He walked the horse over to her and Daisy. "Summer, I'd like you to meet Milo. Milo, this gorgeous lady is Summer. We're going to walk her around the paddock for a couple minutes, then take her for a nice, slow walk along that trail that leads to the stream on the northern border."

"Are you sure I'm ready for that?" she asked, more than a little uneasy.

"You'll be fine, I promise. Daisy is a dream. She doesn't spook easily, and she knows the way like the back of her…hoof. Milo and I will lead the way. At a slow walk, it'll take about twenty, twenty-five minutes to get there, and trust me, it's a stunning spot."

Summer took a deep breath and nodded. "All right, I'm game." To Daisy she said, "I'm trusting you, girl, to get me there in one piece."

Reese laughed. As promised, he and Milo led her and Daisy slowly around the paddock, until she started to feel somewhat comfortable.

"Think you're ready to head out?"

She chewed on the corner of her bottom lip, her anxiety mounting as she stared off in the direction he'd indicated. "I guess. Maybe. I don't know."

He walked Milo up beside her and gave a reassuring smile. "You'll do great. Just sit straight in the saddle, as you have been, and keep a firm grip on the reins, but make sure there's slack. I'll be right there in case you need any help."

"Okay. Let's do this before I lose my nerve." *Sit straight, firm grip with slack,* she silently chanted as Daisy followed Milo and a grinning Reese from the paddock.

Thankfully, as promised, the ride was peaceful and uneventful. Though she had a feeling her butt would be sore the following day, even at such a slow gait.

A soft rushing could be heard as they rounded a bend, and Summer gazed around in astonishment. *How beautiful!* A clear running stream, no more than fifteen to twenty feet across, ran along the right side of the trail, canopied by a thick awning of trees, some already turning golden or a deep red, and surrounded by a lush carpet of sweet-smelling grass. An overabundance of purple, yellow, and white wildflowers perfumed the air. Some she recognized, like the purple and white columbine she loved so much, orange poppies, red clover, and yellow buttercups. Others she was seeing and smelling for the first time, like the fragrant little red buds that grew right along the shore and resembled trumpets.

Reese dismounted and came over to help her down. She wobbled slightly when her feet hit the ground, and the backs of her thighs and butt were a bit sore, but overall, not as bad as she'd feared. He grasped her hand and led her to the edge of the burbling stream, and it was then she saw the tiny silver fish swimming in the crystal clear waters.

Tears stung her eyes, startling her. Embarrassed, she turned away for a second to get her emotions under control. What the hell was wrong with her? Sure, this place was a veritable paradise, but that's not something that should make her weepy. And her period wasn't due for a couple weeks yet. Maybe it was just the thoughtfulness of him sharing this lovely spot with her.

"Gran used to bring us here a lot when we were kids," he finally said, releasing her hand to remove his hat and swipe his fingers through his hair. "We'd splash around in the water, but not until after she'd caught all the fish she wanted for that night's supper. Mostly, she'd just watch us run around and play. James and I were so happy when Gran brought us here to live for good."

That surprised her. She turned to peer up at him. "I assumed you both grew up here."

"Nope. Lived in a sky-rise apartment in downtown Chicago until I was about nine. My parents were always traveling, so Meara basically raised us until Gran stepped in. Our grandfather had passed the year before, so I think she was lonely."

He sat down on the bank and stretched his legs out, booted feet crossed at the ankles, his hands braced behind him. The black T-shirt he wore stretched taut over his muscular chest and arms. Reese McMillan was about the sexiest sight she'd ever seen, and her heart did a little flip when he gestured with a nod for her to sit down beside him. She did, but sat cross-legged.

"Your parents…they must have been, like, super rich." She made a rueful face. "Sorry, that sounded really bad. I just, I've never known anyone who had money like that. It's a foreign concept to me."

He smiled. "I'm an open book, you can ask me anything. And no, my parents aren't rich, they were cut out of my grandmother's will years ago. Gran's mother, great-grandma Millie, was the only child of a wealthy Texas cattle baron who died fairly young. Millie wasn't a big fan of Texas, so she sold her father's ranch and headed to Colorado where she met my great-grandpa Mitchell. They built Double M over a hundred years ago."

"Millie and Mitchell…so that's what the Double M stands for."

He gave an affirmative nod. "I'll have to show you a photo of them sometime. They were a pretty striking couple."

"I'd love to see it. I thought the name of your ranch had to do with your last name having two Ms."

"Nope. My great-grandparents' last name was Stanford. They had Gran, who married Daniel Alger, and they had my mother. Dad is the McMillan."

"Got it." Summer picked a stem of red clover and twirled it beneath her nose, a little in awe—and a little envious. "You're a fascinating guy, Reese McMillan. Wish my life had been half as interesting."

"You say 'had' as if it's over. You're barely in to your twenties, woman. You have a lot more living to do."

She peeked at him through her lashes. "It's certainly gotten more exciting since I met you. Though, I'm still not sure if that's good or bad."

He leaned in toward her and caressed a slow path from her knee, up her thigh, and back again. "Maybe it's a little bit of both."

Chapter Thirteen

Summer's pulse sped up to dizzying speeds. *Good Lord.* She felt like a teenager alone with her boyfriend for the first time. Which, after the passion they'd shared last night, seemed utterly silly.

Taking a deep breath, she covered Reese's hand with hers and met his lazy-lidded gaze. She wanted him to kiss her, but he simply stared at her, as if…

Was he trying to coax her into making the first move? She had last night, but it'd been more of an impulse than anything else, and the darkness had somewhat emboldened her. She didn't know if she had it in her to just lean over and kiss him in the light of this beautiful day.

She needn't have worried.

He gave her leg a soft squeeze and whispered, "Come here."

As if drawn by a magnet, she rose up on her knees and was immediately wrapped in his tight embrace.

Reese fell back onto the grass and pulled her on top of him. Holding her gaze, he smoothed his strong hands down the length of her body, from her shoulders, down the curve of her spine, over her butt, to the backs of her denim-clad thighs, stroking a dizzying path up and down until she melted into him like softened butter on warm bread. Then he captured her face with both hands and kissed her. On some level, she knew things were progressing way too fast. They barely knew each other, hadn't even been out on a date, yet this was the second time they'd shared a passionate kiss.

And she couldn't have pulled away at that moment if her life depended on it.

The press of his mouth was light at first, testing, teasing, as if waiting to make sure she was ready and willing. To answer his unvoiced invitation, she ran the tip of her tongue along the seal of his lips. He moaned, a deep, masculine sound, and opened for her. She slid inside, a little hesitant as she brushed his tongue with playful strokes. One of his hands splayed across the back of her head, and he deepened the kiss, taking over the reins as he expertly rolled them over until he was lying on top of her, his hard length pressing her into the soft carpet of lush grass.

Summer wrapped her arms around him, reveling in his slight quiver. She gripped his back, holding on for dear life as he kissed her with a passion she'd only ever dreamt about. He ran his tongue across hers, flicking and tasting, sliding and exploring. Every inch of her tingled, throbbed, and she suddenly resented the barrier of their clothes. The thought of lying naked beneath him, making love in this magnificent paradise, was breathtaking.

He broke off the kiss to run his hot mouth across her cheek, down the column of her throat, nipping and sucking gently as his hand slipped beneath the hem of her shirt. Her pulse sped up, and she arched her neck, giving him better access. His fingertips traced a fiery path up her stomach, across her ribcage until he cupped her breast. Her nipples hardened and her fingers clenched in his hair. She wanted him. So much. But…

At that moment, Summer realized she wasn't quite ready for that next step. And if she didn't put a stop to it, he'd be deep inside her within minutes.

"I-I'm sorry, but I'm not ready for this." She dropped her arms to her sides and released a hearty sigh. "We've literally only known each other for a few days."

He flipped over with a pained groan and swiped his hand through his hair. Turning to face her, he smiled apologetically and reached over to gently cup her cheek. "I'm the one who's sorry." His voice dropped to a low purr. "You're just so damn beautiful."

"Thank you," she murmured, flattered, yet… "Though I'd like to think I have more to offer than just…the way I look."

"You are, without a doubt, the most interesting woman I've ever met. You're funny, smart, strong-willed. And you're an amazing mother."

Tears stung her eyes. Why it touched her so much to have this man recognize how important it was for her to be a good mother, she didn't know. But it did. "Funny might be a stretch."

He grinned and swiped at the corner of her eye. "So, why don't you tell me a little bit about Summer. I mean, I know some of your history, but I don't know much about you personally."

She gave a shrug. "I was born and raised in Redemption, Wisconsin, I'm an only child, and my parents own a small grocery store. They're what you might call religious fanatics. Extremely conservative. I wasn't allowed to have friends, or date, I had to work at the store after school every day, and all day Saturday."

He grasped her hand and gave it a soft squeeze. "Sounds lonely as hell."

She frowned as she thought about Sharlot and Hannah, the two girls who had embraced her in sixth grade, and remained her friends until she'd moved away, even though she hadn't gotten to see them very often once they'd graduated high school. "Well, I did have a couple of friends, but I haven't seen or spoken to either in years."

He gazed at her, eyes lowered in contemplation, as if trying to process everything she'd shared with him about her less than happy childhood. "Have you ever thought about contacting them? Your friends, I mean?"

Summer had thought about it many times. She'd love to tell them about Katie, see what was happening in both of their lives. But she was so afraid her parents would somehow find out and come to Colorado, force her to go home. Which was silly, she knew. She was a grown woman now, they couldn't force her to do anything. But still, the thought alone of them showing up in Golden was unsettling.

She shrugged. "Maybe someday. I just...I don't want my parents to find out where I am."

He propped himself on his elbow and grasped her hand. "I don't mean to pry, but...I know you've struggled on your own. Would it be so bad to let your parents help you?"

Her throat tightened as she remembered their ultimatum. Her chest felt near to bursting with repressed fury. "I can't even imagine letting them into my daughter's life. They are the two most judgmental people I've ever known."

He squeezed her hand, lending silent support, which was just what she needed to continue.

"I was seventeen when I became pregnant. My parents told me they were going to send me to live with my aunt up in Michigan, and then force me to give my baby up for adoption."

"Jesus."

"They were embarrassed, afraid of what people would think." The memory of the way they'd looked at her, as if she were something that had crawled out of the baseboards, caused a surge of pain and resentment to rise up, leaving a chill in her bones. "When I refused, my father threatened to have Nico—Katie's father—arrested for statutory rape. Nico talked me into running away with him, promised me the moon and stars…promised to marry me."

She gave a soft, self-deprecating laugh. In some ways, it seemed like just yesterday she'd been so full of anticipation, so eager for the future. In others, it felt like a million years ago. "I don't regret my decision. There was no way I was going to give up my baby. I may not be able to spoil Katie, but she's happy, healthy, and I love her more than I ever thought possible."

"What about…your ex's parents? Are they in the picture?"

"Nico never really talked about them, but I know he was estranged from them." She shrugged. "I'm not sure if they even know about Katie. It was just sort of unwritten that we didn't talk about our parents."

He gazed at her in silence for a moment, and she would have given anything to know what he was thinking. But then he leaned in and kissed her, gently, yet thoroughly, and all other thoughts escaped her. When he pulled back, a big, fat raindrop struck her in the face.

She sat up with a laugh, and that's when she noticed how dark the sky had become. "I thought it wasn't supposed to storm until later tonight…?" The scent of rain hung heavy in the air.

Reese quickly stood and helped her to her feet. Within seconds, a steady downpour started, and she panicked.

"I just had my first riding lesson. I-I don't think I can ride her back in"—she gestured helplessly at the sky—"this."

"Don't worry. You can ride with me. Daisy will follow along."

He mounted Milo, then gave her a hand up. No sooner had she wrapped her arms around him then he flicked the reins, and they took off at a ground-eating trot.

The ride back was as fast as it was exhilarating. Body tingling with awareness, heart bursting with contentment, she snuggled against his warm, broad back and hung on tight as the glistening, beautiful landscape flew by.

She'd be sore for a few days—man, was her ass taking a beating—but *wow*, would it be worth it.

They were both soaked to the bone by the time they rode up to the stables. Daisy, she was relieved to see, had indeed followed them home.

Home. Wouldn't that be something, to be able to call a paradise like this home? She wondered if Reese knew just how lucky he was.

A stable hand came out and took Daisy's reins, leading her inside while Reese dismounted. He reached up for Summer, and she slowly slid into his arms, happier—and wetter—than she'd been in a very long time. He cautiously set her on her feet just as the hand came back for Milo.

"Thanks, Ronnie."

The older man waved but didn't look back as he disappeared inside.

Reese wrapped an arm around her and nodded toward the house. "Think you can make it? You must be pretty damn sore after that."

She tested her legs, and yeah, she *was* rather tender, especially her backside. But she should be able to walk. The first step caused her to grimace and stumble, and he immediately swung her into his arms.

"I had a feeling. Come on, let's go get dried off. You and Angie are about the same size, so I'm sure she'll have something you can change into. And knowing Meara, there'll be a pot of fresh coffee waiting for us. I'm pretty sure she made shortbread this morning, too."

A cup of coffee sounded like absolute heaven. She linked her fingers behind his neck, relishing the warmth of his body, even through their drenched clothes. "Sounds great. By the way, I'm stealing Meara."

Reese stared in wonder, along with his brother and sister-in-law, as Summer not only got Meara to sit and have coffee with them, but also let her serve everyone. It truly was a first, one-of-a-kind happening, and he felt an odd sense of pride as the dear old woman leaned back and watched Summer as if she'd sprouted wings and a halo.

As soon as he'd gotten the sopping wet blonde inside, he'd had her take two pain relievers, then explained a few minutes under a hot shower would help loosen those muscles up a bit. She'd been a little hesitant at first, but both Meara and Angie backed him up, so she'd gratefully relented. And talk about a difference. She'd come back down those stairs with a relieved smile and barely a kink in her step.

Angela sat on one of the cushioned armchairs, sipping her tea and nibbling on freshly baked shortbread, while James drank his coffee and watched her like a hawk. He worried about his brother. The stress he was under over this difficult pregnancy, combined with the long hours he spent working, both out on the range and at his desk dealing with everyone from suppliers to lawyers, was taking its toll. If he'd only let go of the reins a bit, let Reese help out more on the business end, his stubborn brother could relax more.

He met Summer's gaze as she topped off Meara's coffee. She stared at him with an eagle eye, as if she knew something was bothering him. His chest expanded as an odd sensation gripped him. Not ready to examine it too closely, he sent her a reassuring smile and decided to simply focus on how happy he was since the Hanson girls entered his life.

Summer set the coffee pot back on its burner and took the seat to his left. She picked up her coffee and took a cautious sip before helping herself to a wedge of Meara's buttery shortbread. She broke off small bites and popped them into her mouth, licking the crumbs from her fingers as if she didn't know how sensual the gesture was. She had to know, though. A woman couldn't be that sexy and *not* know.

"So," his sister-in-law said, a definite gleam in her eye, "How was your first riding lesson?"

Angie and Meara shared a knowing smile, one he was pretty sure meant trouble for him.

Summer cast him a meaningful sidelong glance before responding. "I have to admit, it was a lot better than I thought it would be, sore butt and all. I'd never been on a horse before, and within ten minutes, I was riding one by myself. To be fair, Daisy did most of the work," she added with a sheepish grin. "She's as gentle as Reese promised."

"Daisy is a dream," Angela agreed. "I learned how to ride on her as well, and I doubt I rode half as well as you did."

"What, are you kidding me?" James interjected, beaming with pride. "You were a natural. As is our daughter."

"It's true." She swung her proud gaze back to Summer. "James bought a pony for her to ride, and she's amazing…not that we let her do more than walk him around the paddock."

Reese caught Summer's attention. "I think Katie would do well on him as well. Maybe next time?"

"I'm sure she'd love that, thank you."

He nodded, suddenly wishing they were alone again so he could pull her into his arms and kiss her.

The landline rang. James was closest, so he reached back and answered it.

"Hey, Cal, what's up?"

Reese watched with growing dread as the color literally drained from his brother's face.

"Yeah. Okay. Sure. Thanks, I appreciate the head's up." James hung up the phone, and affected a smile for his wife and Meara. "Sorry, business. I have to take care of something, shouldn't take me too long." He stood and leaned over to kiss his wife. "You want me to help you upstairs, or would you like to visit for a while?"

She eyed him curiously—Angie knew her husband very well, and obviously suspected something was up. But she returned his smile and lifted her tea cup. "I'd like to visit for a little while longer. You go, take care of business. I'll make it upstairs just fine."

"Don't worry, bro. I'll help your lady upstairs when we're done here."

James nodded, but he held Reese' gaze a second longer than necessary, raising the hairs on the back of his neck. As soon as he was able to, he'd head to the study and find out what had James so spooked.

"So," Oblivious to the tension, Meara's gaze moved between Reese and Summer. "I get the distinct impression something romantic might be brewing between the two of you."

Summer sputtered and coughed. She'd been in the middle of taking a sip of her coffee when Meara spoke.

Reese hid a grin as he gave her a gentle thump on the back. "Well, now, don't hold back, Meara. I really hate it when you pussyfoot around."

Summer gave a self-conscious laugh, her cheeks pinkening as she dabbed at her mouth with her napkin and cleared her throat. He found her embarrassment adorable as hell.

"Come on, you two. Throw us a bone," Angie teasingly goaded. "You know how boring my life is these days."

Reese glanced at Summer, trying to gauge how she felt about going public. Not that anything serious was going on. They liked each other; there was a mutual attraction. But that was about it. They hadn't even gone out on a real date yet.

She met his gaze, those big blue eyes full of question.

He wasn't exactly sure what came over him, but suddenly he couldn't resist the urge to lean over and kiss her on those lush lips.

She gasped. He pulled back, smiling at her as he said to no one in particular, "Does that answer your question?"

Her answering smile was so bright it lit up the room, and as she gazed up him, happiness melding with uncertainty, his heart did that funny little flip thing that was becoming less scary by the minute.

What the hell? he decided. Time to make that next move. "Summer, how would you like to go out on a date with me?"

Chapter Fourteen

Meara clapped her hands and twittered with delight, while Angie squealed and did a little happy dance in her chair. "Now that's what I'm talking about," his sister-in-law exclaimed.

He was grateful for their support as Summer nodded. "I would love to. But…I can't believe I have to admit this…I've never been on a real date."

The admission surprised him. That scumbag ex of hers had never even taken her out on a proper date? Reese had wined and dined many women over the years, but he knew without a doubt this was going to be the most important date of his life. He definitely wanted to give Summer a night she'd never forget.

"Then I guess I'd better plan something pretty special. How about Friday?"

"Friday would be great. Wait…Katie and I are supposed to make you spaghetti Friday," she reminded, a tinge of disappointment in her tone.

"Tell her you're postponing the spaghetti dinner so she can have a sleepover here," Angie suggested with lightning speed. "She'll be thrilled, trust me, as will Molly. She has bunkbeds in her room, and more than enough toys and games to keep them busy until they pass out from exhaustion."

"And I'll make them a special dinner," Meara chimed in. "Anything they want—chicken fingers, sloppy joes, tacos, you name it. Plus, a sundae bar for dessert." The older smiled from ear to ear.

"I don't know what to say," Summer murmured as she bounced her gaze between the three of them. "You're all so incredibly generous. Katie loves all those things, and she's definitely not a picky eater. I'm sure to her this place is like Disneyland. But…she's never slept anywhere other than her own bed. I'm a little afraid she might get scared when it grows close to bedtime."

Reese hung his arm around the back of her chair. "No problem. We'll drop back here after dinner, see how she's doing, then head back out for the rest of our date."

Angie waved her hands excitedly, making him chuckle. She seemed to be more enthusiastic about this date than he and Summer.

"I know the perfect place to take her for dinner." His sister-in-law locked gazes with him, her eyes brimming with excitement. "Indulge Bistro." She put her hand to her chest as if she'd just died and gone to heaven. "Oh, my God, the chicken gnocchi is amazing. And so is the seafood cioppino."

"I was actually thinking the Briarwood. Great food, nice atmosphere." And he could reserve a secluded table for them in the back of the restaurant.

Angie nodded in vigorous approval, then turned to Summer. "Their filet is the absolute best, and they have a Kahlua chocolate bread pudding that's to die for."

Reese shook his head. His sister-in-law sure did love to eat. And it wasn't only the pregnancy. She'd always had a strong appreciation for food, one that went well beyond the norm. In fact, James took her out at least once a week, whether it was breakfast, lunch, or dinner.

A glance at Summer caused his smile to fade. She was staring into her coffee mug as if the mysteries of the world could be found there. "You okay? Listen, it's your night. If you don't care for either of those places, we can go anywhere you like."

"Oh, of course. I didn't mean to plan your date," Angie quickly assured with an apologetic flutter of her hands.

Summer looked up and attempted a smile, though he got the impression she was a bit overwhelmed. He recalled her telling him that she and Katie rarely ate out. Heck, the pizza they'd had last night was a rare treat, she'd said.

"It's just… Both those places are so expensive. I mean, couldn't we go somewhere a little more casual?"

Yep, that was the problem all right. He grasped her hand and brought it to his lips. "I don't want you to worry about that. This is a date, and I asked you, which means I pay for everything. And trust me, I can afford to take you anywhere you'd like to go."

He could see the hesitancy still swimming in her eyes, but she gave a slow nod followed by a genuine smile. Funny how he could already read her facial expressions.

"I wouldn't mind going to see a movie. I've never been inside a movie theatre and always kind of wondered what they look like."

He could only stare at her, a little stunned by the admission. A quick glance at Angie and Meara confirmed he wasn't the only one surprised.

"I mean, unless you don't want to go to the movies," she quickly added.

"No, I love a good movie, especially on the big screen. Popcorn, candy, soda…you." He smiled. "Doesn't get much better. I'm just surprised you've never been to a movie theatre. Not even as a kid?"

She shrugged. "My parents were pretty frugal. We didn't even own a TV when I was little. I was about thirteen when they finally bought one."

Hell, he couldn't even imagine. It really brought home just how good a life he and James had always had. Made him feel almost…guilty for having so much when some people had so little.

Determined to treat her to the night of her life, he grasped her hand and announced, "Dinner and a movie it is. And if there's time, maybe a walk down by the river."

"I had no idea you were such a romantic." Summer gave him a teasing glance over the rim of her coffee mug.

"There's a lot about me you don't know," he retorted with a playful wiggle of his eyebrows.

After a moment, Meara, who'd been unpredictably quiet, pushed back her chair and struggled to stand up. Reese came around the table and gave her a hand, a move he knew she wouldn't appreciate. To his surprise—and concern—she didn't argue.

Instead, she gave him a grateful pat on the back once she was up and steady on her feet. "I'd best start cleaning up. Dinner'll be ready in an hour." She smiled at Summer. "You and Katie are welcome to join us. There's pot roast in the slow cooker, and we're having it with mashed potatoes, carrots, corn, and fresh rolls."

"It smells incredible, and I appreciate the offer. But we have nearly half an Alberti's pizza waiting for us in the fridge, and I wouldn't want it to go to waste."

"Ooh, I love Alberti's," Angie said, closing her eyes for a moment and swaying in her chair.

"Well, I made plenty," the older woman assured. "Maybe you can take some home tomorrow?"

"That would be great. Thanks so much."

The beat of two tiny pairs of feet pounding down the stairs echoed overhead a few seconds before Katie and Molly came rushing into the kitchen.

Katie ran straight for her mother. "Momma, guess what? Molly has *bunkbeds*! She said I could sleep on the top one because Peanut Butter—that's her stuffed turtle—he's afraid of heights. But Jelly's not. And she has horses painted on her wall, a white one, and a brown one, and a black one, and a yellow one, and she has lots of games, way more than me, and six dolls, and like…a thousand stuffed animals!"

Summer pulled her up onto her lap with a laugh.

"My God," Reese teased. "Did you get all that out in one breath?"

Katie nodded, grinning.

Molly leaned into Angie's side and gazed up at her beseechingly. "Can we have a sleepover, Mom? Please, please, please? I never had one afore, and neither has Katie."

"*Be*fore," her mother corrected. "And as a matter of fact, we were just saying how nice it would be if you had Katie over for a sleepover this Friday."

His niece's eyes rounded with excitement. "Really?" She ran around the table and grabbed her friend's arm. "We're gonna have a sleepover Friday!"

Katie slid off her mother's lap and the two clasped hands and started dancing around.

Summer leaned in close to him and whispered, "I think it's time for us to head home. Though I have a feeling Katie won't agree with me."

"I don't agree with you either," he teased. "But I understand. And at least I know I get to see you tomorrow."

She looked down at her coffee cup, then back up, worry darkening those bright blue eyes. "Sure you won't get tired of me before we've even gone on our first date?"

He gently grasped her knee beneath the table, wanting more than anything to pull her into his arms and kiss that silly concept right out of her head. "Impossible."

She smiled, and all he could do was stare at her like some lovesick fool. He cleared his throat and forced his attention back to the girls, who were now racing around the kitchen playing tag.

"All right, kiddo, time to head home," Summer announced. "Go grab your backpack, please, and don't forget to clean up any mess you helped make in Molly's room."

"We already did," Katie informed her as she and his niece raced out of the kitchen and back up the stairs, surprisingly, without an argument.

"Thank you both for everything," Summer said to Meara and Angie. "I'll see you all in the morning." To Meara, she added, "That shortbread was amazing."

"I've been making it for years." The older woman set the stack of dirty plates in the sink and turned on the faucet before glancing back over her shoulder. "I'll add pecans and shaved chocolate next time. Heavenly."

"That does sound good." Summer rose to her feet. "Can I give you a hand?"

Meara turned back to the sink and added a squirt of dish soap. "I've got it covered, young lady. Save your energy for morning. Don't forget, we're gonna tackle the rest of those windows."

Summer shared a quick grin with Reese. "I haven't forgotten. In fact, I'll make sure to get to bed a little early tonight."

"That a'girl."

Reese chuckled. It pleased him to know Meara and Summer had such a great rapport.

As soon as Katie returned, he walked them out to the car.

Once Summer had the little peanut buckled in the backseat, she turned to face him, uncertainty flickering in her eyes again.

"You all right?"

She nodded. "I just… This is all so new to me. Are we…are we dating?"

Relief filled his chest. Hell, yes, they were dating. And the thought didn't bring on a panic attack, like it had in the past. He snaked an arm around her waist and pulled her in close. "As far as I'm concerned, we are. You?"

She gave a tentative nod. It became clear to him that she had trust issues, not that he could blame her after all she'd been through. He supposed he'd just have to prove himself, something he'd gotten a lot of practice at over the past five years.

He leaned down and kissed her, a soft, unassuming press of his lips to hers. She leaned into him, but pulled back, casting a sidelong glance toward the backseat.

Message received. No PDAs in front of the little one. "See you tomorrow."

She gave a decisive nod this time, as if she'd just come to some sort of conclusion. A soft smile curved her lips. "See you tomorrow." She got in the car, started it up, and drove off.

Reese watched until her little red car disappeared down the driveway and out of sight.

No sooner than he walked back into the house his cell phone buzzed. He pulled it out and frowned. A text from James: *Come up to the study.* A bad feeling swelled in his gut. It wasn't like his brother to be cryptic.

Thankfully, Meara and Angie were still in the kitchen, so he was able to slip upstairs without being seen.

The study door was closed, but since James had summoned him up, he knew it would be unlocked. He opened the door and closed it softly behind him. His brother sat behind the desk in the process of tossing back a whiskey. Reese felt a little sense of déjà vu.

"Should I be concerned?"

"Not about this." James poured another and gestured for him to sit. "Just got off the phone with Mom."

Not at all what he'd expected to come out of his brother's mouth. He sat. "Let me guess. She and dad already blew through their yearly allowance and need an advance."

James shook his head. "They're divorcing. Mom caught Dad with another woman. Found out he's been seeing her for over twenty five years."

Reese could only stare at him as the news sank in. "Huh. Wish I could say I was surprised. The only thing that's surprising is they've lasted this long."

Reese wished he cared enough about either of them to feel any real sympathy. But James Sr. and Lillian McMillan were two of the most selfish people on the planet, and pretty much strangers to their own children. Hell, they hadn't even made the time to return to Colorado to meet their granddaughter, who was already five years old. Sure, they Facetimed here and there, mostly on holidays. But what kind of people didn't want to meet their own grandkid? And hell, it's not like they lived across the globe. They owned a loft in SoHo. Reese should know, he and James paid for it.

His brother finally downed the second whiskey before slumping down in the chair. "There's more."

He'd have laughed if James' expression wasn't so grim. "I can hardly wait."

"Dad and this woman have children together. Twin daughters. Mom said they just turned twenty two."

Okay, *now* he was surprised. The old man had been hiding these girls for over two decades? *Jesus*. Disappointment, resentment, and a whole host of other emotions rose up for a civil war in his chest as the enormity of the situation struck. "Is this for real? I mean, Mom *has* been known to stretch the truth for her own benefit."

"I hear you. But she was crying so hard I could barely understand her. She said Dad's mistress is the one who told her about…our sisters."

"Well, what the hell did he have to say for himself? Has he…always known about them?"

James leaned forward, bracing his forearms on the edge of the desk. "I got the impression he's always known about them, though I doubt they've seen much more of him than we have. He isn't answering his phone. Mom said he begged her not to file for divorce. Swore this was the first time he's been with the other woman in years, and only because he and mom had gotten into some huge fight. But…he had to have been taking care of them financially all these years, or why else wouldn't this woman have come forward and sued him for support?"

"Which also explains why they always blow through their allowance so damn fast."

"He's cut off as of this fuckin' minute," James declared, pouring and tossing back a third whiskey.

With a nod of agreement, Reese shoved to his feet and started pacing. No mystery why the old man kept the girls a secret—money. Mom and Dad were completely dependent on the very generous yearly allowance he and James gave them. Dad even more so, as it turned out.

"What about Mom?"

James' top lip curled with distaste. "Unless we want her moving in here with us, I suppose we'll have to keep up with her allowance."

Reese shuddered. He could barely stand to have a five minute phone conversation with the self-absorbed woman. Having to see her day after day, feed her insatiable need for sympathy and self-assurance indefinitely? No thanks. "I think you know what my vote is."

James tried to hide a grin, and suddenly, they both started laughing.

"I'm pretty sure Meara would kill her before she even unpacked her bags," he pointed out.

"Hell, Angela'd help her hide the body."

They both chuckled again. No one liked their mother, particularly not Angela, who had no use for a woman who could *"consciously abandon her own children."*

He caught a whiff of Meara's amazing Guinness pot roast. "Wow, smell that? Dinner must be just about ready. Think I'll go wash up."

"I'll be right down," James said as he picked up the phone. "I'm gonna give the old man one more try."

As Reese headed down the hall to the bathroom, he thought about Summer and how different she and his mother were. His mother, who'd had loving parents and every advantage in life, grew up to be a cold, spoiled, self-centered woman who had zero maternal instinct. While Summer had been raised by militant-style religious fanatics, had very little growing up, and was one of the most loving, caring people he'd ever met. She worked hard, loved her daughter fiercely, and would do anything necessary to take care of her.

Which she did as a single parent.

Because of him.

Chapter Fifteen

"So, what are you planning to wear tonight?"

Summer stiffened at the innocently asked question—something that had actually been on her mind all week long. Angela no doubt had a closet full of gorgeous outfits, so it would never occur to her that Summer had pretty much nothing to wear for her and Reese's first date. She'd been able to salvage the peach blouse, thankfully, which happened to be the only decent piece of clothing she owned. But it wasn't exactly something to be worn on a date.

"I don't know." She turned to meet her friend's curious gaze. "I'm torn between my dark blue jeans and Green Bay Packers T-shirt, or my black jeans and white Polo."

At Angela's horrified expression, she laughed.

"Why do you think I wanted to go someplace casual for dinner?"

The pregnant brunette pushed to her feet and waddled to her closet. She opened it with a flourish, and started sliding hangers across the wooden rod, stopping to toss a few items onto the bed as she went along.

Summer watched with a sense of disconcertment, her face warming with humiliation over the offer she knew was coming.

Once finished, Angela turned to face her, a gleam of excitement dancing in her eyes. "You've only got an inch or two on me, so I assume we wear about the same size. A couple of these I haven't even worn yet, and I have a feeling they'll look much better on you than me." She searched through the pile, pulling out three dresses that each looked as if they'd costed more than her car was worth...not that it was worth all that much.

The brunette held up a sleeveless, royal blue, V-neck mini dress. "I bought this from a catalog, but it turned out to be too snug in the cleavage area for me," her buxomly friend admitted with a grin. "I'm glad I didn't return it, though. I think it would look fabulous on you."

She turned it around, revealing the dress to be backless.

"Um...I'm not sure... I mean, it's gorgeous, but..."

"Too sexy?"

"Maybe a little."

Angela chuckled and tossed it aside. She picked up a little white number with a pleated, bell-shaped skirt, long sleeves, and cutouts at the shoulders. Also beautiful, but not quite her style.

She gave her head a reluctant shake. "Listen, this is so incredibly generous of you, truly. But I...I think I'd feel more comfortable wearing my own clothes. I actually do have one nice blouse I can wear."

Angela dropped the dress on the bed and carefully lowered herself to sit on the edge. "When I first came here to Colorado, I had very little to my name," she quietly revealed. "I had spent almost every penny I'd saved buying Reese's half of the ranch."

Summer frowned. "Reese sold you his half of the ranch?" The thought astonished her. He truly seemed to love this place. "But...I thought this was his home."

"Oh, it is! I sold it back to him when James and I got married. Which is a long story, and not really mine to tell. The point I was trying to make is I didn't always have such nice things to wear. The first time James bought me a dress, I felt...well, probably much the same as you're feeling now. A little uncomfortable, a little embarrassed, like a fish out of water."

Summer gave a soft, self-deprecating laugh. Her friend had certainly hit that humiliating nail on the head. "That's most of it. Also…Reese is going to know anything that nice didn't come out of my own closet."

Angela waved that away. "Trust me, Reese won't even give it a thought, especially since he hasn't seen any of these dresses. Reese wants to take you somewhere special and pricey, so let him. You guys can do burgers for your second date."

"Why do I get the feeling you don't lose many arguments?"

Her friend summoned her over with a knowing grin and a crook of her finger to start trying on dresses.

"Momma, you look like a Disney princess," Katie exclaimed as she skidded to a halt in front of Summer. "But why? Where are you going?"

She crouched down to eye level with her daughter. "Don't you remember? Reese is taking me out for dinner. And you're having a sleepover with Molly." She ruffled the little sweetie's hair and rose to her feet.

"I remember, we're gonna have the bestest time!" She bounced up and down. "And Meara's gonna make us mac 'n' cheese again."

"She also bought all the fixings for sundaes," Angela announced as she waddled over to join them. "Now, I bet a certain brother-in-law of mine is waiting impatiently for you down in the living room, so time to make that entrance."

More nervous than she cared to admit, Summer gave her daughter a quick side hug for courage. Then she glanced in the mirror that hung over the dresser, wondering if she should redo her eye liner, which was a little heavier than she normally wor—

"Your hair is gorgeous, and your makeup is perfect," her friend assured her.

"You look very pretty, Momma," Katie assured her, slipping her hand into Summer's. "Now, come on. Boys get mad if they have to wait."

She almost laughed, but her daughter looked quite serious. "And who told you that?"

"Tommy Odell. He got so mad when he had to wait in line for a cupcake. Julie's momma brung 'em for her birthday."

"Ah." She shared a look with Angela, whose eyes danced with mirth.

"Well, big boys are used to waiting on their ladies," Her friend carefully explained. "So we don't have anything to worry about. Reese will be smiling from ear to ear when your mom walks down those stairs."

Summer took a deep breath as Angela preceded her from the room. She and Katie followed behind, swinging their clasped hands as they always did. When they reached the staircase, Summer realized her hands were shaking and grasped the railing. Never in her life had she been so nervous to make an appearance.

She glanced down into the foyer and her breath caught as her gaze landed on Reese. The man was simply gorgeous. He wore black slacks, a charcoal gray, button up shirt, and a black sports coat that fit him to perfection. He stood when he saw her, slowly, as if a little stunned.

Maybe her friend had been right about the sexy dress she'd talked her into wearing. The red cocktail dress was similar to the gorgeous royal blue number she'd first suggested, only it wasn't completely backless. But it fit her like a glove, emphasizing every curve on her slender frame. Angela had topped it off with a thin, black cape she'd insisted was fashionable, yet would keep her plenty warm enough on this mild October evening.

She was also lucky they wore almost the same shoe size, only a half-size off, or Summer would have had to wear her red sneakers instead of the strappy sandals loaned to her. She had very little experience with heels, but discovered she had a certain knack for them.

She owed her friend big time and would definitely find a way to make it up to her.

Katie dropped her hand and skipped down ahead of her, leaving all eyes on Summer as she slowly, carefully, made her way down the staircase.

Reese stepped forward to meet her, his hands crammed into his front pockets as his gaze raked her from head to toe. "You look incredible."

"Thank you. So do you."

They stared at each other for a moment, and Summer was contemplating running back up the stairs when he reached out and grasped her hand.

"You ready?"

No. "Yes."

She waved Katie over and crouched down…as best as she could in the short dress. "I want you to be on your best behavior tonight, okay? When Angela tells you it's time for bed, no arguments, got it?"

She gave a solemn nod. "Yes, momma."

After a quick hug and a peck on the cheek, Katie ran back to Molly's side, and the two started giggling as they took off into the kitchen.

Meara just managed to swing out of their way as she entered the foyer. She gave her head an indulgent shake before turning to Summer. "Don't you worry, the girls are going to have a wonderful time. And they'll be so tired after a few hours of running around, they'll be fast asleep by the time you guys get back."

"Thank you, Meara. I appreciate it. And I know she couldn't be in better hands."

The older woman beamed. "I'm happy to help. Spending time with the kids is always a joy. You look lovely, by the way." She turned to Reese. "And you look quite handsome. Have a nice time, and don't worry about rushing home." With that, she headed back into the kitchen.

Reese smiled and held out his arm. "I suppose we'd better head out. The movie starts at six."

Angela handed her the little red clutch she'd borrowed before giving her shoulders a quick squeeze. "Have fun. And Reese, no ranch talk."

He chuckled. "Got it."

He escorted her outside, but instead of heading for his monstrous pickup truck, he led her to an expensive-looking black sports car. *A Porsche*. The sleek vehicle was stunning, and a surge of jealousy rose up like bile in her throat, surprising her—and shaming her a bit. Summer was well accustomed to her lower-class status, though, like everyone else, she longed for some of the finer things in life. But she'd never been the jealous type, and didn't like the feeling one bit.

Reese opened the door for her, and she shook off the negative energy as she carefully slipped into the front passenger seat.

"James bought this for Angie as a wedding present," he explained once he slid in behind the wheel. "But it's not really her style, so it mostly just sits in the garage. I thought you might prefer it over my truck for the date."

Summer couldn't hide her amazement. "Wow. Pretty fancy wedding present. If she didn't like it, why didn't they just return it?"

He turned the key, and the car purred to life. "She didn't tell him she didn't like it, didn't want to hurt his feelings. By the time she finally told him, it didn't make sense to return it as they would have taken a loss. Vehicles depreciate in value as soon as they leave the lot."

"I didn't know that."

As he backed out of the driveway, she glanced around the luxurious interior with awe. Summer could hardly believe she was sitting in such an expensive car, let alone imagine owning it. The reality of just how wealthy the McMillan's were hit her with the force of a gale wind, nearly stealing her breath.

"So, ready for the night of your life?"

Chapter Sixteen

The movie, a psychological thriller, had been amazing, keeping Summer on the edge of her seat until the very end. As Reese escorted her back to the car, the buzz of excited chatter fading into the distance, she silently admitted he'd chosen well—her first experience in a movie theater, and it was everything she'd imagined and more. They'd shared popcorn, sipped soda. He'd even bought a bag of cotton candy, which they devoured like little kids.

He unlocked the passenger door, and opened it with a flourish.

"Thank you, sir," she replied with a playful bat of her eyelashes as she grasped his hand.

Once they were on the road, he told her, "After thinking about it, I decided the Briarwood might be a tad too formal for a first date, so I made reservations at the place Angie suggested, Indulge Bistro. I think you'll enjoy it. The food is fantastic."

"I'm sure I will." Her face warmed at the thought of just how much money this date was costing him. If he were any other man, she'd be suspicious of his intentions. But she truly didn't think Reese was *that* type of guy. Heck, he probably had women throwing themselves at him all the time.

Something acidic bubbled up in her stomach. The thought of him with other women didn't sit well at all.

They arrived and were promptly seated at a table in the back of the modernly elegant little restaurant. Summer asked for water, while Reese ordered a bottle of imported beer. When the waiter asked if they would care for an appetizer, she told Reese to choose something since she was too embarrassed to admit she didn't know to pronounce some of the items on the menu. He ordered calamari, then told the waiter they would wait a bit before ordering their entrees.

The waiter delivered their drinks, poured Reese's beer into a glass, then took his leave. Reese held his glass out, and she smiled, following suit.

"To the first of hopefully many good times." They clinked glasses, and a niggle of doubt once again invaded her thoughts. She suppressed it…Reese wanted more from her than just *"many good times."* They had a connection, something undefinable, unlike anything she'd ever experienced before. And her gut told her the feeling was reciprocated.

Your gut has lied to you before.

He watched her as they each took a sip, his eyes gleaming with what she assumed was masculine appreciation. Ignoring her inner warning, she warmed under his exploratory perusal, unable to drag her gaze away. A spark of desire flared to life, a frisson of awareness dancing across her sensitive skin. A slow burn started in her core, moving languidly through her limbs as his gaze grew more intense. She recalled the intoxicating kiss they'd shared the other night, and her pulse sped up with anticipation—

The waiter appeared, startling her, the haze of sensual enchantment dissipating into the ether. He set two small plates on the table along with their appetizer, which came with two sauces.

"Thank you," they said in unison. The server nodded and took his leave.

Summer took a quick sip of her water and focused on her lap as she silently ordered her racing heartbeat to calm the hell down. She'd been so focused on the sexy man sitting across from her…it was as if he'd cast some sort of spell over her.

When she looked up, she was startled to discover him still watching her.

"You okay, sweetheart?"

Not even close. "Perfect."

He studied her a moment longer, then smiled and picked up one of the battered little Os. "These are one of my favorites," he said before popping it into his mouth.

She watched him chew with anxious uncertainty before swallowing her pride to ask, "What *is* calamari, exactly?"

"Fried squid."

"You mean…like Squidward?"

He laughed, a deep, masculine explosion of sound.

Her face heated. Thank God Katie wasn't with them, she thought as a grin tugged at her lips.

"I'm afraid so. Go on, try it, you'll like it. I promise."

Though her stomach clenched at the thought, Summer eyeballed the crispy fried rings with determination. She breathed deep, exhaled, then picked one up and pushed it between her lips. The man had gone to a lot of trouble to plan this date, and the last thing she wanted to do was hurt his feelings.

"Mmm." Surprised to discover she loved the crunchy bite—the calamari itself wonderfully tender—she eagerly plucked another off the plate.

"Good, huh? I'm glad you like it." He slid several of the tasty little morsels onto one of the small plates, adding a dollop of the red sauce before handing it to her. "Try it with the spicy marinara."

Struck by a sudden wave of insecurity, Summer chewed slowly, watching him as he enjoyed the fried treat with gusto. He seemed so at ease in this upscale atmosphere, and all she could think about was how out of place she felt.

As if sensing her inner turmoil, he reached across the table and grasped her fingers. "Have I told you how beautiful you look tonight?"

"Thank you," she murmured, then felt an irrational need to point out, "This isn't my dress. Angela borrowed it to me because I didn't have anything appropriate to wear. I mean, I do have one nice blouse, but it's…" Embarrassed by her ridiculous rambling, she gave her head an exasperated shake. "Sorry. I guess I'm a little nervous."

He gave her fingers a gentle squeeze. "To be honest, so am I. I wanted to knock your socks off, and I think maybe I've overdone it a bit."

"Oh, no, this has been one of the best nights of my life," she assured him. And it was true. With the exception of the day Katie was born, she couldn't remember ever feeling so lucky.

The thought quickly set off an alarm bell in her head, but she ignored it, refusing to give in to the negativity trying to worm its way into her brain. "No one has ever gone to so much trouble for me before. It's…it's nice."

Before Reese could respond, the waiter returned. "Are you ready to order, or would you like a few more minutes?" He sent a smile back and forth between them.

Reese eyed her for a moment in curious scrutiny, then announced, "I'm really sorry, but we won't be able to stay for dinner after all." He pulled out his wallet and handed the guy a fifty. "Keep the change."

"Oh. Well, thank you, Mr. McMillan. I'm sorry you can't stay. Hope everything is all right."

Reese stood and held out his hand to her. "Everything is perfect. I just came to a realization."

The waiter smiled and nodded. "Very good. You both have a good night." He started stacking the dirty plates as Reese led her from the restaurant.

Curious about this 'realization,' Summer waited until they were seated in the car before asking him about it. "So, not that I'm complaining, but I *am* kind of hungry."

He chuckled as he started up the engine. "Don't worry, we're going to have dinner. I just realized I should have taken you to my favorite spot instead of somewhere you felt out of place."

"Picked up on that, did you? I'm really sorry." She didn't know whether to feel embarrassed or relieved.

He made a left out of the parking lot heading west, then reached out to grasp her hand as he'd done in the restaurant. "I can be pretty clueless, but yeah. You kept glancing around as if I'd taken you to a nude beach instead of a nice restaurant."

She laughed. "Sorry. I didn't mean to come across as ungrateful. I'm just not used to such…fanciness."

"You were the most beautiful woman in the restaurant. And 'ungrateful' isn't a word I'd ever use to describe you."

His kind words warmed her heart. She met his gaze for a brief moment, wanting nothing more than to lean over and kiss him. Lord how she wanted to kiss him.

"Maybe you should give Angie a quick call, see how the girls are doing…?"

"Good idea." She slipped her cell from the borrowed clutch purse and dialed her friend's number.

Angela answered on the second ring. "Great minds! I was just about to call you."

"Everything's all right, I hope…?"

"Oh, fine," her friend assured her. "The girls ate, played with their stuffed animals, took a bubble bath in the Jacuzzi tub. James just helped me upstairs, then hurried back down to watch a movie with them in the den. Meara headed to bed right after the bath-time fun."

She laughed softly, imagining how much fun Katie must be having. "Sounds like quite the night."

"And I'm hoping your night is going just as well…?"

She cast a quick, sidelong glance at Reese, who, thankfully, had his eyes on the car ahead of them, and not her. "Definitely." She would have said more, but felt a tad awkward talking about the date—which they were in the middle of—while said date was sitting right beside her.

Angela must have understood because she chuckled. "Well, listen, you guys have fun and don't worry about Katie. She's having a great time, and they'll probably fall asleep watching movies anyway, James right along with them."

"You guys are the best, I can't thank you enough."

"You can thank us by not worrying and simply enjoying yourself." With that, her friend hung up.

As she slipped her cell back into the purse, Reese asked, "So, is everything okay? The girls having a good time?"

"They're having a wonderful time. I just wish there was some way I could repay you all for everything you've done for us."

"You do that every day by helping Meara and Angie."

He didn't mention they were paying her to do so, but she decided not to look that particular gift horse in the mouth. She did, in fact, love everything she did, especially learning how to keep the books. She knew Angela had taken a few business courses, and she thought she'd like to do the same. One day, after she'd saved up enough money, that is.

Fifteen minutes later, they pulled into the parking lot of a place called Smiley's. She'd never heard of it, but it appeared to be pretty casual. And it was right on the river, which made the view phenomenal.

He opened her door and held out his hand. "Smiley's has the best burger in town. And their fries are freshly hand-cut and thick, just the way I like 'em."

"Sounds good. Though I've only ever eaten at fast food places, so the best burger I've had since moving here is my own."

"Yeah? Maybe you could make me one of these amazing burgers someday."

"I'd be happy to. I'll even spring for hamburger buns," she teased as he escorted her across the parking lot. When he cast her a confused, sidelong glance, she explained, "I'm old school. I eat everything on white bread—hamburgers, hotdogs, sloppy joes."

He laughed. "White bread works for me. No need to buy any fancy buns on my account."

They reached the door, and he opened it for her. Soft country music spilled out, and as she stepped inside, the most delicious aromas wafted under her nose. A tall, reed-thin woman with chin-length blonde hair approached with a welcoming smile, and Reese asked for a table on the side of the restaurant facing the river. Ever the gentleman, he waited until she sat down before taking his own seat across from her.

"Your waitress will be right with you." The hostess told them before strolling back to the front of the restaurant.

"It smells *so good* in here," she said, glancing around with interest. The roughhewn log walls were tastefully covered with framed hunting and fishing photos, while unpolished beams ran the length of the ceiling and framed each doorway. Since hunting was big back home in Wisconsin, she felt right at home with the rustic décor.

Reese took a cursory look around. "It's not as busy as I thought it would be. Not that I'm complaining."

The waitress approached the table, set a glass of water down in front of each of them, then handed over the menus she'd had tucked under her arm. "How are you folks doing this evening?"

"Very well, thank you," Reese said with that great smile of his. Summer managed to drag her gaze away from him and smiled at the woman as well.

"Wonderful. Can I get you something from the bar tonight?"

Reese gave the menu a quick perusal. "Actually, I think I'll take a root beer."

The waitress turned to Summer. "And what can I get for you?"

"Root beer sounds perfect. Thank you."

She nodded and made a notation on her order pad. "I'll be right back with your drinks.

"Is it just me," Summer whispered once the waitress was out of earshot, "or are you feeling a little sense of déjà vu?"

He gave a soft chuckle. "I'm feeling pretty damn lucky, actually."

"Oh?"

He reached across the table and grasped her fingers. Reese McMillan was turning out to be quite the romantic. "I'm sitting across from the prettiest lady in all of Colorado."

She playfully rolled her eyes. "Thank you. Though you may need to have your eyes examined."

He stared at her for a moment, eyes slightly narrowed, as if trying to figure something out. "You really have no idea just how gorgeous you are, do you?"

She cleared her throat and had to force herself to hold his gaze. She was uncomfortable with compliments, always had been, and swiftly changed the subject. "So, the best burger in town, hey?"

An hour later, after a wonderful dinner—that did, in fact, include one of the best cheeseburgers she'd ever eaten—and even better conversation, Summer knew she was dangerously close to falling in love. Reese was funny, smart, thoughtful, kind. The gentleness and patience he'd shown her daughter told her everything she needed to know about what kind of man he was. And what kind of father he would be to Katie…if things happened to move in that direction.

And despite his sister-in-law's warning, he'd told her all about his love of the Double M and his desire to open a full-service dude ranch. She'd had no clue what a dude ranch even was, and listened with rapt fascination as he explained, in complete and vivid detail. The longing in his voice, the determination in his tone, leaving no question in her mind he would make his dream a reality one day.

Maybe she'd even be around to see it.

"I don't want this date to end," she quietly admitted after the waitress dropped off the bill. As much fun as they'd had, Summer yearned for a little alone time with him. Maybe he'd even kiss her again before they headed back to the ranch to pick up her car.

He pulled out his wallet and stuffed several bills inside the small black folder. "Well, we haven't had dessert yet. Since you already checked in on Katie, why don't we go grab something sweet? Ice cream, or maybe we could head to The Cheesecake Factory."

Before she lost her nerve, she took a deep breath and said, "I still have Popsicles at my place."

Chapter Seventeen

Reese paused as he rolled her 'Popsicle' comment around in his head. If she were anyone else, he'd be pretty certain it was an invitation for…more. And damn, did he want more. But with Summer, he couldn't be sure. She'd made it clear the other night she wasn't ready to sleep with him, which he completely understood. Hell, they'd only known each other a week.

And she *had* voiced concern about the cost of the date. Maybe she was simply trying to save him a buck. He almost laughed out loud at the thought.

"Popsicles sound good to me. Got any orange ones left?"

A shy smile curved her lips. "Plenty. Katie's favorite is green, and I prefer red or purple."

Liking where this was heading, he escorted her from the restaurant. He'd take it slow, let her set the pace. He didn't want her to think he was expecting anything other than the proffered Popsicle. But if she *had* changed her mind about sleeping with him, wild horses wouldn't be able to drag him away, so strong was his need for her.

Once behind the wheel, he cleared his throat and strived for a casual tone. "So, your place for popsicles. You sure?" He wanted to give her an out, just in case she'd had a change of heart since making what had to be an impulsive suggestion.

"I'm sure. Unless…you'd prefer something else?" She glanced down and studied her lap.

Reese just barely caught the flash of insecurity in her eyes as she worried her bottom lip. So badly he wanted to pull her across the console and show her exactly what he wanted. "There's nothing I'd like more right now than…a Popsicle. I just wanted to make sure it's what you want, too."

She finally met his gaze, but just barely. Her shyness was a surprising turn-on.

"It's what I want."

He reached over and grasped her hand. Her smile seemed to ignite as he stroked her thumb with his own.

Reese made it to her apartment complex in record time. He followed her in, then closed and locked the door behind him as she set her purse on the kitchen table. Without glancing back, she opened the freezer.

He shrugged out of his sports coat and hung it on the knob of the door, undid the buttons at his wrists and folded his sleeves up a few inches. An odd sensation gripped him as he watched her shut the freezer and spin back around, a mesmeric little half-smile curving her lips. She handed him an orange Popsicle, and he saw she'd chosen red for herself.

She peeled down the plastic wrapper, slowly, almost as if teasing him. It wasn't until she caught his gaze that his suspicion grew. She opened her mouth, slipped the cherry-flavored ice rocket inside, and sucked gently, twirling it around, slowly pulling it in and out with a throaty "Mmm."

Unsure of what to do—eat his dessert, or drag her into his arms—he decided on the former, still a little unsure of her motives. He certainly didn't want to jump to a conclusion that could have lasting consequences. After everything Moretti put her through, he knew she was far from ready to put her full trust in anyone.

He unwrapped his treat and silently scolded his racing heart and hardening body.

It struck him that he'd never given any other women this much thought. If he wanted someone, he made a move. None of this overthinking and indecision. And not that he was conceited, but he rarely got turned down. It was just something he'd become accustomed to. Hell, he knew it had more to do with his bank account than his looks. The fact that he wasn't a troll was no doubt a huge plus.

But with Summer, he wanted more than just sex. And Lord, he'd never imagined feeling something like that before. It confused him, knocked him off his game. He wanted her, yet…he wanted their first time to be perfect. For her. He certainly didn't want her to feel obligated to sleep with him because he'd taken her out on a date. And, shit. Was that what was going on here? Did she—

"Are you okay?" she suddenly asked, eyeing him with concern.

He cleared his throat. "I'm great, why?"

"You're frowning at your Popsicle like you're mad at it."

He glanced at the thing in surprise. Forcing his features to relax, he chuckled. "Sorry, just… thinking about family stuff."

She paused, a slight frown marring her own brow. "Nothing to worry about, I hope?" She headed over to the couch, perched on the edge, and gestured for him to join her.

He sat down beside her, hip to hip, draped his left arm across the back of the couch behind her, and took a small bite of his Popsicle. While he couldn't admit the true path of his thoughts, it *would* be nice to talk to someone about his parents. Though he wasn't exactly sure how much to share. This was James' business, too, and his brother was notoriously private.

"I didn't mean to sound nosy, it's just… If you want to talk about anything, I'm happy to listen."

He stared at his slowly melting frozen treat as he searched for a way to start the conversation. He looked over and nearly groaned as he watched her work her Popsicle as if it were the most delicious thing she'd ever consumed. How desperately he wanted to kiss those red-tinted lips.

"Reese?"

He cleared his throat. "My parents are getting divorced."

She drew in a sharp breath. "Oh, my God... I'm so sorry. Are you okay?"

"I'm fine. I can't stand either one of 'em, so it's hard to work up any real emotion over it. And I'm sorry if that sounds harsh, but, believe me, you won't meet two more selfish, narcissistic people than my parents."

Her eyes softened with compassion. He knew she must be thinking about her own mom and dad, and her own dysfunctional relationship with them. While Reese had had James to ease some of the loneliness, Summer had taken on the brunt of her parents' authoritarian nature all alone.

"Crappy parents. Hell of a thing to have in common, hey?" She glanced at her treat as if in surprise, then hurried and licked up what was about to drip.

"I'm sure we'll find we have plenty of great things in common as we get to know each other better. I mean, we both like calamari. That's huge in my book."

She giggled, a girly yet oh-so-sexy sound he loved. "Once I got the image of Squidward out of my head, I was fine. And you're right, it was amazing."

"I could eat a plate every single day."

They finished their sweet treats at the same time. Summer got up to toss their sticks and wrappers, and when she came back, instead of sitting back down beside him, she straddled his lap, grasped his shoulders, and met his gaze with laser-focused intensity.

The breath froze in his chest; he settled his hands uncertainly at her waist. They stared at each other for what seemed like days, and he was trying to regain the ability of speech when Summer spoke.

"I know I said I wasn't ready for…*this* yet. But…" Her voiced dropped to a near whisper. "I haven't been with anyone since…well, it's been just Katie and I for over five years now, and I love my daughter. She's been my main—my *only*—focus, since the day she was born. But then I met you and realized…I want more. Which sounds selfish now that I've said it out loud."

She heaved a breathy sigh, her gaze wavering with indecisiveness. Reese hated that she was feeling such guilt over something as normal and primeval as needing love and comfort. If there was one thing he had learned about her in the short time he'd known her, Summer was a deeply sensual woman. It pleased him on some masculine level to know she hadn't been with anyone in all these years.

He slid his hands slowly up her waist, her arms and shoulders, caressing every silky inch with seductive intent until he had her face cupped gently in his palms. Those beautiful blue eyes, so conflicted, yet so full of longing, as if begging him to deny her absurd conclusion.

"There isn't a single selfish bone in your body." He leaned in and kissed her, softly, a kiss meant to reassure. "You're an amazing mother, sweetheart. You always put your daughter first, which happens to be one of your most attractive qualities. But you have needs like everybody else." His tone grew raw as desire gripped him. "Katie is safe and sound, and a million miles away right now. There's just you and me here." He ran the pad of his thumb along the soft curve of her cheek.

She stared at him, her gaze dropping to his lips, back up to look him in the eye, then back to his lips, as if waging some inner battle. When she leaned in and kissed him, Reese swallowed a groan of relief. He'd never wanted a woman more, and didn't know how he'd find the strength to walk out of there if she changed her mind. But he would. For Summer, he'd wait as long as he had to, no matter how long it took.

Ah, hell…was he falling in love? Is this what it felt like?

He wrapped his arms around her and deepened the kiss, slanting his mouth across hers with hungry urgency, teasing the seam of her lips before pushing inside to plumb the hot depths. His hands roamed at will, kneading and caressing a path from her shoulders, down the elegant curve of her spine, to the flair of her hips. He rested his hands on her outer thighs, his thumbs gently stroking her silken skin. Impatient with need, he grasped the hem of the sexy red dress and worked it up her slim frame.

Summer lifted her arms and let him pull the dress over her head, then reached back for the clasp of her bra as he quickly unbuttoned and stripped off his shirt. He caught and held her gaze for a brief moment, as she unhooked her bra and slid it from her shoulders. He could feel her awkwardness in the slight quiver of her hands, and knew she was struggling with self-confidence.

To him, her insecurity was crazy. Summer Hanson was the most beautiful woman he'd ever laid eyes on, her lithe body unequaled.

As soon as she dropped the satiny, black undergarment to the floor, naked except for a pair of tiny matching panties, he cupped her soft breasts and reclaimed those lush lips, ready to show her just how desirable she was to him.

She twined her arms around his neck and plastered herself against his chest, her light, floral fragrance sweeping over him like a warm caress. He continued to smooth and stroke her honeyed skin, awed by the silky texture, eager to taste and touch every inch of her. He loved kissing her, the wet slide of tongues, still cold from their sweet treats, the sexy little hums in the back of her throat.

Tunneling his fingers into those golden tresses, he cupped the back of her head and slanted his mouth across hers to further deepen the kiss. The sensuous back and forth glide of their tongues made him hungry for more as her passionate response and soft moan of arousal surged through every cell in his body, making him drunk with need. He coaxed her head back until she was draped over his arm, those glorious, pink-tipped orbs just begging for his attention.

He captured one nipple with gentle pressure, licking the pebbled peak with the flat of his tongue before sucking gently, and softly thumbing the other, teasing the tip with light flicks. She moaned, arching into him in silent plea, her intoxicating scent amplifying his need with dizzying intensity. He was so damn hard his cock strained painfully behind the zipper of his dress slacks. Struggling for control—a task completely foreign to him—Reese gripped her hips and maneuvered her to her feet, then stood up before her.

Summer reached out to grasp his zipper, and he watched through lust-hazed eyes as she slid it down his swollen length. He helped her remove his slacks, then his boxer briefs, toeing off his socks as she wiggled free of the tiny black panties. Since he knew the bedroom only contained Katie's small bed, he was about to ask if she preferred the couch or the floor when she whispered, "Do you have...protection?"

He would have smiled over the tremor in her voice if he wasn't so desperate to be inside her.

Stepping back, he reached down for his pants, removing his wallet, and one of the little packets he'd stuffed in there while getting ready for the date. He almost hadn't bothered, but decided if and when they did need it, he would be ready.

She took a deep breath, eyeing the condom as if mustering her confidence. Her nerves were unmistakable—and a surprising turn-on. She knelt on the carpeted floor and held a hand out to him. Heart racing, he grasped it and knelt before her, drinking his fill of the blonde beauty before wrapping his arms around her and slanting his mouth across hers with eager impatience. He cupped her ass with one hand, and the back of her head with the other while guiding her down to lie beside him.

Hooking her leg over the back of his thigh, she plastered herself against him while returning his kiss with growing fervor. He let her set the pace, her tongue teasing at first, growing more bold as her soft fingers caressed the small of his back, tracing a slow path down the curve of his spine as her tongue eagerly mated with his, the sexy little sounds she made in the back of her throat driving him wild. He squeezed and molded the soft globes of her perfect backside while her palms glided up his arms, over his shoulders and down his chest, slowly, smoothing her way across his abs and down further…

When those long, sleek fingers closed around his hard shaft, he nearly came in her hand, like a teenager with his first erection. The thought brought a smile to his lips.

"What?" she whispered, her tone hesitant. She released him, sliding her hand back up to his chest.

He kissed her and leaned back to meet her gaze. "I was just thinking what a lucky guy I am."

She made a sound that was a cross between a laugh and a groan. "Now, why don't I believe you?"

"So suspicious." He moved his lips to the shell of her ear, tracing it with his tongue.

"Reese?"

"Hmmm?"

"Don't…have you changed your mind?"

He lifted his head and stared at her. Had she lost her damn mind? "Changed my… Why would you think that?"

"You don't…seem to be in much of a hurry. Nico…"

When she dropped her eyes and didn't finish her thought, he had a sudden urge to beat the hell out of that idiot. He cupped her cheek and lifted slightly. "I promise you, darlin', I've never wanted anyone as much as I want you. But I don't want to rush. I want our first time to be memorable."

He rolled so she was beneath him, then gazed down at her. Those gorgeous blue eyes were darkened with desire, her lips swollen and pink. When her tongue darted out to moisten her top lip, he nearly lost it. He needed to slow things down, and fast, or he'd end up disappointing her—and embarrassing himself.

He recaptured her lips and reclaimed her supple breast, stroking and teasing her nipple with tiny flicks before moving down to replace his hand with his lips. Her breath caught as he drew the velvety bud into his mouth, and he grew drunk with need as the satiny tip pebbled in his mouth. She stroked his head with light strokes, as if hesitantly urging him on.

He trailed his hands down the soft curves of her waist and hip, his fingers caressing a slow path to her flat belly. He splayed them across her trim stomach and slid down until he could spread her slightly quivering thighs, eager to taste every silky-smooth inch of her.

She tensed. "Uh…what are you doing?"

He gave a low chuckle and met her gaze with surprise. "Sweetheart, I know you're not exactly…experienced, but…you must know—"

A soft, awkward sigh was followed by, "Of course, I *know*…I just… We never… Oh, my god, I must sound pathetic. And I keep bringing up my ex. It's a miracle you haven't raced out the door."

He pressed his lips to the tender flesh just above her bellybutton. "You sound like someone whose only lover was a selfish idiot." He placed a soft kiss just below her bellybutton. "And I plan to rectify that tonight."

She grinned. "And he was fast. Like...really fast."

Reese held back a satisfied smirk. "That must have sucked."

Her grin turned into a hard giggle. "Right?"

A smile broke free, though now he'd have to make sure he didn't humiliate himself. Never had before, but damn, he'd never wanted a woman as much as the beautiful blonde beneath him.

Starting at the spot just below her breasts, he kissed a slow path down the delicate flesh of her belly, over her sexy little bellybutton, splaying his fingers across her damp, dark blonde curls before sliding between her slick folds and sinking a finger into her tight, hot passage. She clenched around him with a soft cry, but Reese was on a mission. To pleasure her like she'd never been pleasured before. Call it plain old male pride, but he planned to wipe every damn memory of that loser ex completely out of her head. And heart.

He slipped one hand beneath her ass for better access, then his mouth joined his fingers in the mission to bring her to orgasm. A series of soft sighs escaped her as he licked her tight little nubbin with light flicks of his tongue, while slowly working his finger in and out of her with slow precision.

Her soft sighs became groans of need as her hips lifted to his hungry mouth. Her arousal was incredible to watch, her intoxicating scent aphrodisiacal. His dick throbbed painfully as he laved her swollen flesh with increasing speed and pressure, reveling in the sweet taste that was uniquely hers, until she arched into him with a lusty cry of release, her hands clenching in his hair, her hips trembling as she came with surprising abandon. He watched her through hunger-filled eyes, so magnificent she was in the throes of her pleasure.

Reese found the condom and tore it open, sheathing himself in record time. If he didn't come before he was deep inside her it would be a miracle.

Summer's satiated smile was mesmerizing as she held her arms open to him. His chest grew tight as he gazed down at her. The blonde bombshell with a heart of gold. He held himself poised above her. "You okay?" he whispered, searching her face.

"I'm great. You're…amazing."

He kissed her, guided himself to her glistening core, and entered her with gentle care. It nearly killed him to go slow, but he knew it had been awhile for her and didn't want to pound her into the floor. Instead he sank into her welcoming heat with a long, hoarse groan.

She wrapped her legs around his thighs, her hands stroking his back, his arms, his shoulders. Reese tried to keep a slow and steady pace, but as she lifted to meet his thrusts, carnal instinct took over, and he couldn't hold back any longer. Though he'd wanted to make her come again, he knew it was doubtful he'd last that long.

But as their hips rocked together with desperate need, her nails clenched into his back and she convulsed around him, releasing a guttural cry as she reached climax for a second time, the heels of her feet digging into his ass as he drove into her with furious abandon. Reese came hard, a rough, soul-deep shout tearing from his throat. They moved together, riding every last wave before collapsing into a tangled heap of sweating bodies.

Sated in ways he'd never imagined until meeting the amazing woman beneath him, he rolled to his back and pulled her into his side. She snuggled against him with a hearty sigh of satisfaction, and he tightened his hold on her, happier than he'd ever been in his life. When she pressed her lips to his shoulder, Reese squeezed his eyes shut, assaulted by a whole host of emotions—fear, exhilaration, happiness, contentment…fear.

He brought her hand up and kissed her fingers while trying to make sense of it all. He'd had sex with more women than he could count, some he couldn't even remember their names or faces—not something he was proud of—but he'd never felt anything like this before. Maybe he should bite the bullet and talk to James, who had a little more experience with that particular emotion than he did.

He got up to dispose of the condom, and when he returned, she was lying on her stomach on the couch in a very risqué pose, that pert, sweet ass just begging for his hands. He grew instantly hard just thinking about all the ways he wanted to pleasure her.

Kneeling on the floor beside her, his ran his hand over the gentle curve of her hip with slow strokes, exploring her soft flesh until she was a quivering puddle of need. He wanted to make her come with his mouth again, have her sit up and lean back, spread those creamy thighs wide, giving him full and total access. But he wasn't sure if she was up for that again so soon.

"You're the most beautiful woman I've ever known," he murmured as he slowly worshiped her lithe body with long, slow strokes. She hummed softly, and as if reading his mind, she sat up and reached for him. He had another thought, of her riding him, slow and easy, then fast and hard, and it nearly stole his breath, so badly did he want her.

With a soft sigh, she drew her fingertips lightly across his chest, back and forth, in a lover's caress. "Reese?"

"Mmm?"

"Was that…memorable?"

Chapter Eighteen

Summer waited with growing uncertainty for Reese to respond. She knew what they'd just shared had been incredible—at least for her. But she wanted...no, *needed* to know Reese felt the same. Not that she expected some kind of declaration or anything. But she certainly wasn't the casual sex type, so she sure hoped it had meant something to him as well.

She was about to tweak his chest hair when his brows pulled together and he sat beside her on the couch. "Are you kidding me? Memorable would be an understatement, sweetheart." He leaned in for a quick kiss. "I think the more important question is, was it memorable for you?"

She was tempted to teasingly demure, but her uninhibited response had surely been all the answer he needed. Hopefully, her face wasn't as red as it felt. "Seared into my brain for eternity."

He grinned and leaned in for another kiss. He tried to coax her into straddling his lap, but she had other ideas—like getting even. She slid down to kneel between his thighs. Those sexy brown eyes darkened as he realized her intent, and he smiled reassuringly while reaching out to tuck a stray lock of hair behind her ear.

Not quite confident enough to hold his gaze, she refocused on the long, rigid length jutting out from the apex of his thighs. Determined to please him, she stroked a slow path up his muscled legs, teasing and caressing as she moved closer to his impressive erection. Lord, the man was magnificent. She wrapped her fingers around him, drawing a groan from deep in his chest.

Gaining confidence, she leaned in to run her tongue across the silken head, then swirled around and around while leisurely milking her hand up and down his smooth, hard flesh—silk-covered steel.

Peeking at him through her lashes, Summer was thrilled to discover him watching her with laser focus through passion-narrowed eyes. She worshiped him with her lips and tongue, licking a path down and around his thick sex, cupping and caressing his balls. His hands came up and tangled in her hair as another low groan reverberated deep in his chest.

"*Fuck*, that feels good," he muttered, his voice raw, husky.

Emboldened by his praise, she took him into her mouth, sucking on the head much as she had her Popsicle—only he tasted so much better—then worked her way down his stiff length, her throat stretching until she'd taken him all in. Determined to pleasure him as he had her, she worked her mouth back up, using her lips and tongue to drive him wild, licking every inch of his turgid shaft, while stroking him with a quick, steady rhythm.

His hips lifted as his whole body tensed like a tightly strung bow. She'd anticipated he'd come in her mouth, but he pulled her up and kissed her, quickly putting his big hand over hers and stroking hard and fast, showing her how to finish him off. She worked him with a tight fist until he tore his lips free from hers and came with a hoarse shout.

Once his breathing slowed, he chuckled softly. "Damn, sweetheart, that was a surprise."

She grinned, incredibly pleased with herself. "You're welcome."

He grasped her ass with both hands, then positioned her so she straddled his lap. "I need to wash up, but unless you're sore, I do have another condom…?"

He continued to caress and stroke her, and her nipples hardened as she ached for him to be inside her again. Eager to try something different—before she lost her newfound confidence—she said, "I've never been on top. Is it like riding a horse?"

"More like riding a stallion," he teased.

She could feel him growing hard again beneath her and was truly was impressed by his stamina. The man was so incredibly sexy, he'd turn her into his sex slave at this rate.

The apartment buzzer rang. Reese broke off the kiss and frowned toward the door as a rush of anxiety hit her. Katie! She struggled to sit up as whoever was in her lobby starting buzzing with urgency.

She shot to her feet as Reese cursed and followed suit. He grabbed his slacks and headed into the bathroom while she raced into the bedroom to grab her robe.

"It's got to be James. Something must have happened," she declared while tying the sash and hurrying to the door.

Reese, who'd donned his pants, but hadn't bothered to button them, gently grasped her arm. "Let me get it. James wouldn't show up here without calling first, and he certainly wouldn't press on the buzzer like that."

She nodded, her heart in her throat. Though what he said made sense, and of course he knew his brother better than she did, an overwhelming feeling of dread washed over her, and she couldn't seem to shake it as Reese went to open the door.

She heard a curse, then, "Where the hell is Summer?"

Dread gripped her at the sound of that rough voice. *Nico?* But he still had five years left to serve on his sentence!

"I think you need to leave." Reese, his low tone surprisingly dark, menacing.

"Wait…McMillan? What the fuck are you doing here?"

More conversation she couldn't quite make out, then, "Summer! What the hell is going on here?"

"I said you need to leave." Reese again, his voice hard, angry.

Nico's words finally registered, and a shiver of dread raced up her spine. He'd called Reese by his last name. They knew each other. But…how could that be possible? And why wouldn't Reese have told her?

Making sure her sash was tied tight, she took a deep breath, then strode into the hallway to confront her past—and what she'd started to hope would be her future.

Nico, much to her surprise, looked quite different than the last time she'd seen him at the Jefferson County courthouse. His hair had receded a bit, he'd put on some muscle, and there was a hardness in his gaze that hadn't been there before.

Mustering her courage, she crossed her arms over her chest and demanded, "When did you get out? And why the hell did you come here?"

His slow smile made her skin crawl as he looked her up and down. "Damn, baby, you look great. I've missed you like crazy."

"I asked you why you're here, dammit. When did you get out? And how?"

A scowl wiped away his appreciative stare. He glanced at Reese—whose enigmatic expression was impossible to read—and a sneer curled his upper lip as his gaze returned to her. "Yeah, I can see you weren't expecting me. Care to tell me what this cocksucker's doing here? Do you have any idea who he is?"

Reese had gone surprisingly quiet, and when she looked at him, an almost apologetic light shone from his eyes. He moved to stand beside her, finally saying, "Can we go back inside and talk? I can explain—"

"Explain *what*?" Nico angrily interjected as he took a step forward. "How you and your boy, Mark, set me up? How you're responsible for me having to leave Summer and our baby girl for five fucking years?"

She looked up at Reese, silently begging him to refute her ex's ridiculous claims. How could he have had anything to do with—

"Look, I didn't have a choice," he told her, an admission in every sense of the word. "And I didn't know about you and Katie. He never mentioned either one of you, not once." He shot Nico a scathing look, then swiped his hand through his hair, his frustration palpable. "Sweetheart, can we please go inside and talk?"

"What's to talk about, rich boy?" Nico demanded. "I did five years in prison because of you. Missed out on seeing my baby grow into a little girl, on marrying the woman I love."

"Are you delusional?" Summer demanded, incredulous. "You had no intention of marrying me, and we both know it. You were sleeping around, probably from the moment we hit town. You made a fool of me, left me alone with a baby to raise, no money, no job. I can't even believe you had the nerve to show up here."

Nico dropped his arms and flexed his hands, twisting around to eyeball Reese as if anxious to take a swing at him. He finally turned back to face her. "I made mistakes, I can admit that. But I want to make it up to you. Make it up to Katie Bear. Start a new life together." He jabbed a finger in Reese's direction. "He's a coke head, baby. That's how I met him. His buddy Mark's dad was the sheriff. They called me one night to score, and it turned out to be a big fucking setup."

Summer's heart constricted with pain as her gaze locked on Reese's. His silence was damning as he stared at her. "So, it's...true? You're a drug addict?"

He grasped her hand. "No. I was, years ago. But something happened that...set me straight. I haven't touched that shit in over five years. I swear to you."

She wanted so much to believe him, he seemed sincere, but...her head was spinning.

"I heard he slept with his brother's fiancé," Nico promptly announced. "Mark's sister, Paige. And his brother walked in on 'em. What kind of a scumbag fucks his own brother's girl?"

"You son of a bitch!" Reese lunged and grabbed him by the throat.

"Reese, please, let him go! I just want him to leave."

He gave her ex a shove and released him. Nico dropped to his knees, but recovered quickly and unsteadily stood back up.

"Where's Katie?" he rasped, glaring at her. "I don't want this sonofabitch anywhere near my daughter!"

"I've been more of a father to her than you ever were," Reese shot back.

"Yeah? And who the hell's fault is that?"

"You were a dealer when I met you. *That's* the reason you're not in Katie's life."

She stepped in between them, unable to handle another display of machoism. Not now. All she wanted was for Nico to leave so they could head back to the ranch and check on her daughter. She knew Katie was safe and sound, and likely sound asleep by now, but just taking a peek in at her would help to settle Summer's nerves.

"Enough already. Please." She glanced around as it suddenly dawned on her that her neighbors could very well be listening. "I don't need everybody knowing my business. Nico, you need to leave."

"I want to see my daughter. Dammit, Summer, I have rights."

"Katie doesn't even know you," she shot back in a furious whisper. "I have to talk to her, prepare her for this."

"You make it sound as if we've never met. I was in the hospital room when you delivered her. I held her even before you did. I adored that little girl, and you know it."

Anger surged through her as her blood boiled. If he truly loved his daughter, he wouldn't have put them all in jeopardy. She glared at him through narrowed eyes. "What I know is she wasn't even two months old when you were taken away in handcuffs. When the cops tossed our apartment looking for drugs, it took me hours to clean up, and Katie cried the entire time. All she knows of you, all you are to her, is the guy in the picture."

His face twisted with fury. "You bitch!" He grabbed her by the upper arm so hard she cried out in pain.

"You're a dead man!" Reese roared, and punched him so hard he crumpled to the floor like dead weight.

She stared down at her ex in horrified silence, fearing Reese might have killed him. But then Nico moaned and slowly sat up. Gingerly fingering his left eye, he shoved back to lean against the wall.

"I think you broke my fucking eye socket." He glared up at Reese with venomous hatred. "You stole five years of my life, now you're sleeping with my girl and playing daddy to my kid? You're gonna pay for this, you arrogant asshole. I'm pressing charges."

He'd just pulled out a cell phone when the apartment door directly across from hers flew open.

Mr. and Mrs. Giles stood staring at them in wide-eyed horror. The elderly couple glanced from Nico, to her, to Reese—who still hadn't buttoned his pants—before announcing, "The police are on their way. Good Lord, what in the world is going on here?"

Nico shoved the cell back in his jacket pocket and struggled to his feet, his expression smug as he glowered at Reese.

Mortified, she spun around and raced into her apartment to throw some clothes on, her mind a whirlwind of utter disbelief. How could such a wonderful night have taken such a horrible turn? One minute she's soaring to the heavens, the next she's freefalling into hell.

"It's me," she heard as Reese came in right behind her. When she came out of her bedroom, he was waiting for her by the door, fully dressed, his sports coat slung over his shoulder, his gaze cautious. It seemed as if he wanted to say something, but then he opened the door without a word and escorted her back out into the hallway.

Nico was on his feet again, Mrs. Giles hovering in front of him, trying to get him to apply an ice pack to his eye. Summer could only imagine what kind of bullshit story he must have told, because both she and her husband were glaring at her as if the word 'slut' were emblazoned across her forehead.

Thankfully, the police arrived within minutes, as the tension had become almost too much to bear.

She'd probably have to move, though she had no idea where she'd go. Hell, she didn't even know if she'd still have a job after all this, and she sure as hell couldn't afford anything else in town. Maybe her landlord would allow her to move to another building…

The first officer, who was a good head taller, and fifty pounds lighter, than the second, walked straight up to Reese, brow raised in curiosity. "McMillan? What's going on here?"

Reese cast a sidelong glance at her neighbors. "Would it be all right if we went inside to talk?"

The officer gave a curt nod. To the older couple, he said, "We'll be over to take your statements after we're done here."

"Oh, well, we didn't see anything, so there's not much we can tell you," Mr. Giles explained. "Just heard a kerfuffle and figured we'd better call you."

"We appreciate it, sir. Ma'am. Enjoy the rest of your evening."

Nico handed the ice pack back to Mrs. Giles with his trademark smile. Both she and her husband gave Summer one last judgmental glance before slipping back inside their apartment. Though she'd certainly have plenty of questions to field tomorrow from the nosey twosome, right now, all she wanted was to get this over with so she and Reese could head back to the ranch to check on Katie.

And have a conversation with him she wasn't sure she wanted to have.

Once they were all inside her apartment, Reese closed the door and moved to stand beside her. Nico glared at him while fingering his eye, which was starting to swell a bit and turn colors.

"Okay," the taller officer began, "Who would like to speak first?"

Nico jabbed a finger in Reese's direction. "This asshole attacked me, and I want him thrown in jail."

"And this sonofabitch put his hands on Miss Hanson, squeezed her arm so hard she cried out," Reese countered, arms crossed. "You put your hands on a woman, you're lower than horseshit and deserve what you get."

"He's lying!" Nico shot back. "I didn't touch her. Tell him." He gestured at her.

Did the idiot really think she would lie for him after...*everything* he'd put her through? She rolled up her sleeve, revealing a pinkish-purple bruise that wrapped around her upper arm. Summer bruised easily, so it looked much worse than it was. But Nico *had* squeezed pretty hard, and she certainly didn't want Reese to be taken away by the police for trying to protect her. She'd have to call his brother, explain everything that had happened. How humiliating would that be?

"If *you* press charges," she quietly informed him, "then *I'll* press charges." And having just gotten out of prison, they both knew he had a lot more to lose than Reese. Not to mention the officer and Reese obviously knew each other and seemed to be on friendly terms.

By the tightening of his mouth, Summer knew he had just come to those same realizations.

He stared at her, hard, confused, as if…as if he had no idea who she was anymore. She'd grown a lot in the time he'd been away. No longer the subservient teenage girl he'd known, but an independent, grown woman. She'd raised their daughter for five years without a lick of help from him, and with little help from anyone else. Not that she and Katie lived a life of luxury. Lord knew she wished for better for her daughter—and herself. But she'd done the best she could, and Katie was happy, healthy, and thriving.

Finally, his lip curled, and he shook his head in disbelief. "So it's like that, huh? Just another notch on rich boy's cowboy boot."

Reese took a threatening step forward, but the second officer quickly moved between them.

"Come on, McMillan, hit me in front of the nice officers. Show my woman what a tough guy you are."

"I'm not *your* anything," Summer swiftly informed him, truly repulsed by the thought of this man ever laying a hand on her again. "You're not a damn thing to me anymore."

"You don't deserve a woman like Summer," Reese added, disgust evident in the curl of his lip. "You never did."

"Well, neither do you, rich boy. But I have a kid with her, you don't." Nico's expression grew smug, his swollen, black eye a sharp reminder of just how off the rails this night had gone.

"And how do you know that?" she asked, striking back at him for making her doubt her own self-worth. "Like you said, you've been gone a long time."

"Well, if you do, it isn't with him. McMillan bangs a new chick every other week, which means you two haven't been together long enough to have a kid. Don't get me wrong, honey, you know I think you're gorgeous, but no way this guy's changed *that* much. He dates supermodels and actresses, not poor local girls. You're a novelty, nothing more."

Her face grew warm as her self-esteem took a nosedive. Supermodels and actresses? As much as she wanted to rub it in his face just how wrong he was, it *had* only been a week since she met Reese. And though she really didn't know all that much about him, the one thing she did know, thanks to Angela, was that he'd never been in a serious relationship. Ever.

Reese cleared his throat and stepped back, thankfully not rising to the bait. To the taller officer, he said, "Jake, can we hurry this along, please? The lady's had a long night."

"Self-important asshole," Nico muttered.

The officers ignored him. The one he'd called Jake said, "As long as nobody wants to press charges, I think we can call this one a misunderstanding." He shot a pointed look at first Nico, then Reese. "Deal?"

Nico crossed his arms over his chest. "Fine. But I want to see Katie before I leave."

Frustration gripped her. She didn't want to talk about this in front of the police. "She's not here, she's sleeping over at a friend's house."

He glared at her so hard she worried her head would burst into flames. After a quick glance at each officer—was he trying to garner sympathy?—he angrily stormed past her into the kitchen to retrieve a pen and a slip of paper from the junk drawer. After writing something down, he slapped the paper on the counter and set the pen on top of it.

"My cell phone number. I want to see my daughter, Summer. If I don't hear from you by Monday, you'll be hearing from my lawyer."

Chapter Nineteen

As Nico locked eyes with him in silent victory, rage simmered in Reese's gut, bitter and all-consuming. He wanted to chase after the bastard and beat him into the ground. If that sonofabitch cost him Summer...

Lord, what he wouldn't give to start the night over again.

Everything had been going great. He'd never felt such chemistry with a woman before, and not just sexual, but on every level imaginable. He knew this was different from anything he'd ever felt before. Terrifyingly different. And he was almost certain Summer felt more for him than just a physical attraction. But after everything she'd learned tonight, and the awful way she'd learned it... Fuck, what a total piece of garbage she must think he is.

Though the only thing she was probably thinking about at the moment was getting back to the ranch to check on Katie.

"Hey, Jake, I really appreciate the discretion. Moretti is the lady's ex, and apparently he made early parole. She wasn't expecting him, and as you probably picked up on, he wasn't happy to find me here."

Reese cast a sidelong glance at Summer to gauge her reaction; she was staring at the ground as if praying it would open up beneath her. He didn't feel right sharing her private business, but it couldn't be helped. He needed his friend to know what was going on in case Nico started harassing her. Officer Jake Teller was a total hard-ass, but he was also a champion of women. Reese knew he'd make sure to drive past whenever he was in the area, maybe ask some of his fellow officers to do the same.

His old high school buddy gave a curt nod of understanding. To Summer he said, "Miss, if you have any more trouble, call the station and we'll send someone right out." He handed her a card.

She took it with slightly shaky fingers. "Thank you. I'm sorry to have bothered you. Both of you," she added, addressing Teller's partner.

"No bother at all," Jake assured her in his no-nonsense tone. "McMillan, I'm sure we'll talk soon."

As soon as they left, Summer raced into the bedroom, returning seconds later wearing the same light blue hoodie she'd had on the first time he saw her. Hard to believe how much had changed in those seven short days. She slipped into her sneakers, then retrieved a grocery bag from the kitchen and collected the red dress, cape, and heels she'd borrowed from Angie.

"If you don't mind, I'd really like to go check on my daughter."

"Of course."

He didn't speak again until they were on Route 6. "Sweetheart, I'd really like a chance to explain…everything."

When she didn't respond right away, a boulder of fear settled on his chest, making it hard to breathe. The thought of losing her when he'd only just found her was unthinkable. The woman occupied his headspace from the moment he crawled out of bed, to the moment he crawled back in. What kind of music did she listen to? What was she like as a child? Her favorite sport? Her favorite ice cream flavor? What did she dream about?

And now that they'd slept together, those feelings had intensified into something possessive, primal. Just the *thought* of Nico—or anyone else—putting their hands on her made him batshit crazy. And jealousy wasn't an emotion he had any real experience with, so he had no idea how the hell to deal with it.

"After I've checked on my daughter." She cast him a swift, sideways glance. "I just need to see her. I know she's okay, but… I just need to see her."

"I get it, no worries." He smiled to reassure her. "We're only about ten minutes from the ranch."

Reese pulled into the driveway and drove until the darkened path became lit by the motion-detector overhead lights James had installed a few years back. The massive, six-stall garage was to the left of the main house, and after hitting the button clipped onto the visor, he pulled in and parked in the last open spot.

Grateful for the late hour, he escorted Summer into the quiet house and directly upstairs to Molly's room. She swiped away a tear as they reached the top of the staircase—an action he was pretty sure he wasn't supposed to see. So badly he wanted to take her in his arms, reassure her she had nothing to worry about, that he'd hire the best attorney money could buy for her and Katie. But the woman was prideful, and already uncomfortable with having accepted his and his family's help. He couldn't imagine she would agree to take anything more from him.

Certainly not after tonight's bombshells.

But Moretti was as self-absorbed as they came. Once he realized he couldn't win her back, he'd make her life a living hell. Drag her into court, force Katie to spend time with him. Sure, the guy was her biological father, but if he truly gave a damn about her—or her mother—he wouldn't have been selling drugs out of their apartment, possibly putting their lives at risk.

Forcing his troubled thoughts to take a back seat, he slowly opened Molly's bedroom door, and managed another reassuring smile as he motioned Summer inside.

His niece was snuggled under her My Little Pony comforter, soft, steady snores pouring from her mouth. He grinned. The little chainsaw was almost as loud as her father. He realized the top bunk was empty, and that Katie was sound asleep right next to her log-sawing bestie. If they weren't the cutest damn thing he'd ever seen he didn't know what was.

He stepped out of the way so Summer could move in for a closer look. She reached out to touch her little girl, but then pulled back as if afraid she might wake her. After a few more seconds, she nodded her thanks, and quietly slipped from the room. He knew she was thinking about having to tell Katie about her father, and it was probably killing her.

Once they were back downstairs, he said in a low tone, "There's this old, wooden swing on the back porch that my grandfather made for my grandmother. They used to sit out there year 'round to watch the sun set. I was hoping we could head out there to talk."

She crossed her arms and met his gaze with a self-assurance he found as fascinating as it was surprising. Summer Hanson may be soft-spoken and gentle, but she had a sexy inner strength that captivated him.

"I saw the swing, it's beautiful." She nibbled at her bottom lip before adding, "Okay."

Relieved, he gently grasped her hand and escorted her into the kitchen. He pulled two bottles of water from the fridge and handed her one before opening the sliding glass door that led out to the back porch.

Summer ran her fingers over the padded burgundy cushion before sitting on the edge of the swing, her knees touching, her denim-encased legs slightly apart. She twisted the cap on her bottle of water, took a small sip, then recapped it and set it on the porch by her feet.

Reese sat down beside her, careful to leave some space between them. He didn't want her to feel crowded in any way. Perched on the edge of the seat the way she was, he feared she might jump up and run for the hills at any moment.

"Look, I need you to know I had every intention of telling you about my connection to Nico."

"Then why didn't you?" she immediately countered. "It's not like you haven't had plenty of opportunities." She stared across the dark sky toward the mountains beyond, her incomparably beautiful face bathed in moonlight, a slight frown marring her brow. He wanted to reach out and smooth it away, but knew she wouldn't appreciate the gesture.

"I wanted you to get to know me first. My past isn't pretty. I've…done some things I'm not proud of. But I've worked hard to turn my life around, and I've been clean for over five years. I'd like to think that counts for something." He gave a self-deprecating shrug. "With the exception of James and Meara, I've never needed to explain myself to anyone before. This is, uh, very new to me."

She turned slightly, but didn't quite meet his gaze. "So, it's true then? You slept with your brother's fiancée?"

He'd half hoped she would have forgotten about that. It was the last thing he wanted to talk about since it showed him in the worst possible light. But she deserved to know the whole truth, especially if he was going to be not only in her life, but her daughter's as well. He took a long pull off his water, wishing like hell it were a bracing shot of bourbon.

"Yes. And it was the lowest moment of my life." He took a deep breath and settled back into the swing's comforting embrace. "Her name is Paige. I was friends with her brother, Mark. James is a hard worker, he's always put the ranch first, and Paige didn't like it. So she started hanging around with me and Mark.

"We did a lot of partying, and on one particular night,"—he quietly cleared his throat—"that I wish I could erase from existence, Paige and I ended up in bed together. Some of that night is still fuzzy, but the look in my brother's eyes when he opened the door and saw us... Sobered me right up. And it's something that still haunts me. Needless to say, he wouldn't speak to me for a very long time. I think the reason he finally forgave me is I inadvertently stopped him from making the biggest mistake of his life. I'm also the reason he met Angela, even if the reason wasn't exactly…ideal."

Summer was quiet for a moment as she absorbed everything he'd said, and his pulse sped up as he waited for her to respond. He suddenly realized she held power over him, and the thought was unsettling.

"She mentioned you'd sold her your half of the ranch, but then she sold it back to you after her and James were married. She said the story wasn't hers to tell, so that's all I know."

Great, as if he didn't already look like the world's biggest asshole. But she deserved the entire story, and judging by her tone, she wanted to know.

"I was at a casino in Atlantic City playing poker in a private, high stakes game. I needed money to cover a bet, so I offered to put up my half of the ranch, but it was a cash only table. Angela, who was the dealer, offered to buy it. I have no idea how she was able to come up with all that cash so fast, but she did. One of the players was a lawyer and wrote out a quick contract for the sale. I won the hand, so I did a little celebrating. Figured her plan all along was to sell it back to me for a profit. But by the time I went looking for her, she was gone."

He smiled ruefully, remembering the surge of panic that had gripped him when he learned she'd already left for Colorado to claim her prize. A prize worth, at that time, over a hundred times what she'd paid for it.

"But…if you were clean by then, and trying to make amends to James, why the hell were you in Atlantic City gambling away your great-grandparents' life work?"

She stood, suddenly, crossing her arms in a self-protective manner, her disappointment a tangible barrier between them. He thought she might storm off, but then realized she wouldn't go anywhere without Katie.

"I'm sorry." She dropped her hands to her hips and gave her head a slight, almost imperceptible shake. "That was uncalled for. I just…I don't understand how you could risk losing this incredible place on the draw of a *damn card*."

Shame gripped him, scorching a path up his neck and face. Having never wanted for anything his entire life—maybe with the exception of his parents' attention when he was a young kid—he'd never looked at his situation through the eyes of someone who'd grown up with so little.

He stood as well, staring off into the distance for a moment—his future, which he would never take for granted again—before turning to look at her.

"My brother owns fifty-one percent of this ranch. I thought if I could win enough money to buy the one percent from James, he'd see I had changed, that I wanted to become equal partners—like we already would have been if I hadn't been such a screw-up. Not one of my better ideas, but thankfully it all worked out in the end."

She turned to face him, her entire face now in shadow. "It's just hard for me to believe you could do such a thing…which might seem unfair since, truth is, I barely know you. But after everything Nico put me through, as cliché as this sounds, I swore off men. I had a little girl to raise, and rent to pay. Those were the only two things that mattered. Then I met you and thought…maybe all men *aren't* assholes. Tonight, when I realized you knew my ex, and *how* you knew him, it threw me. I just…I don't want to go down that road again. And I can't take a chance on Katie getting hurt."

He closed the short distance between them and grasped both her hands. He'd never needed anyone to believe him—believe *in* him—more than he did right now.

"Sweetheart, I swear to you, that's not who I am anymore. I was young and thoughtless and resented James for things that weren't even his fault. I made one bad choice after another, until I almost lost my brother. But that all seemed like another lifetime ago until I met you. I've spent the last five years working my ass off, and it would kill me if I lost you because of stupid past mistakes."

He pulled her close and slid his arms around her. Though he wasn't sure what to expect, he breathed a silent sigh of relief when she didn't pull away. "I realize we haven't know each other very long, but I like you. *A lot.* More than I ever thought possible." He stroked a slow path from her slim hips to her shoulders, desperate to make her understand just how much she meant to him. She shivered, and he hoped it was his touch that elicited such a response, and not the chilly night air.

When she remained silent, he threw caution to the wind and gently grasped her face with both hands before pressing his lips to hers. Just a soft touch, testing the waters. Resting his forehead against hers, he whispered, "Come up to my room, spend the night with me."

She sighed and brought her hands up to splay against his chest. But instead of leaning into him, she stepped back and shook her head. "I'd be lying if I said I didn't want to. But I think we need to put the brakes on this…whatever it is between us." He opened his mouth to argue, but she rushed to add, "Reese, please. I know that's not what you wanted to hear, but it's what I need right now. My head is spinning and…all I can think about is Katie. How am I supposed to tell her this awful person is her father?" She said the last word as if it were poison on her tongue.

He propped his hands on his hips and hung his head, wishing there was something he could say to dissuade her. Disappointment rose up in his throat until he thought he might choke on it. He knew she was right, and hell, it's not as if she didn't have plenty of reason not to trust him.

"Look, I don't want you going back to your apartment knowing Nico is probably watching for you. Please spend the night, even if it's not with me. The room across from Molly's is a guest room. I'll stay out of your way, if that's what you want. Just…please stay."

She looked as if she might decline his offer, but finally gave a hesitant nod. "Thank you. I appreciate it."

With a heavy heart, he escorted her back inside.

Chapter Twenty

After tossing and turning most of the night, Reese still managed to drag his sorry ass out of bed before dawn to help the men put up a new section of fencing in the east pasture. He skipped breakfast, only stopping in the kitchen long enough to gulp down a quick cup of coffee, and fill his thermos. James, who was just shoving the last bite of his toast in his mouth, grunted a "Morning," before pushing back from the table, grabbing his own thermos, and leading the way out to the garage.

They both had plenty on their mind, he knew, so he closed his eyes and enjoyed the short ride out to the site. John and one of the newer hires—Cam, he was pretty sure the guy's name was—were already waiting for them, leaning against John's ancient, red Ford pickup. They all exchanged greetings, then quickly got to work.

Once the sun was high in the sky, the conversation started to flow, as did the dirty jokes. Reese wasn't in the frame of mind for such talk, but he smiled and managed a few chuckles as they listened to John's boastful claims of a threesome the night before with identical twins. James glanced over and gave him an eye roll, which prompted a genuine laugh out of him.

"So," John said as he hammered a metal fence post into the ground, "Word is Reese here's nailing that hot blonde who works up at the house. That true, boss?" He shot Reese a wink, then said to no one in particular. "Man, I bet she gives good head. Can you pass her my way once you're done with—"

Reese hauled back and swung, smashing his fist into John's face with such force the guy went down like a lead balloon.

"Don't you *ever* talk about her like that again, understood?" White hot rage coursed through him like a blast of adrenaline. He flexed his throbbing hand and walked off, desperate to get his anger under control. Not something he was used to having to do since he'd always been pretty even tempered. But Summer brought out a protective side of him he hadn't known existed. With Nico, it had been gut-wrenching jealousy, with John, blind rage over a careless comment.

"What the fuck is wrong with you?" James demanded as Cam rushed over and handed John a bandana to wipe his bloody nose.

All three stared at him as if he'd lost his ever-lovin' mind. John was one of his closest friends; the guy was like a brother to him and James. And yeah, they'd been making crude jokes like that for years. But when the comments were suddenly directed at Summer, it triggered something primal in him—just like the night before.

His anger dissipated as remorse set in. John couldn't have known his feelings for Summer were different than any woman he'd dated in the past, otherwise he never would have made those comments, of that Reese was certain. He gave his throbbing hand a shake and met his friend's wary gaze.

"I think you broke my goddamn nose," John muttered, his shock evident as he examined the bloodstained bandana.

"I'm sorry. It's just… Look, she's a hard-working, single mother struggling to keep a roof over her and her kid's head. She doesn't deserve to be talked about like that."

"Hell, I didn't mean nothin' by it. Just trying to lighten the mood." John started to push to his feet; Reese and James both grabbed an elbow and helped him up.

"I'd better get you to the doctor, have that looked at."

"Actually, Cam, why don't you take John to Urgent Care," James said. "Reese and I have business to take care of."

The Double M's newest hire gave a hard nod. "You got it, boss."

Once they were on their way, James dipped his head toward the truck. "Get in." His tone brooked no argument, not that Reese would've given him one. He owed his brother an explanation; his actions could have led to a lawsuit, if John were that sort of guy. He wasn't, but it could have just as easily been Cam he hit.

James started the truck, but didn't put it in gear. He sat for a moment staring out the windshield as if collecting his thoughts. Then he turned slightly and demanded, "Would you like to explain to me what the hell just happened?"

"You heard what he said about Summer. What if he'd said something like that about Angie?"

"Angela is my *wife*. You've been on one date with Summer. I get that you like her, but that was quite the overreaction. And all because he made a crude comment? Hell, John's been talking shit like that for years. Usually, you're talking right along with him."

"I know."

"So, I'll ask again, what the hell happened?"

Reese blew out a hard breath and explained everything that had happened the night before, told him about his connection to Summer's ex and the horrible way she'd found out about it. How the guy thought he'd pick up with Summer and Katie as if five long years hadn't passed—which no way in hell Reese would let that happen. He just needed the stubborn woman to give him another chance so he could make things right.

"I hate them living at that apartment. The guy's always been a creep, selling drugs out of there right under her nose, sleeping with that slutty friend of Paige's. He's probably just watching the place for a chance to catch her alone. I don't trust him. But…she made it clear she wants me to keep my distance, at least until she figures things out." He closed his eyes and leaned his head back. "Nico told her about me and Paige. She looked at me like…fuck, like I was pond scum. And I am."

"You made some mistakes, no one's gonna give you a pass on that. But you've worked hard to put all that shit behind you. Eventually, she'll realize that and come around." After a few seconds he asked, "Do you love her?"

Reese scrubbed his eyes with the heels of his hands, then sat up and let out a whopper of a sigh. "Hell, I don't know. I have no idea what love feels like." Only he was pretty sure he knew *exactly* how it felt. He cast James a sidelong glance. "How did you know you were in love with Angie?"

"The morning I woke up and realized she was gone?" James turned to meet his gaze. "Never been more scared in my life."

Reese nodded, and they both turned to gaze back out the windshield.

"Listen, why don't you drive down to Austin with Andy to pick up that new stallion. It'll give you a couple days to clear your head, and a couple days for Summer to miss you."

Reese managed a smile, though the last thing he wanted to do right now was leave. He'd no doubt spend the entire time worrying about that asshole ex of hers. But maybe James was right, on both scores. Sure would be nice to come home and find out she'd missed him.

"If I do, will you have Angela invite Summer to stay here at the ranch till I get back? I'm not sure I could leave knowing Moretti had open access to her. It's possible he still has a key to the place."

"Don't worry, I'll make sure she and Katie are safe. If she doesn't agree to stay here, I'll hire someone to watch her place round the clock. Deal?"

"Deal."

James gave him a thump on the shoulder, put the truck in gear, and headed back to the ranch.

Summer had planned to head home after breakfast, but Katie and Molly tag teamed her, begging to stay for lunch because Meara was making chicken soup and grilled cheese sandwiches. Since she wasn't all that eager to go back to the apartment knowing Nico was probably waiting for them, she'd relented. Besides, everything Meara made was ten times better than anything she could make, so it was a win-win for all of them.

"So, don't keep me in suspense," Angela whispered as they sat at the kitchen table sipping coffee. "I want to hear all about your date."

"It was…good. And I brought your dress, cape, and shoes back, though I accidentally left them in the car. Thanks again for lending them to me."

Angela's eye widened with stunned excitement, as if she'd just told her they'd eloped or something. "Did you guys…do it in the car? On your first date? I have to admit, that's pretty hot." She chuckled, then bit her lips to stifle herself when Meara came back from checking on the girls.

She gave her head a vehement shake, casting a surreptitious glance at the older woman before taking a quick sip of her coffee.

Meara brought the pot over and topped them both off, then sat down with a soft groan and filled herself a cup. "So, young lady, how was your date?"

Angela grinned at her, the shit. And as much as she wanted to tell them exactly what they were hoping to hear, she knew it was only a matter of time before they discovered the truth.

"The date was great, actually. Until I found out Katie's father made early parole."

"No way! Seriously? How did you find out?" Angela's wide-eyed, open-mouthed dismay would have been comical had the situation not been so serious.

"He showed up at my door right after…" Her words trailed off as it suddenly dawned on her just what the older woman might think of her if she knew she's slept with Reese on their very first date. "We decided to head back to my place for popsicles." Oh, God, how lame that must sound.

But Meara simply regarded her with concern, her kind eyes crinkled with worry. "Darlin', I'm not so old that I don't understand why you and Reese wanted…popsicles. I'm just glad my boy was with you when your ex showed up."

Relieved to know the older woman wasn't sitting in judgment, Summer admitted, "Me, too. But…I'm afraid it got ugly." She explained to them everything that had unfolded, ending with Reese insisting she spend the night at the ranch. "I slept in the guest bedroom."

A frown marred Angela's brow. "Look, I understand why you're upset with Reese for not telling you he knew your ex. But if you think about it, you can understand his point. You did, in fact, do exactly what he was afraid you'd do—think the worst of him."

Somewhat surprised by her friend's censure, Summer rose to her feet and moved to gaze out the picture window. Tears stung her eyes then started free-falling as she realized what these two must think of her, how judgmental she was acting toward a man who had never shown her anything but kindness.

She heard a chair squeak and then Meara was taking her into her arms. Angela was right behind her, and suddenly she was ensconced in one big, loving embrace.

"There now, young lady. Nothing wrong with a good cry. And you surely have reason to be upset. A night of such promise ending like it did. And of course, Angela and I understand your reservations. It must have been quite a shock to learn Reese was once capable of such stupidity."

Angela let out a soft snort, which made Summer smile. Meara released her and moved over to the sink. She wet a paper towel and handed it to her.

"But," the older woman continued, "Under his older brother's guidance, he's become a new man. Loyal, caring, hard-working. James is quite proud of him, and so am I. Whoever ends up capturing his heart will be very lucky indeed."

"Reese has definitely made his share of dumb ass mistakes," Angela chimed in as she lowered herself back onto the chair. "But he's not the same arrogant idiot I met all those years ago. He works hard, and he's a savvy businessman according to James. Many of the deals that have made the largest profit over the past few years have been the ones Reese negotiated. The Double M is at least triple the size it was when I first arrived, maybe bigger. And he's always been amazing with Molly, who adores her uncle like nobody's business."

Angela swiped at her eyes with the wet paper towel, her doubts slowly fading away as they described the man she had come to know—before Nico showed up at her door and painted Reese in the worst possible light. He'd been so generous with her, and with Katie. And though she still harbored some reservation, her gut told her the man she'd made love with last night, the man who had spoken to her with such raw honesty, was exactly who he said he was.

The kitchen door swung open, and both McMillan brothers strode in. James came around the table and kissed his wife, while Reese pause only long enough to cast her a hesitant smile before hurrying out of the room. She heard his heavy footsteps on the stairs and wondered if there was a particular reason the two had come back to the ranch so early in the day.

"I'm sending Reese on a business trip to Austin," James explained, answering her unspoken question. "He'll only be gone a couple of days. We'd like you and Katie to stay here at the ranch until he gets back. I know Angela would be grateful for your company, and Molly will be thrilled."

Disappointment settled in her chest like a huge weight. She'd hoped they could talk later, once Reese finished his workday, and now he was going to leave still believing she thought the worst of him. Her face warmed as she met James' sympathetic gaze. "I assume he told you about my ex?"

He gave an almost apologetic nod. "We just want you and Katie to be safe."

Angela grasped her husband's hand. "I think it's a great idea. We can watch movies, eat until we burst." Her eyes lit up. "I'll make a cake! I found a recipe I've been meaning to try."

James and Meara's identical looks of dismay were comical.

"Hey, I bet Meara would be happy to bake that cake for you." James cast a meaningful glance at the housekeeper, who nodded furiously.

"I would be happy to," she hurriedly agreed. "Give you young ladies more time to visit."

Angela eyeballed them both in suspicious silence, then turned to drawl, "Mistake salt for sugar *one* time, and suddenly you're banned from the kitchen."

Summer burst out laughing. "Well, I know my way around a pantry well enough, so maybe we can bake a cake together."

Reese joined them a few seconds later, a duffle bag gripped in his left hand. He stood before her, his gaze cautious. "I asked James to invite you and Katie to stay here this weekend, and I hope you'll accept. I'll be back Monday morning." He moved in close and lowered his voice. "I was hoping we could talk again once I get back."

"Me, too." She wasn't exactly sure what she would say, but she knew without a shadow of a doubt that she wanted this man in her life.

Chapter Twenty-one

——— ✦ ———

*M*onday morning arrived with a splash, in the literal sense, as a torrential rainstorm blew in just before dawn. The same line of storms was responsible for Reese and Andy being delayed just south of Santa Fe, and now they weren't due home until sometime in the afternoon.

Molly woke up with a sore throat, though Katie felt fine, so James offered to drive her to school, which Summer very much appreciated. She loved a rainy day, but was a little afraid to drive in such a heavy downpour.

Meara had planned for them to can pie filling, so after a short argument with Angela, who insisted she was perfectly capable of taking care of her own daughter for a few hours, they got busy peeling and cutting apples. Perfect weather for the job. And since she'd never canned before, the older woman was incredibly patient and kind as she explained the process step by step.

They were just about to break for lunch when the school called. A bad feeling gripped her, and she excused herself and stepped outside for privacy. "Hello?"

"Hi, this is Margaret Anderson from Beaumont Elementary. Is this Summer Hanson?"

"Yes, it is." Her pulse sped up, but then she realized Katie must have come down with whatever Molly had.

"Ms. Hanson, we had a gentleman show up here claiming to be Katie's father. He wanted us to release her into his care, said you had okayed it. We, of course, told him we would need authorization from you first. He wasn't happy, stormed out and drove off. I called you immediately."

A ball of fear settled in her gut. "Thank you for letting me know. Since I have you, the only people I authorize to take Katie out of school besides myself, are my employers, the McMillans: Reese, James, and Angela. Their daughter and Katie are in the same class."

She heard clicking, and then, "Got it. I have all three listed."

"Thank you, I appreciate it."

"No problem at all. Have a good day."

"You, too." She ended the call and took a deep, shuddering breath. So, it seemed Nico had no intention of respecting her wishes, not that she was all that surprised. That he'd planned to take Katie out of school and tell her who he was without her being there… The man clearly didn't give a damn about their daughter's feelings, or hers.

Since she couldn't be sure he wouldn't pull another stunt like this, she made the decision to tell Katie herself. She could only imagine how frightened her little girl would be if Nico ended up cornering her in some other way. Another concern was Reese. As captivated as her daughter was with him, Summer wasn't sure how she was going to take the news.

She found Angela and explained about the call from the school. "I have to tell her about her father. I'm going to take her back to the apartment after school so we can talk."

Angela's forehead scrunched with worry. "Maybe you should bring her back here first and wait for Reese to get home. He'd be happy to drive you to the apartment, make sure everything goes smoothly. In fact, maybe it's best if you and Katie moved in here for a while. I'm sure James will insist once he knows what's going on."

She gave an appreciative smile. "What's going on is Katie's father is out of prison and he wants to get to know his daughter. While I'm not thrilled about it, legally, I don't think I can keep him from her. And morally…well, I'm conflicted, but I want to do what's best for my little girl. You and your family have been wonderful to us," she added before her friend could respond. "But I *have* to go home at some point, and I'm sure Reese and Andy will have plenty to do once they get here."

"I know he wouldn't want you going back to that apartment alone, especially if he knew what happened today."

She arched a brow in exasperation. "Then don't tell him. Listen, I have to introduce her to Nico sooner or later. He's already shown up at the school, which means ignoring him won't make it go away. And I don't have the money to take him to court."

Angela's mouth twisted in thoughtful contemplation. "I'm going to have James give his lawyer a call. Cal Henderson is one of the best in the state, and he'd be happy to help, trust me."

Cal Henderson as in Henderson and Smythe? A bubble of laughter almost escaped her. Wouldn't that be quite the coincidence. She opened her mouth to argue, but Angela persisted. "Believe me, Cal is a good guy. He'll be happy to hear you out, give you a course of action."

"What's the chance I'm going to win this argument?"

Angela grinned. "Zero to none."

Summer stood outside the school with only mild trepidation as she waited for the final bell to ring.

She couldn't imagine Nico would be foolish enough to show up and cause another scene, especially in front of a crowd of people. But prison had obviously changed him, so she couldn't rule it out. He'd certainly never put his hands on her like the other night, which still had her a little freaked out. What if he became angry with Katie? The thought was enough to freeze the blood in her veins, and she quickly shoved it to the back of her mind.

When her daughter finally strolled out the front doors of the school, Summer took a quick glance around before rushing forward to meet her.

"Hey, sweetie, did you have a good day?"

A hesitant shrug. "We had cookies for Carly's birthday, but I missed Molly."

"I know, I'm sorry. She still isn't feeling well, so we're going to head back to the apartment today. You've probably missed your bed, hey?" She grasped her hand and led her down the walkway to the parking lot. When she didn't respond, Summer prompted, "Everything okay?"

A sullen nod. "I just…I thought we were gonna live with Molly's family now."

Well, hell. Exactly what she'd been afraid of, Katie growing attached to her friend's wonderfully welcoming family. Sadly, she wasn't alone. Summer had also started to feel as if…as if they belonged somehow.

She gave her daughter's shoulder a gentle squeeze. "The McMillans have been amazing to us, and I get that it's really fun there—lots to do, tons of toys to play with, a big TV to watch your movies on."

"Yeah, but... Reese lives there, and I want him to be my daddy."

That stopped her short. She knew Katie really liked him, but she hadn't realized she was already harboring delusions of fatherly grandeur. Summer captured her little face with both hands and smiled. "Katie Bear, Reese is a very nice man, but he's not going to be your daddy." At least, not anytime soon. "He *is* your friend, though, and he likes you very much."

"Molly's daddy said you went on a date with Reese. I though that meant..." She shrugged.

Thanks a lot, James. "I'm sorry you got your hopes up. I like Reese, and he likes me. But for right now, we're just friends. Understand?"

Another sullen nod, but Katie grasped her hand, and they made their way to the car. She made it home within minutes, and had just parked in her usual spot when a mid-size black car pulled in right behind her. The driver's door flew open, and out stepped Nico, his smile annoyingly smug.

Her heart sank. Dammit, she wasn't ready for this, and hated him for forcing himself on them. If only she'd listened to Angela, they'd be on their way to the ranch right now.

Bile churned in her gut as she braced herself for the inevitable. She turned around and pasted on her most reassuring smile. "Katie Bear, I have a surprise for you. There's someone you're going to meet soon, so remember your manners, okay?"

Her little face screwed up with curiosity. "Who?"

Nico strode up, and had the nerve to blow her a kiss before ducking down to peer at their daughter through the window. His face transformed into something familiar as he stared at the beautiful little girl in the backseat. Katie's eyes grew round as dinner plates as she stared back at the strange man gazing at her with such rapt fascination.

"Ready?" Summer asked, recognizing the fear flashing in those big brown eyes, which just about killed her. She got out and opened the back door, unbuckled her daughter's seat belt, and helped her from the car. Katie leaned into her side, hiding half her face as a small tremor went through her.

Nico came around to meet them. He met Summer's gaze for a quick second, then crouched down and smiled. "Hey, Katie, do you know who I am?"

She shook her head before breaking eye contact, her little face creased with uncertainty.

He reached out and gently chucked her under the chin. "I'm your father."

Katie stared at him for a second, then looked up at her for confirmation. Summer nodded, her chest tightening at the fear swimming in those dark brown eyes. "You okay?"

She cast a quick glance at Nico, then wrapped her arms around Summer's hips and whispered, "But I want Reese to be my father."

Nico heard her. His face reddened, and he glared at Summer as if their daughter's whispered declaration was her fault. Unsure of what to do, the decision was taken from her hands when one of the other tenants pulled into the parking lot. Loathe to have her private business made public, she grasped Katie's hand. "Come on, let's head inside. Maybe have some vanilla wafers and milk…?"

Without waiting for a reply, she led her daughter toward the apartment complex. Nico followed along, thankfully keeping a short distance behind.

As soon as he closed the door behind them, Katie raced into the bedroom and shut the door.

Nico started after her, but Summer stepped in front of him. "Good Lord, she's only five years old and just had a major bombshell dropped on her. Give her a few minutes to let it settle in."

He spun away with a muttered curse and veered into the kitchen. A quick perusal of the near-empty fridge brought a scowl to his face. He slammed it shut, cursed again, and slapped his hand on the counter. "This isn't how it was supposed to be, dammit."

Incredulous, she crossed her arms and leaned a hip against the side of the couch. "Then you shouldn't have pressed it. She doesn't know you, Nico. She's scared."

"I'm her fucking father," he crudely reminded. "Why would she be afraid of me—unless you've been filling her head with bullshit. Or maybe McMillan's been feeding her lies. I don't want that asshole anywhere near my kid again, Summer. I mean it."

"Don't be ridiculous." She cast a quick glance at the bedroom door, then lowered her tone in hopes he would follow suit. "Reese would never do something so petty."

"Yeah?" He cocked a brow. "Tell that to his brother."

"Your name never came up before that night," she countered, ignoring his effort to get under her skin. "And Katie hasn't seen him since, he's out of town on business." Having had about all she could take from this man, Summer straightened and moved to the door. She needed to check on Katie. The thought of her little peanut bawling her eyes out in silence broke Summer's heart. "Look, I think it's best if you leave now. We can try this again once Katie's had time to process...everything."

Indecision etched his brow, and she could only hope he cared enough about their little girl to leave without issue. He seemed to collect himself, then, suddenly, he was standing toe to toe with her, that smile she used to find so sexy in full effect. He reached up and grasped her chin, then kissed her, a full on, open-mouthed kiss meant to seduce.

Completely taken off guard, it took her a few seconds to react. She shoved back and glared at him. The man was delusional if he thought she'd ever want anything to do with him again. "What the hell are you doing?"

"If I have to explain it, I'm more out of practice than I thought." He tried to take her in his arms, and she literally recoiled in disgust. A scowl distorted the face she used to think so handsome. He swept his angry gaze up and down her body. "What, you think you're too good for me now that you're screwing McMillan?"

"This has nothing to do with Reese, or anyone else. I'm not interested in revisiting the past with you. You *sold drugs*, right here in this apartment, with our infant daughter asleep in the other room. It's a miracle someone didn't show up here with a gun to rob you. Or worse." She shuddered, the thought of how bad things could have gotten if not for...well, if not for Reese being forced to help the police.

Nico swept both hands through his hair and held her gaze with laser intensity. "I screwed up. You don't think I know that? Know how much I hurt you, leaving you here alone to raise our baby girl? I'm...so damn sorry. For everything." His tone softened. "I've missed you, baby. Getting back to you and Katie...it's all I've thought about for the past five years. And I know I can make things right if you give me a chance. Maybe even...earn your forgiveness."

A slow throb started just above her right temple. Last thing she wanted to do was continue this conversation, especially with Katie hiding in the other room, probably more frightened than she's ever been. "Whether I can forgive you or not isn't the problem. You want to have a relationship with your daughter, you'll have to be patient. But you and I? Not going to happen. It's been over five years, Nico. I've moved on."

His gaze grew hostile again as he flexed his hands. For a split second, she thought he might actually hit her. Instead, he grabbed her wrists and pulled her into his chest, twisting her arms in the process. She cried out, but her complaint was muffled when he kissed her again, this time with bruising intensity. He tried to force his tongue into her mouth, and she twisted her head to the side, shoving at his chest as hard as she could. He let go, only to backhand her. Summer fell back into the arm of the couch and toppled over, crashing into the coffee table.

Stunned, and more afraid than she'd ever been, she stumbled to her feet, desperate to get to Katie. Nico reached out as if to help her up, his face twisted with both horror and astonishment.

"Jesus, baby, I'm sorry! I-I didn't mean to—"

The door burst open with a splintering crack and Reese rushed in. Her relief was so great tears stung her eyes. She'd never been so happy to see someone as she was at that moment. The feeling was short-lived as his gaze settled on her face, which she knew by his reaction had already started to color.

"You sonofabitch!"

"Reese, please!" she begged, grasping his arm. "Katie's in the bedroom. I'm fine, I swear."

He stopped in his tracks and cursed, casting an eye across the room before pulling her into his side with gentle assurance. She realized she'd been holding her breath, and released it on a silent sigh.

"It's time for you to go," he commanded, his tone low, hostile.

Nico's lip curled. "Arrogant prick. You need to mind your own damn business." He turned his venom on Summer. "I got back in touch with my parents and told them about Katie. They were thrilled to hear they have a granddaughter and can't wait to meet her. I want to take her to New York with me, just for a couple days to—"

"Are you out of your mind?" She cast a quick glance at the bedroom door and lowered her voice. "I'm not letting you take Katie anywhere, let alone all the way to the other side of the country."

"Dammit, Summer, she's my daughter, too!" He smacked his chest as if for emphasis. "You have no right keeping her from me!"

Reese tensed; she tightened her grip on his arm. "I warned you, Moretti. Get the fuck out of here, or I'll drag you out myself."

Nico eyed him with blatant hatred. She knew now that he held Reese responsible for everything that had gone wrong in his life. She also knew that

Reese's choices probably saved her—and Katie—from years of abuse.

He seemed to collect himself, meeting her gaze with sudden disregard. "You have no right keeping my own kid from me. My parents offered to hire me a lawyer, so consider this your official notice: I'm suing for custody."

High-octane fear gripped her as his announcement sank in. She couldn't afford to hire a lawyer, and he obviously knew it, the bastard. His gaze shifted back to Reese, and she realized his intent. The asshole was trying to embarrass her by proving her cowboy wouldn't ride to her rescue.

"No judge in their right mind would give him custody," Reese assured her, giving her a measure of hope.

"My father *is* a judge," Nico countered, his tone smug. "And he promised to do everything in his power to help me win."

Nico's father was a judge? He'd only mentioned his parents briefly, but she hadn't gotten the impression they were very well-to-do. Had he already filled their heads with horrible lies about her? Almost certainly. And if the man truly was a judge, that could give Nico a huge advantage.

"If that's true, what a disappointment you turned out to be," Reese drawled. "No wonder they didn't want anything to do with you."

Nico's mouth twisted into a humorless grin. "Takes one to know one, rich boy. Difference is,

I'm an only child, so"—he shrugged—"no one to live up to. But you'll always pale in comparison to that golden boy brother of yours."

She felt Reese tense and twined her fingers with his in silent support.

"Can't argue with that," Reese agreed. "James is definitely the best guy I know. In fact, while you were rotting away in prison, we were working side by side building the Double M into the second largest privately-owned ranch in Colorado."

Reese brought their twined hands up and kissed her fingers. She knew the gesture was for Nico's benefit, but it warmed her all the same.

"That said," he continued, "consider this *your* official notice. There isn't a chance in hell I'm going to let you, or your father, take her daughter away. They'll have the best legal team money can buy, and trust me when I tell you the McMillan name carries a lot of weight in this state. Until then, you want to see Katie—more importantly, if she wants to see you—it'll be under Summer's terms, not yours." He lowered his voice again to that deadly tone. "Now get the fuck out of here before I break every bone in your worthless body. And if you ever lay on a hand on this woman again, it'll be the last damn thing you ever do."

She could practically feel the scorch of Nico's fury as his hateful gaze slid from Reese to her, and back again. But he held his temper as he swept past them and out the door.

Reese turned to face her. "Look, I know I overstepped—"

Standing up on her toes, Summer grasped his handsome, wonderful face, and kissed him soundly.

Chapter Twenty-two

Stunned by her reaction, it took Reese a second to respond. He slanted his lips across hers and pulled her against his chest, desperate for the taste of her having spent every waking moment since he left for Austin thinking about her. And while he wasn't sure what the reason was for her change of heart, at the moment he didn't care.

She cut the kiss short with a soft, sexy sigh, then pulled back to explain, "I have to check on Katie, but I was hoping we could talk later?"

He cupped her cheek. "I was hoping the same thing."

Summer headed into the bedroom, so he took a look at the door to see how bad the damage was, making a mental note to contact the apartment owner once he got back home.

The jamb was busted, which meant it couldn't be locked. Not that it mattered. He wasn't leaving them alone in this apartment, even if it meant moving in here and sleeping on the floor. After what he witnessed today, there was zero chance he'd ever leave them unprotected again. The thought of what may have happened if he'd gotten home a half-hour later terrified him.

The woman was stubborn, but if she balked, he'd just have to ask for Angie's help. His sister-in-law had a knack for getting what she wanted, and he knew she wanted Summer and Katie safe and sound at the ranch.

The bedroom door opened, and Summer walked out carrying Katie in her arms. She had her legs wrapped around her mother's waist, and her head rested on her shoulder, though he could clearly make out her reddened eyes, and tear-stained face. Those tiny shoulders quaked, and it tore him up on a level he'd never imagined. His heart ached for the little girl whose whole world had just been turned upside down. Christ, he could only imagine her confusion, and how scared she must have been, especially if she'd heard Nico strike her mother. And since Reese had heard it from out in the hallway, it was a pretty good bet she had as well.

"I want you to pack up everything you and Katie need," he said without preamble. "I'm taking you both back to the ranch with me." Just in case the prideful woman wanted to argue, he added, "There's no way I'm leaving you here alone again."

Katie's head popped up. She rubbed at her eyes, then gazed at him as if he'd just offered her the key to some magical kingdom. Summer's expression was inscrutable.

He took slight advantage of her daughter's reaction to add, "Angela and Meara have both come to depend on you, and since you already work there, you'll save a fortune in gas money."

He nodded for emphasis. Summer did the lip twist thing.

"Momma, I-I don't wanna live here no more. I wanna live with Reese and Molly, and Meara, and Molly's momma and daddy, and Daisy, and Peanut Butter cuz Jelly misses him."

Summer laughed, a light tingling of sound that never failed to affect him. "I get it, sweetie, I get it."

Katie slid from Summer's arms and grinned up at him, as if she knew she'd helped his cause. "I'm gonna go tell Jelly!" she announced before racing back into the bedroom.

"She's telling Jelly, can I assume that makes it official?"

Another soft laugh, but this time her eyes were full of gratitude. "If you're sure it's all right with James and Angela, I gratefully accept your generous hospitality. At least, until I can find another apartment. But I have one stipulation."

"Woman, if you're about to insist on paying rent,"—he wasn't exactly sure what was about to come out of his mouth, but knew it wouldn't be appropriate for little ears, and changed course— "I'm going to be highly insulted."

She pursed those luscious lips again, and he couldn't help but chuckle. "We'll talk about it later. And Reese...thank you. For everything."

He responded with a brisk nod, worried his voice might crack if he tried to speak.

Summer packed a huge, very old suitcase, two duffle bags, plus several plastic bags, while Katie stuffed every toy she owned into her backpack. The realization that all her toys fit into one child-size backpack broke his heart, and he decided to rectify that as soon as he could. Though Summer would have his hide if he suddenly bought out a toy store, so he'd have to pace himself.

She took one last glance around, as if this might be the last time she saw the place. And if he had anything to say about it, it would be. But he knew, despite all that had happened with Nico, Summer and Katie had five years' worth of memories in this little apartment, so he let her look her fill while he took the opportunity to put their luggage in her trunk, and send his sister-in-law a text to let her know what was going on. Angie's smartass reply? *"Maybe there's hope you after all."* Grinning, he gave his head a shake and headed back to collect the two people who had become as important to him as breathing.

"Make sure you pack anything of value. The lock on the door is busted, so I wouldn't leave anything important behind."

Her eyes brightened as she nodded toward Katie. "The only thing I have of value is this little girl standing beside me."

Their gazes held, and he realized, like an arrow of clarity straight to the heart, he'd fallen in love with her. He knew it as surely as he knew his own name, and while the revelation nearly took his breath away, he managed to stay firmly on his feet, packing away his new discovery to mull over later. Right now, he needed to get them home and settled in.

He held the apartment door open. "Ready?"

Summer nodded before repeating to Katie, "Ready?" Her vigorous nod earned a laugh from her mother, who grasped her hand and led her outside.

Reese closed the door behind them, then followed her to her car, and opened both driver side doors. "I already have everything in your trunk."

"Thank you, I appreciate it." Summer tossed her purse on the passenger seat. "I have to admit, I'm more than ready to get the heck out of here."

He helped Katie into the car before stepping back to meet Summer's gaze. "Glad to hear it. I sent Angie a text to let her know what's up. I'm sure Meara's getting rooms ready for both of you as we speak."

"Just one room is fine for us," she insisted as she buckled Katie into her seat. "I don't want to impose anymore than I already have."

"Neither of you are an imposition. Besides, you're doing us all a favor, truth be told. Angie's basically bedridden, and you know Meara can sure use the help. James and I try, but she won't hear of it. Told us to run our own business and leave her to run hers. Frankly, we're both a little afraid of her."

"You're both afraid of Angela, too," she teased as she climbed into the driver's seat.

"I will neither confirm nor deny that absurd statement." She arched a brow while starting the car, and he teasingly admitted, "Okay, maybe a little."

She laughed and put the car in gear. "Meet you at the ranch?"

"I'll be right behind you." Reese hopped in his truck, turned her over, and pulled out behind them, feeling in that moment like the happiest man on earth.

Just as he'd predicted, Meara had Summer's room ready by the time they arrived, and it was the one he'd had her stay in Friday night, right across from Molly's.

"Once Molly is feeling better, she's hoping Katie will stay in her room," the older woman explained.

"Are you sure?" Remembering just how comfortable this bed was, Summer ran a reverent hand over one of the four, perfectly fluffed pillows before spinning around to face them. "It's more than big enough for the both of us."

"But momma, I wanna sleep in Molly's room." Katie propped her hands on her hips, the stubborn lift of her chin almost identical to her mother's. "She said I could have the top bunk."

"Besides," Meara chimed in, "A young woman like yourself should have *some* privacy."

"I just don't want to make extra work for you."

Summer walked around the bed to gaze out the window, which overlooked the flower garden and wooden gazebo his grandfather had built. Reese knew the view was stunning, even at this time of year. Much better than the parking lot view she had to look at through the windows of her apartment.

"Nonsense. You work here, so you'll be helping out plenty. I think we can even find a small chore for Katie to do." She gave the little cutie a pat on the shoulder. "Molly helps me and her mother with the laundry. I bet you can help me fill and empty the dishwasher."

"I can, I know I can!" Katie gazed up at Meara in worshipful wonder, as if she were the most amazing person on the planet. Reese knew the feeling. Meara had a way of making everyone feel needed and important. Hell, he and James still looked at her like that.

Summer turned to face the older woman. "Thank you, Meara, so much. Katie and I will be a big help, won't we, sweetie?"

"Yep. And I already know how to do chores. Momma lets me help cook, and wash dishes, and fold the towels. Can I sleep in Molly's room?"

Both women chuckled. Summer said, "Yes, but not until she's feeling better, okay?"

"It'll probably just be a night or two," Angela assured them as she waddled into the room. "Molly's feeling much better, but I'd like to keep her home one more day just to be sure.

Because Katie hadn't left her mother's side since they'd arrived, she and Meara thankfully hadn't asked about the very visible bruising around Summer's eye. But when Angela suddenly needed to check on something with James, Reese suspected she was filling his brother in that something had happened at the apartment.

"No worries, we understand." Summer smiled down at her daughter. "This room will be fine for us, right, sweetie?"

Katie nodded, but her eyes were bright with disappointment.

"The bed in here is very comfortable," Angie assured them. "I'm sure you and your mom will sleep like logs."

Reese didn't want to know how Angie knew how comfy the bed was since he'd never known her to sleep in there. No doubt her and James had christened every room in the house. Reese would wait until he and Summer were settled in their own home before doing the…

Whoa. Slow down, cowboy. You don't even know how the lady feels about you yet, not really.

Meara gave her hands a clap. "So, dinner will be ready in about half an hour."

Reese sniffed the air. "Tacos?"

Her face lit up. "With black beans and cilantro rice."

"Sounds like heaven." He looked at Angie. "James in his office?"

"Yeah, he had a couple of calls to make."

He nodded his thanks. To Summer, he said, "Well, since you're in good hands, I need to check in with my brother. See you at dinner?"

Her face pinkened just the slightest bit. "Wouldn't miss it."

Reese smiled, then walked out of there before he gave in to the urge to kiss her. If not for the fact she probably would've killed him, he just might have. But he knew she'd have enough questions thrown at her once the two women got her alone. Angie and Meara would want every last detail as to how she got that bruise. He just hoped they stopped there, and didn't go on to plan Moretti's disappearance.

He rapped on the door before swinging it open. James sat back in the big leather armchair, crossed feet up on the desk, cell phone pressed to his ear. He gestured for Reese to sit, and he could tell by the eye roll that he was talking to one of their parents.

"I'm not saying they aren't welcome, I'm just saying this isn't a great time. Angela is due in less than two months and she's not supposed to be on her feet for more than ten minutes at a time. And we have a couple of new houseguests, so Meara's got plenty to do. I won't add to her already full plate. Listen, Reese just came in, and we have business to take care of. I'll give you a call back later in the week. Yeah. Sure, I get it. Okay, bye." He ended the call, took a deep breath, and then dropped his feet to the floor and tossed his cell on the desk.

"I take it he wants to come for a visit, bring our newly discovered sisters with to meet us?"

"Not him, he's too busy trying to win mom back to have time for us. Or his granddaughter. He wants us to invite the twins for a visit so we can all get to know each other."

Reese shrugged, not exactly adverse to the idea. "They're family, and it's not their fault they got stuck with a self-centered jackass for a father, any more than it's ours. I'm okay with it if you are."

"I'm fine with it, just not right now. I'd like to get through the next couple of months before having to deal with any more drama."

"I hear you. You doing okay? Angie looks like she's feeling better."

"She is, and so am I, thanks for asking." His brow lifted, "The question is, how are you? She told me Summer is sporting a pretty nasty shiner. Is her ex still breathing?"

"I knew she took off to tattle." He gave his head a rueful shake and dropped down onto the leather sofa. "Lucky for him, Katie was there, or the motherfucker would've left on a stretcher. He also threatened to sue her for full custody, which is what I need to talk to you about. Think Cal would represent her?"

"I'm not sure, but I can ask him. He specializes in corporate law, but even if he doesn't, I'm sure he can recommend someone for you."

"I need the best lawyer money can buy. No way in hell I'm gonna let that piece of shit take Katie away and drag her back to New York like some prize."

James leaned forward and propped his forearms on the desk. "He's an ex-con. No judge in his right mind would do that. Relax."

"You don't understand. Moretti's father *is* a judge. He could have friends here in Colorado, who knows? All I do know is that it would kill Summer to lose her little girl. There's no way I can let that happen."

James' expression sobered. "It won't happen, I promise. I have business dealings with at least three sitting judges here in Jefferson county, and several more in Denver. And again, if Cal can't represent her, he'll make sure to find us the best custody lawyer in Colorado."

Reese's shoulders sagged with relief. "Thanks, man. I appreciate it, more than you know."

"Nah, I'm pretty sure I know. I recognize the look. You've fallen hard and fast, little brother.

Reese didn't even try to deny it. "Yeah, I have. And you know what? Despite all this Nico bullshit, I'm happier than I've ever been. I just have to figure out a way to prove to that stubborn woman we belong together."

"Something tells me you won't have to convince her too hard."

"For the sake of my sanity, let's hope you're right."

Chapter Twenty-three

Watching Katie blossom while chattering excitedly with Reese, and Meara, her new favorite person, about everything from her new favorite movie—Alvin and the Chipmunks, which she'd watched for the first time with Molly and James Friday night—to the new white bunny her teacher brought in for the class, was such a major relief. Especially after the incident at their apartment.

Once Nico left, she'd found Katie hiding under the bed, curled up in a ball and sobbing quietly into Jelly. It took her a few minutes to coax her out as she didn't believe "the mean man" was gone. Summer swore to her it was Reese in the other room, and finally she'd shimmied out and launched into her arms. Clearly, if her chattiness at the dinner table was any indication, her daughter was made of stern stuff, as they say. And for that, she was grateful.

After enjoying one of the best meals she'd ever had—cilantro rice, who knew?—she gave Katie a quick bath, then got her settled into their new bed. Her little girl had had quite the day—they both had—so she rubbed her back until her excited chatter died down into soft snores.

Leaving the small desk light on just in case she woke up, Summer shrugged into her hoodie and quietly slipped from the room, closing the door silently behind her before heading down to the kitchen where Reese said he'd be waiting.

A man of his word, he stood in front of the windows gazing out into the darkness. His moonlit expression was hard to read, though his body language seemed relaxed. The man was so darn gorgeous he took her breath away. His hair was damp, so he must have showered, and he'd changed into a pair of light gray sweatpants, and a darker gray, long sleeve thermal shirt. He looked like he belonged on the cover of a magazine, and the image of him like this would be forever emblazoned in her mind, regardless of where things ended up between them.

He turned to face her, his smile so potently sexy it should be registered as a lethal weapon. With an inner eyeroll over her silly thoughts, she stepped up beside him and gazed out into the darkened night. "What are you looking at?"

"The moon is full tonight. I've always thought it was one of the most beautiful sights I've ever seen." He turned back to meet her gaze. "Though it pales in comparison to the view in here."

She's pretty sure a blush tinged her cheeks, but she managed to give a playful wave. "Go on, stop."

He moved in, slowly, as if testing the waters. She knew they needed to clear the air, but right now she wouldn't mind if he took her in his arms, maybe even kissed her. Instead he reached out and gently touched his fingertips to the bruised side of her face. His eyes darkened and his smile faded.

"I bruise easily, remember? It doesn't even hurt, I swear."

"I just...I can't help thinking what could have happened if I hadn't gotten there when I did."

She grasped his hand and twined her fingers with his. "But you *did* get there in time, so let's not think about that. Or him. I'd much rather talk about us. I mean, if you're still interested in there being an us...?"

He slid his arms around her and pulled her tight against his chest, his chin resting on her head. He held her so close she could feel the racing of his heart, while the clean, masculine scent she'd come to recognize as uniquely his enveloped her in its seductive embrace. She closed her eyes, savoring the moment as he held her with such loving care.

"Sweetheart, there's nothing I want more. It's been killing me knowing I may have screwed up the only relationship I've ever wanted to be in."

"Is that where this is heading then, a relationship?" she whispered against his shoulder.

He pulled back and gently recaptured her face. "I sure as hell hope so," he professed before kissing her, his lips soft on hers, and way too brief as he pulled back to declare, "I'm crazy about you, Summer. And I adore Katie. I want you in my life, if you'll have me. I know my past concerns you, but—"

"It doesn't. Not anymore. And not the way you think." She caught her bottom lip between her teeth, searching for the best way to explain why she'd reacted the way she had. "When Nico announced how and why you two knew each other, all I could think was, 'Here we go again. Drugs and cheating round two.' I knew I couldn't handle another experience like that, and I certainly didn't want Katie getting hurt down the road. She was just a baby when Nico went to prison, so obviously, she doesn't have any memories of him...well, until today. But she adores you, in case you couldn't tell, and it would break her heart if you suddenly weren't in her life anymore."

His hands slid down to her shoulders, his eyes full of remorse as he, she assumed, searched for the right words. "I'm so sorry you found out the way you did. It should have come from me, I know that. I was just so afraid of scaring you off. I knew right away my feelings for you were different than anything I'd felt before. And in case there's any question, the adoration is mutual. Katie's amazing, any man would be lucky to call her daughter."

Tears stung her eyes, and one slid free. He swiped it away with a gentle swipe of his thumb. "Thank you. I can't tell you how much that means to me."

"I meant it. She's an incredible little girl."

"And that's what makes you so wonderful. You're nothing like Nico. I know it with absolute certainty. You screwed up, but you got your life back on track and you didn't blame anyone else for your mistakes. That makes *you* pretty incredible in my opinion."

A slow smile spread across his face. "Damn, when you say it, I almost believe it. Though 'wonderful' might be a reach."

She glanced toward the back door, eager to try out his grandparents' swing again. Only this time, they could relax and enjoy it. She dipped her head toward the back porch. "Can we?"

He seemed surprised by the request. "You bet." With a hand at the small of her back, he escorted her outside, took a seat in the middle of the padded swing, then pulled her onto his lap.

Laughing softly, she snuggled against him and gazed out toward the moonlit mountains, breathing in the fresh scent of pine, which mingled heavenly with the purple and yellow flowers that still bloomed around the porch and along the walkway. "It truly is one of the most beautiful views I've ever seen."

"I couldn't agree more."

That deep, sexy tone turned her head, and she discovered him staring at her. Their gazes locked for a second before he leaned in for a quick kiss. But she wanted more, so much more. Summer cupped the side of his clean-shaven face and slanted her mouth beneath his. She'd been dreaming about kissing the man all weekend long, and she didn't hold back as their mouths meshed with urgent need.

She loved him. The realization hit her like a bolt of lightning. It scared the living hell out of her, and she wasn't ready to tell him yet, but she'd somehow managed to fall head over heels in love with a man she'd known less than two weeks. The thought was ridiculous, and yet she'd never been more sure about anything. Living under the same roof would give them the opportunity to see how compatible they were. The thought of sneaking into each other's rooms brought a blushing grin to her face.

He pulled back, but she couldn't really make out his expression. "Damn, did I already lose you?"

A giggle escaped over her naughty musings. "I was just wondering which bed was more comfortable, the one in your room, or the one in the guest room I'm staying in."

His hands slid down to her hips and he gripped her tight. "I mean, if that's a challenge, we can try both to be sure. But my money's on my bed." He leaned in to add in a teasing whisper, "And it's a California King, so nice and roomy."

"Katie sleeps like the dead," she told him, wanting nothing more than to drag the sexy man up to his room and prove his boastful claim. Not that she doubted his big ol' bed was just as comfy as he said. But reality quickly returned.

"Wait, what are we thinking? It's only like eight-thirty. Meara, Angela, and Reese all must still be awake."

"So…?"

She glared at him, but with no real heat. "Sooo, I can't imagine Meara would approve of us sleeping together while there's small children under the same roof."

His brow scrunched. "James and Angie do. What's the difference?"

"The difference is they're married. Of course, they sleep in the same bed. Can you imagine if one of the girls accidentally walked in on us? I'd be mortified. Angela thought we did it in your truck, though I assured her we didn't. You know where I wish we could go? Back to that gorgeous spot you took me to last week."

He chuckled and gave her a quick kiss. "Woman, I could get whiplash trying to follow your train of thought. But yeah, I'd planned to take you back there before the weather turns, only this time with a couple of blankets and a picnic basket."

"And an umbrella," she teased.

"Definitely an umbrella. I'd actually like to take you and Katie both there one day. If not this year, then in the Spring. I think she'd have a lot of fun learning to fish."

He was talking about the future, which both thrilled, and frightened her. What if the spark that burned so hotly between them now, died a quick death? She couldn't imagine that happening, at least on her end. But she knew he'd never been in a serious relationship before, maybe he'd discover she wasn't the one after all. Maybe—

"I love you."

Her head shot up. "What?"

"I love you. I…I hadn't planned to say it. I mean—"

"We've only known each other a little over a week."

"Exactly. But come Saturday, it'll be two weeks, and then three weeks, and then a month, six months, a year. The only thing I know for certain is that I want you in my life. I *need* you in my life. Every woman I've dated in the past, I knew right away there was nothing there. Nothing lasting, anyway. But when you stepped out of your car that day, I felt alive like I never had before. And it's only grown stronger since. You and Katie have made me happier than I ever thought possible. And yes, I know that sounds corny as hell, but…Summer Hanson, I love you."

Her eyes glazed over with tears of joy, though her brain refused to celebrate. "But…I'm nobody special. What will your family think?"

He shifted, his handsome face suddenly awash in the glow of the full moon. "My family thinks you're amazing, and trust me when I tell you they're all hoping this will happen." He caressed her unbruised cheek, his smile reassuring. "It's soon, I get that. Too soon. But you're the only woman I've ever said those three words too, and I have no intention of giving up just because you aren't ready to—"

"I love you, too," she admitted before losing her nerve. "I was afraid to say it because you've done so much for me, I didn't want you to think it was part of some…ploy. Especially after you told Nico you'd pay for my attorney."

"It never would've crossed my mind, darlin', you're as genuine as they come. And I *will* pay for your attorney. No way in hell you're heading into a custody battle without the best representation available to you."

"It's not that I don't appreciate your incredibly generous offer, because I do. I just… The thought that anyone might think I'm sleeping with you for your money kills me. I've never been beholden to anyone before, and I already owe you so much."

A sound rumbled deep in his throat that smacked of frustration.

"I can afford it, and you can't. That's a simple fact. And if Moretti's telling the truth about his dad being a sitting judge, that might give him some credibility. I get that you're independent and self-sufficient. Besides being an incredible mother, those are the qualities I admire most about you. But sweetheart, in this, you need help. You can't possibly be willing to take a chance on losing custody of Katie because you don't want to owe me. And I care about both of you too much to let that happen."

She gazed back out across the rolling hills to the mountains beyond as fresh tears pooled in her eyes. Though his words hit home in the worst way, he was absolutely right. If she didn't swallow her pride and allow him help her, she just might lose her daughter.

Summer straddled his lap and met his darkened gaze, wanting to convey just how much she wanted and needed him, and how much she appreciated him and everything he'd done for her. And planned to do. She wanted nothing more than to lose herself in this wonderful man's arms—and if they had to be quiet as church mice, well, that would only add to the excitement.

"You are the most incredible man I've ever known, and I gratefully accept your offer to help." She leaned in to nip at his bottom lip. "So, is that offer to head up to your room still good?"

Chapter Twenty-four

Blissfully. Happy.

Those were the exact two words Reese would use to describe himself if anyone asked how he was. He'd spent the last five weeks getting to know Summer, and Katie, and he was more in love than he ever thought himself capable of. The Hanson girls were the best thing that had ever happened to him, and he planned on pulling out all the stops to prove he was just as good for them.

Summer had even allowed him to spoil them a little bit...within reason. Katie had never been to the zoo, had never been to a carnival, not that she had ever lacked for anything important. Summer, he knew, had devoted every possible minute of every day to her little girl, and they were rich in ways Reese was only beginning to understand.

But watching Katie's face light up the first time she held out a palmful of pellets to feed a deer was something he'd treasure for the rest of his days.

She, of course, insisted on feeding them all—deer, goats, llamas, sheep. And when they got home from the zoo, she'd asked to feed Daisy a peppermint since she still had some left from when she was sick. Reese suspected veterinarian school might be in her future.

As for Summer, he'd accidentally discovered her birthday was the day before Halloween, which the proud woman had never even mentioned, so he'd booked a night in the Presidential suite at the Four Seasons in Denver, and she'd nearly lost her mind, spinning around in slow motion with her mouth hanging open. He knew she'd never seen such a grand hotel, and it really drove home just how blessed he was.

And while the suite certainly was unforgettable, it was the delicate, heart-shaped gold locket he'd gotten her—complete with a picture he'd had Angela take of him and Katie inside—that brought her to tears. They sure had enjoyed every minute of their very first romantic getaway, and Reese smiled over a couple of particular memories with pure male satisfaction.

He'd also hired a lawyer for her, Cal's partner, Doug Smythe, who he now knew was the job interview she'd missed because of him. Seemed prophetic in a way, though Summer had been a bit anxious to meet with him. But according to Cal, Doug was the best custody lawyer in Jefferson county, maybe the entire state, and that fact was enough to get Summer on board. In fact, they were hoping to hear from him today with a court date. The waiting had been stressful, and they were both more than ready to get this over and done with. If Nico was granted visitation, they'd deal with it. And if the guy truly loved his daughter, he'd give up on his fantasy of having a future with Summer, and concentrate on getting to know the amazing little girl he was damn lucky to have.

But Reese was uneasy. Moretti was a ticking timebomb, already angry over his lot in life, blaming Reese for the loss of his freedom, and the loss of his family. It was doubtful he'd ever take responsibility for his own actions. But the real headscratcher? He hadn't contacted Summer once about seeing Katie. After all his big words about her being his daughter, too, and wanting his parents to get to know her, he hadn't called once in the past five weeks.

Slim arms snaked around his waist, drawing him from his troubled thoughts. "Ready to decorate the cupcakes?"

He turned and took her in his arms. Summer and Meara had baked five dozen cupcakes earlier, and they had three kinds of frosting as the girls couldn't decide between vanilla and strawberry. Chocolate was a must. "Ready, willing, and able, with an extra emphasis on willing."

She grinned, her eyes flaring slightly. "I know, right? If Meara wasn't standing guard, I'd have stolen a big spoonful of chocolate frosting. And I know why hers tastes so much better than mine. Coffee." She said it as if it should have been as clear as the nose on her face.

"Coffee, huh? Makes sense, I guess."

"I'm definitely stealing the idea. Come on." She tugged his arm and they headed into the kitchen.

Molly and Katie were already sitting on stools, chattering up a storm, both with a cupcake sitting in front of them and brandishing a small, resealable bag filled with frosting. They had rainbow sprinkles, chocolate jimmies, and Reese's personal favorite—crushed Oreos.

Meara leaned a hip against the counter, her smile doting as she watched them.

Reese clapped his hands together. "So, I hear it's time to frost some cupcakes."

Katie bounced on her seat, her eyes big as poker chips. She held up her makeshift pastry bag. "Reese, look! Meara put two kinds o' frosting in my bag so I can make swirls."

He met the old girl's gaze with admiration. "Great idea. Can I have chocolate and vanilla in my frosting bag?"

She gestured toward a big white bowl on the counter beside her. "Take yer pick. I have the flavors in separate bags, as well as some with chocolate and vanilla, and some with vanilla and strawberry."

Once everyone was seated, the fun began with a flurry of frosting and decorating. Meara stayed to collect the cupcakes as they finished them, refilling the plate of unfrosted four times until every last cupcake had been decorated. They each ate one with a glass of milk, then Meara reminded the girls they promised to bring some for the class on Monday. She had them pick out two dozen of their favorites, then packed them up in carriers to stay fresh. The rest were put under several domed cake plates.

"Wanna go watch a movie?" Molly asked her friend as she slid from her stool. "You can pick the first one, and I'll pick the next one."

Katie nodded and followed suit. "But don't pick Alvin cuz I wanna pick Alvin."

Molly gave an exaggerated eye roll. "Fine, but next time I get to pick Alvin."

They raced from the kitchen, through the house, and down into the sunken den in what had to be record time. He shook his head in amazement. "It's a miracle they don't leave burn marks on the carpeting."

Meara chuckled as she stared off after them. "I can't remember ever being that quick on my feet. A hundred years ago, maybe."

"I wasn't allowed to play much with the other kids," Summer shared as she rose to her feet and squeezed one last glob of frosting onto her finger. "That's why it's so wonderful to watch Katie and Molly build such a tight bond. She's never been happier, and I am forever grateful to all of you for everything you've done for us."

She caught his gaze and stuck her finger in her mouth to slowly and thoroughly suck the sweet buttercream off. Reese fought the urge to toss the sexy witch over his shoulder and race upstairs to his bedroom. The woman was a seductress the likes of which he'd never known. One sidelong glance, one sexy gesture, and he was putty in her hands.

She playfully licked her lips, a promise for later, before carrying the few dishes over to the sink. "Meara, why don't you let me clean up the kitchen. You've been on your feet all day, and there's not much to do now that the cupcakes are put away."

Meara thought on it, then gave an affirmative nod. "Young lady, I think I'll take you up on that. Thank you."

"Thank *you*." Summer gave her a quick side hug. "Now, please, go kick up your feet and relax. We've got this, right, Reese?"

He grinned and cocked a brow at Meara. "She's good, huh?"

"Very. She'll keep you on your toes, which is exactly what you need." The older woman cast him a quick wink, then lumbered past them out of the kitchen.

Summer turned the sink water on and soaped up the dish sponge. Reese capped the sprinkles and other toppings, put them back in the cabinet, then came up behind her and lightly grasped her shoulders. "You're amazing, you know that? Meara was exhausted, but the old girl's stubborn." He grinned. "Seems every female under this roof could fall into that category."

"Good thing you McMillans aren't afraid of strong women."

He could hear the humor in her voice. She challenged him every day, and truth was, he loved it.

"You know, if you hurry up, we can sneak upstairs for at least a good hour while the girls are watching their movie."

She craned her neck back to peer up at him, that delectable throat just begging for his lips. "I'm on it."

Forty minutes later, they were lying in each other's arms in Reese's bedroom, body's cooling in the aftermath of the most amazing 'quickie' to date. They'd really learned to utilize their time, he thought with a self-satisfied smirk. He tightened his arms around her and nuzzled her temple, her ear.

His cell phone rang. With a groan of disappointment, he pushed up onto him elbow and reached across her to grab it off the nightstand. He looked at the screen—Doug Smythe. Well, the guy did have impeccable timing, that's for sure. He slid his finger across the screen to answer. "Hello?"

"Hey, Reese. Got some good news. Is Summer nearby?"

"She's right beside me. Hang on, I'll put you on speaker." He propped himself up against the massive oak headboard and tapped the speaker icon.

Summer sat up in a rush, clutching the comforter to her throat. A slight blush stained her cheeks, as if she imagined the attorney could somehow see them through the phone. He grinned. She frowned.

"Prepare yourselves, we have a court date: Friday at nine a.m. I'll meet you both at the courthouse by eight-thirty so we have a little time to go over everything. As I already explained, Katie won't appear in court, but Jennifer will on her behalf, so she will be represented. Do either of you have any questions?"

Jennifer was Katie's GAL, or Guardian ad Litem, which was someone who represented the best interests of the child in a legal case. And Jennifer had been wonderful with Katie, answering her questions and calming her fears.

Summer leaned in closer to the phone. "Will the judge make a decision Friday, or will we have to go back to court at some point?"

"The judge will deliver his ruling Friday and the order will be written up."

She met Reese's gaze, the worry simmering in those deep blue depths tugging at his heart. He knew she was used to expecting the worst, but he hoped to show her that good things can and do happen to good people. Also, that she could count on him, truly count on him, to take care of her and Katie.

"Thanks, Doug, if we think of anything else, I'll text you."

"Appreciate it since I'll be having dinner at the in-laws tonight. Until Friday."

He set his cell back on the nightstand and slipped his arm around her. She snuggled into his chest with an anxious sigh.

"In my head, I know everything will be okay. But I can't get rid of that, I don't know, odd sense that something is going to go very wrong."

He kissed the top of her head and gently stroked the curve of her hip, knowing her mind was a jumble of anxiety over this. "Everything is going to be fine, you have to trust me."

"I do trust you, more than I've ever trusted anyone. But realistically, we don't know what's going to happen. I'm not really worried he'll win sole custody; he just got out of prison, and Katie doesn't know him. But Reese, he's hateful, and violent. If he gets anything besides supervised visitation, I don't know what we'll do."

She'd said 'we'll', which was such a huge step for the headstrong, self-reliant woman. She saw them as a team, and that was a major coup in his mind. "I don't see that happening, but if it does, I'll hire someone to keep an eye on Katie at all times. He'll never be alone with her, I promise you."

She turned in his arms and blessed him with the most beautiful smile he'd ever seen. Then she straddled his lap and pressed her palms to his chest. "Think we have time for another round?"

He grew hard as stone in response. "Well, I'm not a betting man anymore, but I'm sure willing to give it a try."

"Good to know."

Chapter Twenty-five

As if history was repeating, it started to rain as soon as Summer and Reese left the ranch to head to the courthouse, just as it had the first time she was supposed to meet with Doug Smythe. And while the circumstances were quite different this time, a nervous energy surged through her, making it difficult to relax. A lot more was riding on the outcome of this meeting than the last one.

Reese grasped her hand and gave it gentle a squeeze. "Everything is going to be fine. It's even raining, which is good luck."

She swung her head and frowned at the obtuse man, too anxious to take any comfort in his reassurances. "That's only if it rains on your wedding day. Any other time it's a bad omen." She turned back to stare out the windshield. "It was raining the day I missed my interview because a certain clueless cowboy drove through a mud puddle and soaked me from head to toe."

He cast her a sheepish grin. "Yeah, I was kinda hoping you forgot about that. Hey, on the flip side, we have a great story to tell our grandkids someday."

She laughed softly. A calming warmth seeped into her bones at the thought of them growing old together. "Can't make that stuff up, can you?"

He chuckled. "No, ma'am."

They were both quiet for the rest of the ride to the Jefferson County courthouse, which was only another ten minutes away. Thankfully, the rain had let up by the time they arrived since neither of them had thought to bring an umbrella.

The building was just as imposing as she remembered, having been there the day Nico was sentenced, and her steps slowed as her nerves tried to stage a comeback.

"You okay?"

"Yeah, sorry. Just remembering the last time I was here. Never really expected to have to come back again."

"You have everything on your side, sweetheart, every reason to feel confident. You've spent the last five years raising a wonderful little girl, all by yourself, as Jennifer will attest to, while Moretti was serving time for drug possession and other related charges. And this wasn't his first arrest, that

I know for sure. No judge in his right mind would be favorable toward a guy like him. He'll probably be awarded some kind of visitation, like Doug explained, but if that happens, we'll deal with it. Together."

God, how she loved this amazing man. While she still had no idea how she'd gotten so lucky, truth was she didn't much care anymore. "I don't know how I would've handled any of this without you, or how I'll ever pay you back, but...thank you. I love you." She tightened her hold on his arm.

"Maybe we can revisit the French maid's costume...?"

She narrowed her eyes, but coyly added, "It's definitely on the table now. At least, for a special occasion."

As they were walking up the concrete steps, his tone grew oddly thoughtful. "Do you know why I believe in fate?"

"Is this a trick question?" she teased, watching her feet to make sure she didn't miss a step, or slip on the slick concrete.

"Because even if I hadn't been the idiot who splashed you that day," he continued, "we still would have met, at the ranch that Saturday. It was already predestined."

Her eyes misted over as the truth of his pronouncement sank in, and her worries dissipated into the ether. No matter what happened today,

Reese would be by her side, and eventually, everything would work itself out.

As soon as they entered the building, Doug Smythe strode forward to meet them. He shook Reese's hand, then hers, before leading them up to the second floor. Doug made an impressive figure— tall, fit, with graying, dark blond hair, faded blue eyes, and an expensive-looking, dark gray suit—and his confident demeanor certainly helped to put her at ease.

They went over everything that would happen in court, the most likely outcome, which would be limited, supervised visitation. Summer was terrified for Nico to receive visitation, supervised or otherwise. The guy she knew, before he'd gone to prison, while not perfect by any stretch, had been nothing like the angry, hateful man who was quick to temper, and prone to, it seemed, violent outbursts. What if he lost his temper and hurt Katie during one of these visitations?

Doug was escorting them into the courtroom when she caught sight of her ex. And, my God, he looked awful—haggard, angry, and while wearing a nice suit, he looked strangely unkempt for someone about to appear in front of a judge. Didn't even look like he'd dragged a comb through his hair. Not that she was in formalwear, but she had purchased a long-sleeved, silk maroon blouse, a pair of black dress slacks, and a pair of low-heeled dress boots. And while she'd carefully applied just the lightest touch of makeup, Angela had insisted she pull her hair up into a sleek ponytail, and also borrowed her a pair of classic, small gold hoops.

An older couple moved into her line of vision, and she knew without a doubt they were Nico's parents—Katie's grandparents. Nico was a younger version of his father, an absolute spitting image. The only real difference was the touches of gray in the older man's thick head of hair. His mother wore her chin-length, auburn hair in a chic bob, a very sophisticated navy pantsuit with sleek, pointed toe pumps, a pair of gold drop earrings, and a matching necklace. Odd finally seeing them after all this time; she'd never even seen a picture. And they certainly weren't at all what she'd imagined them to be, which was more like her own small-town parents, than the uptown couple before her.

When the woman touched Nico's arm and said something to him, he gave a hard nod, glanced up, and that's when he caught sight of Summer. They held eye contact for only a few seconds, but it was enough to send a shiver down her spine. He didn't look…right. That old saying 'If looks could kill' popped into her mind, and suddenly she couldn't wait to get back home to the ranch, the only place she felt truly safe these days.

Reese leaned in and said in a low tone, "The idiot's wasted."

Before she had time to process the truth of his claim, they were both led inside the courtroom by attorney Smythe. He showed them where to sit, and her pulse sped up as the reality of what was about to happen struck her with the force of a gale wind.

It wasn't long before the bailiff called for everyone to rise, and announced the Honorable Judge Marcus C. Halford would be presiding. Once everyone was seated, the judge spoke.

"Good morning, everyone. So…" He clasped his hands and rested them before him on the bench. "Calling the case of Moretti versus Hanson. We're here to decide the parental responsibilities for Miss Katie Moretti, who is five years old."

Summer's mind went blank, her body numb, the judge's words becoming a jumbled mess as she tried to keep up with everything being said. Her heart started racing, and she pressed a shaky hand to her breastbone. A panic attack?

As if sensing her distress, Reese grasped her hand and held it during the entire proceeding, not that it lasted very long. The judge called Nico first to the stand, and it wasn't long before he—and everyone else in the courtroom—realized Nico was bombed, and strangely jittery, talking a mile a minute. If this is what he'd been doing for the past month, mystery solved on why he'd never contacted her about seeing Katie. And thank the lord he hadn't.

Judge Halford, who, like most justices, had zero patience for such blatant disrespect of the court's time, also showed a small amount of empathy, warning Nico to get his act together or he'd personally revoke his parole. And then he made his decision regarding custody.

"Mr. Moretti, while I do appreciate your desire to have a relationship with your daughter, I also understand Miss Hanson concerns, particularly in light of your behavior today. So, my ruling is as follows: Visitation is denied. But I'm going to give you six months to prove to this court you are ready to be in your daughter's life. That means regular drug testing, having steady employment, and establishing residence. After six months, if the court is satisfied you've done everything you need to do, including staying sober, you will receive one hour per month of supervised visitation with your daughter for six months. If the visits go well, we'll up it to bi-monthly for six months, which is when we'll return to court to…reassess."

Immensely relieved, Summer let out the breath she'd been holding. Reese gave her hand a squeeze.

"I can see you're not happy, Mr. Moretti, but let me be blunt. Not only could I have denied your request entirely, I also could have revoked your parole, effective immediately. With what I saw today alone, consider this your lucky day, sir. Your daughter doesn't know you, and according to her representative, she's afraid of you. That's why we're going to take this slowly. You get one chance, Mr. Moretti, I suggest you take the next six months to get yourself under control and focus on what's important. This court is adjourned." He banged his gavel.

As the judge rose from his bench and headed back into his chamber, Summer chanced a glance at her ex, who appeared to be on the edge of a meltdown. His face was mottled with rage, and his hands were both fisted, his jaw working back and forth as he fought for control. It still surprised her, seeing this destructive side of him.

Reese stood and held out his hand to her. Always such a gentleman, her cowboy. She slung the thin strap of her purse over her shoulder and stood beside him. They spoke with Doug for a few moments, then Reese ushered her from the courtroom.

Out in the hallway, as they waited for the elevator, she realized Nico and his father were in a heated exchange, and loudly enough for those around them to hear.

"...got no one to blame but yourself. How could you show up to court like,"—he swept a disdainful hand up and down—"this? Was that your goal all along, to embarrass the hell out of us?"

"Fucking relax. I just had a few drinks to calm my nerves."

"Yeah, a few too many to think straight, you fool. You're damn lucky the judge decided to take pity on you. You could have screwed up your only chance to be a part of that little girl's life." His father pulled out his cell phone, and added, "You're moving back to New York with us, tonight. And you will do exactly as Judge Halford ordered you to do. We'll fly you out here in six months so you can start to get to know your daughter. Sober and clean. Got it?"

"Fine, Pop, whatever. Can we just get the hell out of here?"

The elevator doors opened and Reese motioned her inside. As she turned, she made accidental eye contact with her ex, whose hateful gaze burned a hole right through her. Summer could barely draw air into her lungs as the elevator doors slid shut.

Reese took her into his arms. "At least we won't have to worry about him for the next six months. I can't believe he was stupid enough to show up to court wasted like that."

She frowned. "But wouldn't he have had to go through some kind of drug rehabilitation program in prison?"

"Maybe, I don't know. Didn't help, if he did. And he's on the verge of crashing. Don't know if they'll make it back to New York before he does, and I don't really care. Let his parents take care of him, get him the help he needs. All that matters right now is getting home so we can celebrate."

She eyeballed him with teasing suspicion. "Is this about that French maid's outfit?"

He laughed. The elevator doors opened, and they stepped out into the lobby. "No, but I reserve the right to reexamine the idea later tonight." He grasped her hand. "Actually, I was thinking we'd grab Katie and head to Alberti's for an Italian feast, complete with cannoli and chocolate gelato. My treat."

He opened the door for her, and they stepped outside. The skies were overcast, the air damp, but for the moment it wasn't raining, so they hurried to the truck and climbed inside before Mother Nature decided to unleash again.

"Albert's sounds good to me. I can eat a dozen cannoli all by myself."

"You're ambitious, which I like. But we both know you'll barely be able to get a second one down, let alone twelve."

She rolled her eyes at the annoying man. "Obviously, it was an exaggeration, you're not supposed to call me out on it."

"Sorry. Guess I still have a lot to learn about women."

"Only one woman," she corrected.

He stopped and turned her in his arms. "Only one woman," he repeated before leaning in to kiss her, a long, leisurely kiss that might have gone on much longer had a sharp clearing of a throat not reminded them they were still in public.

They were on the highway heading back to the ranch within minutes. As soon as they pulled up to the garage, James quickly strode to the car and motioned for Reese to roll down his window.

"Something going on?"

"Angela's water broke. Because she's high risk, her doctor told us to call an ambulance to take her to St. Anthony's. It should be here in a few minutes. Molly wants to go with, so Meara offered to come along, but we didn't know if you'd be all right with Katie coming, too."

Summer's heart leapt to her throat. "Can I go see her? She must be terrified."

James nodded his appreciation. "She's actually handling it much better than I am. And yes, of course, I'm sure she'd love to see you."

She climbed out of the truck and hurried inside. She could hear her friend giving orders all the way from the foyer. She sprinted up the stairs just as Meara was carrying Angela's overnight bag from her room. The older woman beamed as soon as she saw her.

"The newest member of the family is ready to make his or her entrance."

"I heard. Would you like me to take that down to the foyer for you?"

"No, missy, I got it. I ain't so old I can't carry a duffle bag down the stairs. Go, see Angela before the ambulance arrives. She's been dying to know how things went in court today."

"Where are the girls?"

"Molly won't leave her mother's side, and Katie wouldn't leave Molly's. Strong, caring, supportive young ladies, just like their mothers." Without waiting for a response, the older woman lumbered past her down the stairs.

Such high praise coming from one of the most amazing women she'd ever known nearly brought Summer to tears. James and Reese's voice carried up, so she rushed down the hall. The nonstop chatter of two very excited little girls reached her ears as they both eagerly exclaimed how they were going to help feed and burp the baby.

"What about changing diapers, are you both going to help with that chore as well?"

"Ewwwww!" they both exclaimed in harmony.

Angela laughed, but a grimace suddenly contorted her face.

"Girls, I need you both to do something very important, please. Go ask Molly's daddy if there's anything else he needs brought downstairs."

Katie nodded and grasped her friend's hand. "C'mon, the amba'wince is comin'!"

Molly cast an unsure look at her mother, who waved her off. "Go, sweetie. I'm fine. Summer can wait with me until you get back."

As soon as the girls were gone, Angela's face screwed up and the tears she'd been holding at bay streamed down her face. "Thank you," she managed as she swiped them away. "I love my little Molly Waddles, but she's almost as bad as her father when it comes to hovering. And they watch my face like hawks, so I have to hold a smile in place until they leave the room." She gave a pathetic chuckle, which caused Summer to chuckle, and suddenly they were both laughing and crying at the same time.

The ambulance sirens could finally be heard, and Angela turned to face her. "Quick, before they get up here, how did it go in court?"

"Very well, thank God. Though the judge was surprisingly compassionate considering Nico showed up to court smashed out of his mind."

Her eyes and mouth both widened. "No way, what an idiot. What happened?"

Summer could hear the EMTs climbing the stairs just as James strode into the room. He smiled at his wife, though worry lines etched his eyes and mouth.

"How are you feeling?"

"Annoyed," his wife informed him. "Summer was telling me what happened in court, and I want to hear the rest."

James gave his head a bemused shake. "Darlin', you are the most contrary woman I've ever known. Summer can give you all the details *after* this baby is born."

Angela probably would have argued, but she grimaced again, only this time James saw it. He muttered a curse, and everything after that seemed to happen in warp speed until Angela was being lifted into the back of the ambulance.

James turned to Reese. "Are you sure you don't mind?"

He gave his brother a thump on the back. "We'll meet you at the hospital. Go, have a baby."

James gave him a grateful nod, then climbed into the back of the ambulance and grasped Angela's hand.

Determined to think nothing but positive thoughts, Summer got the girls ready and in the car within five minutes. Reese grabbed Meara's wool coat and escorted her out to the Lincoln, which was much easier for the older woman to get in and out of than his big truck.

Once they got to the hospital, time dragged as was normal with pregnancies. Babies came when they were ready, and sometimes that took hours. So, it seemed as if they'd spent an eternity in that waiting room, especially with two highly energized little girls, when James finally emerged through the swinging doors. He looked a little worse for wear, but the worry lines that always seemed to bracket his mouth were finally gone, replaced by a genuinely joyous smile. Which she hoped meant everything went smoothly.

"It's a boy. James Michael MacMillan the 3rd, eight pounds, four ounces, twenty inches long," he proudly announced, earning a hearty congratulatory hug and back-thumping from Reese, and a tearful hug from Meara, who asked, "Since yer beaming from ear to ear, can we assume mother and son are both doing well?"

"They're doing great. Angela's exhausted, but all her vitals are good. She shooed me out to let you all know what was going on."

"Daddy, can me and Katie go see my new brother?" Molly clapped her hands together, and Katie followed suit, as if their combined efforts had double the power.

"You bet." James chucked her under the chin. "Mommy can't wait for everyone to meet Little James." As he swung Molly up in his arms, Katie slipped her hand into Meara's, smiling up at the older woman as if they shared a secret nobody else knew about.

Summer's heart was so full of love and gratitude for this remarkable family. They had taken her and her daughter into their lives and made them not only feel welcome, but as if they were part of the family.

Reese pulled out his phone and glanced at the screen, then said to James, "Hey, I need to give John a quick call. I'll meet you guys back there in a couple minutes. Tell Angie I said congratulations and thank you for my nephew."

James eyed his brother for a brief moment. "Room two-sixteen. Make sure to tell John the good news."

"You got it." He touched her arm. "Why don't you head on in with them, I won't be long."

Something wasn't right, she could feel it. "I actually have to use the restroom, so I'll just wait for you. We can meet your nephew together." She gave Katie's shoulder a pat. "Remember to be on your best behavior, and do not touch little James unless Angela says it's okay."

Once they were out of earshot, Summer asked, "Something's wrong, isn't it?"

She thought he might lie to her, it took him so long to respond. But then he shot a glance in the general direction James had led the others before admitting, "Someone released all the horses from the stables."

Chapter Twenty-six

Reese cursed under his breath as he dialed John's cell. His friend answered on the first ring. "Hey, I'm glad you called back right away. I got a little freaked out when I realized everyone was gone."

"We're all at St. Anthony's. Angela had the baby, a little boy named James the 3rd. Mother and son are both doing well, and so is the proud poppa."

"Oh, man, that's awesome, just fantastic. Please give them both my best." He muffled the phone to shout something to someone else, then said, "Look, I don't know what's going on here, but after Cam and I managed to round up most of the horses, we realized they'd been let out again. Cam thinks it's some punk kids with nothing better to do, and maybe he's right, but... You want me to call the police?"

Christ, last thing James needed was something else to worry about, especially when he was finally able to take a breather after Angie's difficult pregnancy.

"No, let's wait. I'll be home in about twenty minutes. If anything else happens, go ahead and call. And John, you got your rifle, right?"

"Always, boss."

"Good."

As soon as he dropped his cell back in his pocket, Summer insisted, "I'm going with you."

He propped his hands on his hips. "Sweetheart, I have no idea what may be happening, and I'd rather err on the side of caution."

"I'm going with you," the stubborn woman repeated, completely ignoring his warning. "What if it's Nico?"

"We both heard him, he's heading back to New York with his parents. In fact, they're probably already there. Whatever's going on at the ranch, I don't want you anywhere near it, understand?"

"No, and don't talk to me like I'm one of your ranch hands," she demanded in that soft-spoken way of hers, that both frustrated and enticed him. "You're worried, so why are you trying to head back to the ranch by yourself? Has anyone even called the police yet?"

Reese didn't have time to argue, and he reasoned that Cam's assessment was the most logical. After all, what purpose would it serve Moretti to let the horses loose? Definitely seemed more like something a bunch of kids might do than an angry ex. He knew the Miller boys had already been hauled in, more than once, for disturbing the peace.

"Fine, you can come with. But at least promise me you'll stay in the truck until I've had a chance to talk to John."

"I will, I promise."

He eyed her for a second, then texted his brother to let him know they'd had a little mischief at the ranch, nothing to worry about, but he'd asked Summer to come with him, and if he could keep an eye on Katie until they got back, he'd appreciate it. Last thing Reese wanted was for James and Angela to worry needlessly on what should be one of the happiest days of their lives.

They were about a quarter way up the Double M's nearly half-mile long driveway when he recognized John's truck up ahead parked off to the side. His gut told him something wasn't right at the same time he saw John lying prone on the gravel about ten feet from the driver's side door. He pulled up directly behind him, leaving his headlights on.

"Get down," he quietly ordered as he retrieved his Glock from beneath his seat. "Call 9-1-1. You might not get a signal right away, but keep trying. And whatever you do, keep your head down."

With a fearful nod, she slid down onto the floor of the truck.

Reese kept careful watch as he slowly opened his door and stepped down onto the gravel. Gun ready, he cautiously made his way to John's side. Could his friend have had an accident, or was their something more sinister going on? He crouched down to examine him, and realized he had a bleeding wound on the back of his head. He felt for a pulse, and quickly found one, much to his immense relief. His ranch hand had been knocked unconscious, and Reese couldn't think of anyone with a motive to come there to do harm except for Moretti. But where was the bastard?

His answer was swift in coming when John's driver side door flew open and he was staring down the barrel of his friend's Marlin 336.

Nico's wide-eyed, maniacal smile left no doubt that he was coked out of his mind. Had he seen Summer? Did he know she was in the truck? Obviously, this had been a planned ambush. Maybe Moretti thought if he got him out of the way, he'd have a clear path back to Summer and Katie.

Or maybe it was old-fashioned revenge. Either way, he kept his eyes on the rifle, and his own gun down by his side out of sight.

"Thought you were heading back to New York with your folks. Would've been the smart thing to do if you truly cared about Katie."

"Don't you dare say her name!" Moretti's hand trembled with rage, but also because he was wired, which made Reese very nervous. "You're the reason my life went to shit! You and Mark set me up, then walked away scot free. And if that ain't bad enough, what do I find out as soon as I return home? You're fucking my girl, and playing daddy to my kid! *My* kid, dammit, not yours."

"She doesn't know you. And if you do something stupid here, she never will. Not only will my brother make sure you spend the rest of your life in prison, he'll take care of Summer and Katie as if they were family. Because that's what they are now."

Moretti's face twisted with hatred, his eyes practically bulging from his head. Just as quickly, he laughed, a sound born of desperation. He stepped down from the truck and closed the distance between them. "You gotta die, McMillan. It's the only way this can end, the only way to square us."

"If you shoot me, you go back to prison, only this time for life. If you hop on that plane back to New York, get some help and get your life back on track, no harm, no foul. You get to know your daughter, and everyone wins."

"But that's the problem, Rich Boy." Nico's expression was completely devoid of emotion. "I don't want you to win. I want you to die."

He raised the gun and aimed it at Reese's head.

"No!"

The blood froze in his veins at the sound of Summer's voice—the stubborn woman had gotten out of the truck! The reckless move distracted Nico, who swung the rifle toward her.

Reese brought his gun up and fired at the exact moment another shot rang out. A red stain blossomed dead center of Nico's chest. He jerked back, his expression one of shock before he slumped to the ground in a heap. Reese's bullet hit him in the shoulder, which is where he'd been aiming.

Having no clue who the second shooter was, Reese raced toward Summer, who had just jumped down from the truck and stood staring in horror at Moretti's crumpled body. He took her to the ground, rolling her beneath him behind the safety of the truck.

"Obstinate woman," he muttered. "I told you to stay down on the floor of the truck. What if he'd shot you?"

"What if he'd shot *you*?" she threw back at him. "It would've been my fault, I brought him into our lives."

"None of this is your fault. Moretti is responsible for his own actions."

He heard movement from the trees and raised his gun while blocking her head with his forearm. When he recognized the uniformed officer emerging, it was like a lead balloon being lifted from his chest, so great was his relief. He immediately lowered his gun.

"Are you psychic, Officer, or just dropping by for a late-night visit?" He stood up and helped Summer to her feet before kissing her firmly on the mouth. "You okay?"

"I'm fine."

He wasn't so sure. Her unblinking eyes were fixated on Nico's unmoving form. He tried to take her in his arms, but she refused to look away as Moretti's lifeblood drained away. Reese knew the police were trained to shoot to kill, and unfortunately for Moretti, Jake was an excellent shot.

"Your brother called to fill me in. I thought it might be those same kids who let a fox into the henhouse at the Buckley's place. What a mess."

Officer Teller crouched down beside Nico and felt for a pulse. After a few seconds, he made eye contact with Reese and gave a quick shake of his head. Moretti was gone.

"John's injured. Moretti knocked him out cold."

As Jake made his way over to check on John, he spoke into his radio to request an ambulance. "I have one civilian injured, one deceased."

"My God, he's…he's dead?" Summer whispered.

Summer's voice was so small, so haunted, he hated to have to confirm her fears. "Yes. I'm sorry."

She swallowed hard, and finally turned away. He wanted to pull her against his chest and wrap her in his arms, shield her from the fallout that was sure to come. And he *would* protect her, in every way he could.

His main concern was Moretti's parents. Would they transfer their anger to Summer and sue her for custody? Not that they'd have much more of a leg to stand on than their son had. But Moretti's father was a judge, which meant he knew the law backward and forward. They were also Katie's legal grandparents who, thanks to their son, hadn't even known she existed until recently.

He heard moaning and realized with relief that John was coming around. The ranch hand was sitting on the ground as Jake quickly examined his head injury. He had his elbows resting on his knees, and his head in his hands. Reese knelt beside him and took a better look at the bleeding gash. "Do you remember what happened?"

"Christ, someone cracked me a good one. A bottle, I think. I was coming out of the stables, I heard movement behind me, and…that's about all I remember."

"I'm just glad you have a hard noggin. Think you can stand up?" John nodded, and Reese and Jake both helped him to his feet. "The ambulance should be here soon, just lean against your truck until they get here. Wouldn't want you fainting on me."

"Fuck off."

Reese gave him a light thump on the shoulder before returning to Summer, who was once again staring at her ex's prone body.

"Hey, why don't I take you up to the ranch, get you a cup of tea—or maybe something stronger? You look like you could use it, and I'm pretty sure I'm going to need to move my truck anyway."

With a grateful nod, she got back in the truck and waited while he spoke with Jake.

"I'm taking Summer back to the house, this has been a pretty scary experience for her. If you need to take our statements before you leave, do you mind doing it up there?"

"Nope. Get your lady home, I shouldn't be long."

"Thanks, man. And will you please make sure one of the EMTs looks John over, maybe talk him into heading to the hospital to get fully checked out?"

"I'll do my best."

Once Reese had Summer settled at the kitchen table, he poured them each a shot of brandy. It became immediately apparent Summer didn't have much, if any, experience with drinking. She dipped her tongue into the glass, and her face contorted, her shoulders quavering and hands flapping as she all but gagged. He was hard-pressed not to laugh.

She cast him a sheepish-glance before setting the glass down and staring at it as if its contents might jump out at her.

Reese tossed his own shot back, then hers before coaxing her to come sit on his lap, which she did without much prodding. "You okay?" he repeated for what seemed like the dozenth time. He gently stroked her arms, which were cold to the touch.

"I just don't understand why he did this. I mean, I know it wasn't what he'd hoped for, but it was certainly more than he deserved. Nico was given the chance to get to know his daughter, which is what he said he wanted. An hour a month isn't ideal, I get that. But it was a start, and eventually they might have built a bond of some sort. I just…I don't understand."

He wished like hell he had the answers for her. "I won't pretend to be an expert on your ex, but I knew a different side of Nico than you did. He wasn't a very nice guy, honey. And who knows, maybe he never really got clean. It's possible he'd been using in prison, and once he got out, he went right back to it. Especially when he found out you'd moved on—and who you'd moved on with."

She turned in his arms and met his gaze. "I'm just so thankful you weren't hurt. I thought…I thought he was going to kill you."

The last two words came out in a strained whisper as tears flooded her eyes. Her face fell, and she threw her arms around his neck and sobbed into his shoulder, the sounds of her abject misery breaking his heart.

Reese stood and swung her into his arms. He carried her upstairs to his room and lied beside her until she fell asleep, which didn't take long at all. He slipped from the room to message Teller, see if the statements could wait until the following day—thankfully, they could—and gave his brother a call. Glancing at the clock as the phone rang, he was astonished to discover only an hour and a half had passed since he and Summer left the hospital. Seemed like hours had gone by since they'd started up the Double M's driveway.

"Man, am I glad to hear from you," James answered. "What the hell is going on?"

He didn't mince words. "Moretti's dead. Jake shot him. He was the one who let out the horses, more than likely trying to draw me out of the house. Probably too high to realize no one was home until he heard John talking to me on his cell." Reese cleared his throat. "According to Officer Teller, I probably owe you my life."

"Thank God for Jake's excellent timing. I'm so glad I called. It just didn't make sense those kids would drive that far out of town, *and* risk an ass full of shot, just to let some horses loose. But Jesus, I never imagined you could be walking into an ambush." James cursed under his breath. "Everybody okay?"

"Summer and I are both fine, but John was knocked out for a spell. He seems okay, but he has a pretty big goose egg on the back of his head. I asked Jake to make sure he gets checked out, preferable taken to the hospital."

"Good. Listen, the girls are all nodding off, and that includes Meara. I'm going to call a car to take us home, then I'll head back to the hospital myself. I don't want Angela to overdo it tonight, she's exhausted."

"Sounds like a plan, and I'm sure you could use a short break anyway. But you may want to take the path around the pines just in case the ambulance is still there. Summer and I will make sure the girls get to school in the morning."

"Thanks, little brother. We should be home within the hour."

Reese ended the call and slipped his cell back into his front jeans pocket. When he turned to head back to his room, he nearly ran Summer down. "Whoa." He drew her into his arms. "Guess my bedtime skills aren't as great as I thought."

Another sheepish smile. "I knew you must have been waiting for a chance to call your brother, so I faked it."

He cocked a brow. "Hope that's not something you have to do a lot of."

She chuckled against his chest. "No, this was the one and only time."

He kissed her on those luscious lips. "Glad to hear it."

"You never got to meet your new nephew."

This beautiful lady never failed to surprise him. After all that had happened in the last twelve hours—court, Nico's unfortunate demise—she felt bad that he hadn't gotten to meet Little James.

"I figured we'd head to the hospital tomorrow after dropping the girls off at school. Don't know how much you heard, but James is calling an Uber to bring everyone home, then heading back to spend the night with Angie and the baby."

"Sounds like a perfect ending to a perfect day."

He caressed her back with long, leisurely strokes. "You deserved a perfect day, too. I'm so sorry for what you're going through," he whispered against the top of her head. "Whatever you need, I'm here."

She pulled back and gazed up at him. "I know. You always are, that's what makes you so incredible. I just...I have no idea what to say to my daughter. Her father is gone, and all she had was one, frightening interaction with him, and what makes me a little sad is she'll probably be relieved. And who could blame her? Nico was nothing more than a man in a picture who turned out to be a monster. At least, in her five-year-old mind. Makes me feel like I failed her somehow. Like I should have made more of an effort—"

Reese cupped her face, hating where her train of thought was heading. "You did everything right, honey. Everything. Nico showing up at your door that night was regrettable, but on the flipside, what if he'd shown up when you and Katie were home alone? Any way you look at it, nothing that's happened is your fault. Maybe he had reason to feel a certain way about me, but you were a victim of *his* bad choices, not the other way around."

Her smile was so brilliant it lit up the dimly-lit hallway. "You always know exactly what to say. I'm so thankful to have you in my life. I used to think living the golden dream was about wealth and power, and living some glamorous lifestyle. But that's not it at all. It's about being rich in all the ways that matter. Love, family, friends. If that makes sense." Her cheeks pinkened as if embarrassed by her sudden insight.

He smiled, his heart so full of love for this woman he had an overwhelming urge to shout it to the world. "It makes perfect sense. I know I'm a lot richer now that I have you and Katie in my life. I love you."

"I love you, too. And while I wouldn't want you to think my head's been turned by money, can we start buying those fancy hamburger and hotdog buns with the seeds on them?"

It took him a second, but he grinned as he recalled the conversation she was referring to, from the night of their first date. "As long as you keep making mine old-school style, you can have anything you like."

Epilogue

"*Quit giggling, silly, or she'll know we're up to something.*"

Summer clamped a hand over her mouth as she tried not to laugh. Thanks to a big-mouthed Angela, she knew Reese had been planning a surprise proposal for weeks, and he'd obviously enlisted Katie's help, which made her love him even more. She wasn't exactly sure what was going to happen, but since he'd asked Katie to help him bring in dessert, she was pretty sure the plan would incorporate the cupcakes they'd made that morning.

She breathed deep in an attempt to get her nerves under control. That's when she caught movement out of the corner of her eye. She craned her head in time to catch Angela tug Molly back out of sight. A low, masculine chuckle followed, and that was enough to burst the damn. The most amazing sense of belonging washed over her, and the urge to laugh warred with the urge to cry, causing a watery giggle to escape, followed by another, and another.

Reese and Katie finally swept back into the dining room, Reese with his arms casually crossed, and her beaming daughter carefully balancing a tray of perfectly frosted and decorated cupcakes.

"What's so funny, Momma?" she asked, casting a worried glance up at Reese.

"I think I know," he drawled, craning his neck to find the whole family hiding around the corner. "You may as well all come in here so I can do this right."

Molly ran in and stood next to Katie, both girls grinning from ear to ear. Meara lumbered in and took a seat at the dining table. James, with a happily gurgling, six-month old J.J. tucked in his arms, fists and feet both pumping away, followed in after Meara, while a radiant Angela brought up the rear and moved around the table to stand behind Meara, her hands resting on the older woman's shoulders.

Now that the moment had arrived, her laughter morphed into panic as reality set in.

He's going to propose!

Katie looked up at Reese as if seeking permission—he gave her a wink and a nod. Practically bursting at the seams with excitement, she spun back and help up her tray. "The one in the middle is for you."

Summer's fingers were trembling as she picked up the white frosted cupcake with pink and red sprinkles. She met Reese's gaze and thought he looked every bit as nervous as she felt. Glancing back down at the cupcake, she realized something was sticking out of the frosting. She carefully pulled it out, and—

Katie's emoji ring from the gumball machine?

She grinned. "Listen, it's not that I don't love it, sweetie, but…isn't this yours?"

"Yep. Reese didn't want his ring to get frosting all over it, so we compa…compri—"

"Compromised," Reese finished for her. "And you did it perfectly, Katie, thank you for your help." She gazed up at him with hero worship, and he gave her head a loving pat before returning his attention to Summer.

She gasped as he got down on bended knee and presented her with a sleek, dark gray ring box. He opened it with a flourish, and she stared in open-mouth shock at the most incredibly beautiful diamond ring she'd ever seen. Not that she'd seen all that many up close, but she had no doubt this is exactly the ring she would have picked for herself. It sparkled up at her from its velvety maroon cradle.

"Sweetheart, I'm pretty sure I fell in love with you the moment you stepped out of your car last September. And I'm forever grateful to Meara for making me take a second shower that day."

Chuckles filled the room with Meara reminding, "You work with horses, son. Pretty as they are, they stink."

He smiled ruefully, that mischievous grin she loved so much. "That they do. But they're also strong, supportive, loyal, faithful—everything I promise to be for you. I love you, Summer Louise Hanson, please make me the happiest man in all of Colorado and say you'll marry me."

She smiled as tears blurred her vision, her heart so full she thought it might explode from pure happiness. "Yes," she said, which came out as more of a whisper. She swiped at her eyes as applause erupted around them. "I love you, too. So much."

Reese let out a soft whoop, then plucked the gorgeous ring from the box and slipped it onto her finger before grasping her hands and pulling her into his arms. He kissed her, then picked her up and spun her around. And while she would've rather died than ruin such an incredible moment, if he didn't quit spinning, everyone within striking distance would be sorry.

She'd taken the test the morning before, and while she'd been trying to find the right moment to tell him, it seemed fate has chosen for her.

"Cowboy, please put me down before everyone in this room is wearing my supper."

Reese stopped, a quizzical frown chasing away his smile as he carefully set her on her feet. "You okay? It is flu season, maybe—"

"It's not the flu." She could only hope the news was as wonderful for him as it had been for her.

"See?" Meara said to Angela. "I have an intuition when it comes to these things."

Angela gave a solemn nod. "With Molly, you knew even before I did."

After decoding their comments, James burst out laughing.

"What the fu—" Reese glanced down at the two little impressionable faces staring up at him. "What the heck is so funny?" he demanded of his brother.

"Just trying to picture your face the first time you have to change a poopy diaper. And not one of those newborn numbers. I'm talking a year in when the stench could knock out a longhorn—"

"Oh, my god, shut up and let her tell him already," Angela scolded, taking a fussy James Jr. from her husband's arms.

As understanding finally dawned, his eyes grew round with shock. He looked to her for confirmation. She nodded as fresh tears pooled. A napkin was pressed into her hand and she dabbed at her eyes.

"Are you sure? When are you due? I mean, we should probably start planning the wedding right now, don't you think?"

She laughed. "Assuming it was that night down in Durango, I'm guessing mid-November."

A smile spread across his entire face as he grasped her hands again and gently pulled her into his arms. "Sweetheart, how do you feel about a summer wedding?"

Her heart so full she thought she might float away, she replied, "It's the only kind I know how to plan."

Enjoy an excerpt from the Donna Marie Rogers'
USA Today *Bestselling Series*

USA TODAY BESTSELLING AUTHOR

DONNA MARIE
ROGERS

Welcome to
REDEMPTION
BOOK 9

Say You
Love Me

Say You Love Me

WELCOME TO REDEMPTION, Book 9
USA Today Bestselling Series

Will a secret from the past destroy their second chance at love?

Bernadette Mitchell thought she'd put the past to rest. At fifteen, pregnant, betrayed, and heartbroken by the baby's father, she'd made an agonizing decision that she lives with every day. But she's made the best of things...until an unthinkable tragedy turns her life upside down and brings the ghosts of her past back to town.

Officer Mike Donovan is happy to be back home in Redemption where he plans to raise his little girl. He's also on a mission—to win back the only woman he's ever loved. Back in high school, he broke her heart with a horrific ultimatum. If he can convince her to give him another chance, he'll spend the rest of their lives proving they belong together. But when he discovers she's been keeping an unimaginable secret, one that shifts his whole world on its axis, he questions everything he thought he knew about her...about them.

Chapter One

"Can my daddy have this dance?"

Bernadette Mitchell glanced down in surprise as the sweetest little voice she'd ever heard pulled her from her musings. An angel with curly red hair and plenty of freckles smiled up at her; a pair of big brown eyes glittered with hopeful curiosity.

Maddie Donovan.

And the little peanut was even cuter up close, especially dressed in a frilly, lavender satin party dress for Caleb and Lauren Hunter's wedding party.

Just as she opened her mouth to gently decline the offer, a pair of men's black oxfords stepped into view. Bernie slowly raised her gaze past black, pleated dress slacks and a white, collared dress shirt—which fit its muscular owner like a glove—to face the last man on earth she wanted to exchange words with. Mike Donovan...*Officer* Mike Donovan.

The gangly young boy she'd known since elementary school had grown into a ruggedly handsome man, his boyishly crooked smile now devilishly potent as he focused his intense gaze on her. Tall, dark, handsome.

And definitely off limits.

He'd started pursuing her again a couple of years ago, shortly after he and Maddie moved back to Redemption—which had been the first time she'd laid eyes on him since they were fifteen years old. And she'd done a pretty good job of avoiding him...up until now.

Until she'd decided to take a break from the festivities and find a dark corner to sit, catch her breath, and collect her thoughts.

Then her mind had wandered, and he'd managed to sneak up on her. Rather, send his precious little girl over to put her on the spot. The jerk.

"Just one dance. Whad'ya say?"

Lord, that deep, sexy voice was almost more than she could handle right now.

She glanced past him, tempted to make a run for it. But Nino's was packed, so no doubt a whirlwind of rumors would start up, and she certainly didn't want to have to deal with that.

Not again.

"My daddy's a real good dancer," the adorable little stinker chimed in.

A reluctant smile found its way to her lips as she looked from daughter to father and back again. One dance… As long as they didn't talk about anything but the weather, what could it hurt?

Bernie cocked a playful brow at Maddie. "You promise he won't step on my feet? I'm wearing open-toe sandals." She lifted her foot and wiggled it.

Maddie gave a gap-toothed grin and sent those red curls bouncing with a definitive nod.

"Fine, then. One dance." She winked at her before meeting Mike's amused gaze.

"I'll take what I can get." He bent down and gave his daughter a kiss on the top of her head. "Thanks, squirt. Tell grandma to save me a slice of wedding cake, will you?"

The little pixie gave another bob of her head and then skipped off, those little, black patent Mary Jane's beating a quick path across the room until she disappeared into the crowd.

"You should be ashamed of yourself," Bernie admonished as he led her out onto the dance floor. The slow strains of "Wonderful Tonight" by Eric Clapton suddenly flowed through the sound system, and a groan escaped her before she could stop it. *Why couldn't a fast tune like "Celebration" or "Let's Get It Started" have come on?*

"Maybe I should."

He held her hand tight, as if afraid she would bolt, while his arm slid around her, holding her much too close for comfort. His cologne, spicy and seductive, enveloped her, the subtle scent as intoxicating as his deep voice.

"But hell, I've tried everything else. You won't talk to me. You won't accept my calls. When you see me coming, you run in the other direction."

She frowned. "That's a bit of an exaggeration."

"No, it's not. You avoid me at all costs."

"Can you blame me?" she countered in a furious whisper.

"It was fifteen years ago, Bernie. Christ, I was a scared kid and—"

"I don't want to talk about this," she insisted, trying to tug her hand free as emotions long buried bubbled to the surface. *Damn him.*

Frustration knit his brow, and he glanced around as if checking to see if they'd made a scene. He led her off the dance floor, and she had no choice but to follow as he held her hand in a tight grip. She was careful not to make eye contact with anyone as they wound their way through the restaurant and out the front door.

The surprisingly cool, early August night air was like heaven against her heated skin. The overhead street lamps lit the area well enough that she could make out the intensity of his stare as he stopped and let go of her hand.

"We need to talk about this," he insisted, tucking his hands inside the front pockets of his slacks. "*I* need to talk about it. I've been trying to apologize to you forever. I just...I'm so sorry." He stepped closer and reached out, capturing both of her hands. "I was a kid. I-I had no idea what to do or say, and I was scared to death of what would happen once our parents found out. So, I said some horrible things I didn't mean and wished I could take back almost immediately. Only, by the time I'd worked up the nerve to tell my mom...you'd already lost the baby."

Tears pooled in her eyes before spilling down her cheeks. She pulled her hands free and angrily swiped them away. Only she wasn't sure who she was angrier with, Mike, or herself. If only he'd said all this before she'd made the choice she had. The choice she'd felt was her only option at the time.

"Please don't cry," he said in a near whisper. He reached and gently wiped a tear from her cheek. "I screwed up. I was so in love with you...you have to know that."

She swallowed and stepped back, wrapping her arms around herself, more confused and uncertain of her choices than she'd ever been. She wanted to run home and lock the door, hide from the world until...until when? It's not like she could turn back time and erase past mistakes, forge a new path and future. Neither could he. They were both stuck in this mess of their own making.

Only, it went so much deeper than even he knew. And she couldn't tell him. Even if she wanted to— and Lord help her, part of her wanted to confess all—she'd signed papers, sworn to keep her secret forever.

Clearing her throat, she forced her lips into some semblance of a smile. "I appreciate everything you said. You were right, we, uh…we needed to talk about it. I've been holding a grudge, and I guess…well, you know I have a stubborn streak."

"Bernadette—"

"Look, this is all I can handle right now, okay? Please, Mike. This was…good. But it's been a long day, so I think I'm going to grab my purse and head home." She took a couple of steps, then turned and added, "She's beautiful. You're a very lucky man."

Without giving him a chance to respond, she hurried back inside.

Available at your favorite online retailers.

About the Author

USA Today bestselling author Donna Marie Rogers inherited her love of romance from her mother, who devoured romance novels like they were Fannie May candies, and never missed an episode of Little House On the Prairie. And though it wasn't until years later Donna would come to understand her mother's fascination with Charles Ingalls, Donna's love of the romance genre is every bit as all-consuming.

A Chicago native, Donna now lives in beautiful Northeast Wisconsin with her husband and children. She's an avid gardener and home-canner, as well as an admitted reality TV junkie. Her passion to read is only exceeded by her passion to write, so when she's not doing the wife and mother thing, you can usually find her sitting at the computer, creating exciting, memorable characters, fresh new worlds, and always a happily-ever-after.

Visit Donna at:
www.DonnaMarieRogers.com